DRAW YOU IN

VOL. 2:
SECRET ORIGINS

JASPER BARK

(with contributions from comics legend Louise Simonson, who appears as herself in the first chapter)

Let the world know:
#IGotMyCLPBook!

Crystal Lake Publishing
www.CrystalLakePub.com

WELCOME
TO ANOTHER

CRYSTAL LAKE PUBLISHING
CREATION

WELCOME BACK TO THE SECOND VOLUME OF *DRAW YOU IN.* I'M SO GLAD YOU COULDN'T STAY AWAY.
WHEN WE LEFT LINDA, SHE HAD JUST TURNED HER BACK ON THE INVESTIGATION INTO HORROR COMIC CREATOR, R. L. CARVER. BUT, THANKS TO AN INCIDENT ON HER BOOK TOUR, SHE MAY BE HAVING SECOND THOUGHTS.
MAYBE A CHAT WITH A DEAR FRIEND WILL CHANGE HER MIND. AND IF IT DOES WILL LINDA FIND HERSELF UNCOVERING THE SECRET ORIGINS OF HER DARKEST FEARS?
YOU ONLY NEED TURN THE PAGE TO FIND OUT!

CHAPTER 1

SOMETIMES, THE SCARIEST THING you can do is pick up the phone and call.

Linda was back from her book tour and it hadn't ended well. Maybe it was the cumulative effect of everything that had happened during the investigation, but an incident on the last day had triggered her anxiety. Linda's thoughts were like a startled flock of birds, flying in every direction and next to impossible to settle.

She needed comfort and reassurance. She needed to hear a friendly voice on the other end of the phone. She knew exactly who she ought to call but she was afraid.

Weezie was the big sister she'd always wanted when she was growing up. She used to fantasize about having an older sibling, someone who'd stick up for her in fights and explain things like French kissing and why boys were such jerks.

It wasn't until she'd been friends with Walt and Weezie for a good few years that Linda realized Weezie fit this bill. She didn't need help with boys anymore (it was men that were a mystery to her now), but Weezie was full of sage advice and lived experience, and she was always there on the end of the phone when Linda needed to talk things through.

Linda was scared her meltdown with Walt at Comic Con would sour their relationship. She was ashamed of her behavior and didn't want to face up to it. Every time she picked up her cell to call, Linda panicked. Her brain shut down and her hands shook. She had to put down her phone and talk herself off a ledge.

Finally, Linda realized how foolish she was being. This was the longest she'd gone without talking to her friends and she missed them. She'd lost count of the career crises, blown deadlines, and bad break-ups Weezie had helped her through.

Linda wasn't certain what she would have said if Walt had picked up, so she was relieved to hear Weezie's voice on the other end of the line.

She took a deep breath. "Weezie, hi, it's Linda." Then she couldn't stop herself blurting, "Oh heavens, I've missed you. I know I should've called sooner, but things have been crazy."

"I hear you. Life has been nuts here recently, too."

Linda could hear Weezie's dog Loki barking in the background.

"Oy! Just the mailman at the door. Walter will get it," Weezie said. "What's going on?"

"Oh gosh, where to start? I stopped drawing for a little while. The guys at Obsidian, my publishers, were being real dicks, they dropped me from the signing tour I was supposed to do. So, then I got a job doing research for the FBI, and that's a whole other story. I was looking into the pre-code horror artist, R. L. Carver. Anyway, that all got kinda scary—don't ask. But then my book, *Doom Divine*, got picked up by some influencers, which really helped sales, so then Obsidian are all like, 'Oh my God, you've got to come be on this tour now.' And that's kinda what I wanted to talk about. But first, how is Walt? I'm still embarrassed by what happened at Comic Con. He's not mad at me is he?"

Weezie laughed. "Whatever it was, forget it. He probably didn't notice. Or if he did, he's forgotten it already. Ancient minds, and all that." Linda could hear the amusement in her voice.

"It's good to hear from you. What's up?"

Linda sighed. She could feel the tension slip from the muscles in her shoulders. She hadn't realized how worried she'd been about the incident at the Con. Walt and Weezie were some of her dearest friends and right now she needed all the friends she could get. She couldn't afford to mess things up with people so important to her.

"Oh great, thanks, I made a bit of a fool of myself and I just . . . you know, didn't want to leave things kinda strange between us. Anyway, there's something I wanted to ask your advice about, it happened a couple days ago, on this signing tour. I was in Minneapolis. Frank, the owner of the store, had me get up and say a few words before I got to signing and when I was done, this big guy, who was kinda scary, got up and started yelling at me."

"How awful! There are some nutty people out there and there's no telling what might set them off." Weezie sighed. "Did Frank have security? Did he know who the guy was? Did he kick him out?"

She paused. "Wait, you're not worried the guy will come after you . . . are you?"

She was starting to sound worried.

Linda bit her lip. How much should she say? She didn't want Weezie to think she was unhinged.

"Actually, the one thing I'm not worried about is the guy coming after me. That part's kinda . . . complicated. But no, Frank didn't have any security, like a lot of these independent stores he can barely afford to pay his staff, let alone security, you know how it is. No one had seen the guy before. The things he said though, that was what got to me. I mean it was all the usual stuff about how I was single-handedly destroying comics with my woke BS, forcing diversity into stories where it didn't belong and how the industry was ruined the minute they let women creators work on books.

"I mean, I'm used to that nonsense online, where I generally ignore it, but it was different with this guy all up in my face. I was kinda rattled. I thought we'd moved beyond all that caveman stuff. Why should my gender matter so long as I'm telling a good story? How do you deal with this sort of abuse? Was it this bad back in the day?"

Weezie laughed. "Heavens, no. Back when dinosaurs roamed the Earth, there were so few women creators in comics, we were more curiosities than threats. Except for rare cons or signings, we were fairly anonymous. Heck, a few fans were surprised that I *was* a woman. They thought I was *Louis*, not *Louise*.

"Most companies considered diversity in stories a good thing. And since they'd barely invented the Internet, the Troll system hadn't developed yet. No Facebook. No Twitter or Instagram. You'd hear the occasional grumble about 'liberal values' but nothing like the rants you get today.

"It's partly because creators are so accessible now. You have to be, don't you? Publicizing your work is part of the job. Which opens you to real fans, but also to crazies. Usually, trolls are cowards, hiding behind fake names and accounts, swollen with imagined grievance or just wanting to cause trouble. My instinct, like yours, would be to ignore them unless I felt physically threatened. But this guy got in your face. You're sure he's not a real danger?"

"They thought you were Louis, for real? That's a scream. But, yes I'm fairly sure he's not a danger, and thanks for being concerned. I looked him up online and the guy's kinda disappeared. Besides, I have the Feds looking out for me now, so he'd be an idiot to try anything. Oh hey, I can't say too much about it, but I've had a wild time with my side hustle as a special advisor to the FBI. I say, 'side hustle,' but it was kinda my only gig for a while there, until my sales picked up. I guess that's one of the few good things about social media.

"Anyway, I can't say too much about the case I'm working, but one of the things we get to do is interview all these old comic creators about what it was like back in the fifties, before the whole Kefauver scare. It's kind of a deep background thing. What you said about being anonymous really rang true. I mean back in those days they didn't even let the artists sign their work, well Bill Gaines at EC did, but he was the only one.

"But this anonymity meant there was way more diversity in comics than people realize, there was a huge ethnic mix, and there were women creators I never knew about. It's really opened my eyes. I feel like their stories have been left out of comics' history and that's why idiots like the guy in the comic book store think it's always been a boys' club and should stay that way. I guess that's what really got to me.

"Anyway, listen to me ranting, sorry, I guess I just needed to talk to someone who'd understand. But this has all been about me, sorry. How are things with you and Walt?"

"We're good. Working, on a lazy, semi-retired sort of schedule. Sounds like your life is much more exciting.

"You know, ages ago, at a cocktail party, I met a woman who wrote comics back in the day, mostly romance comics. She was pretty cool. Because writers and artists weren't credited, I never knew she existed. But we all *do* know Ramona Fradon, who's ninety-five and still going strong. And Trina Robbins has written books featuring unsung women creators in the early days of comics.

"But how can any case harken back seventy years? Well, never mind. Cold case, I imagine. More like in the freezer. You can't say and I won't pump you, but it does sound intriguing. If you're ever able to tell the tale, I'd love to hear it. A comics mystery. There's a graphic novel in there somewhere!

"Completely off subject, decades back, Walter won a Haxtur Award from a Con in Spain—a large, brass statue with a marble base. I always thought it would make an excellent murder weapon. If I ever wrote a mystery . . .

"Anyhow, I hope you aren't going to get anywhere near actual murder . . . or violence of any kind. Leave that to the professionals! Isn't that what cops always tell the amateur sleuths on TV?"

Linda smiled to herself. It felt good to have someone care about her welfare, to worry about her safety, rather than whether she was delivering pages on time or if she would turn up for her flight to go interview a witness. Her whole professional life seemed to involve people worrying whether she'd be on time. In one of those sudden bursts of overwhelming sentiment, Linda found she was grateful to have Weezie in her life.

She'd been adrift these past few months. Talking to Weezie was like throwing a rope to shore and pulling herself into a safe harbor.

"Don't worry, the only dead bodies I've seen on this case have been illustrations, and yes, parts of this case are really cold. I won't lie, there have been a couple of scary moments, and I did give up on the case because of them. It was a lucky coincidence that the tour came up when it did. But scary things can happen anywhere, doing any job, that's what the lunatic in the comic shop showed me. So, I've decided to go back and finish the case. I hadn't really thought about it till now, but I guess that's why I needed to talk to you, to get all this straight in my mind. As usual, you've been a real help. And I might even write this up as a story, like you suggest, you'll probably get to read the whole thing soon."

Linda knew she was talking too much and making this conversation all about her, and she loved that Weezie let her, but she had one more thought.

"By the way, you should totally write that mystery, I'd be first in line for a signed copy. It kinda reminds me of the ending of *Clue*—'I accuse the comic creator, in the studio, with the Haxtur Award!'" Linda couldn't help chuckling at her own joke.

Weezie laughed along with her. "Just keep your eyes open and stay safe. I'm glad you have protection.

"Wait, Walter's signaling me. It's definitely time to take Loki for his walk and where Loki goes, I go. At least according to my dog. Can I call you back later?"

"Of course, listen, it's been wonderful chatting. Thanks for letting me bend your ear. It's been a big help. Enjoy your walk, say 'hi' to Walt, and pet Loki for me."

Linda rang off and clutched the phone to her chest. It was *so* good to connect with old friends. It grounded her and helped her see the things she hadn't wanted to admit, even to herself. The real reason she'd called Weezie was to make a decision she'd have put off otherwise.

But she had to make the decision now. There wasn't any time to spare. What had happened at her last signing had shown her that. It had also shown her she wasn't going to escape the web of weird incidents until she solved the puzzle at the heart of Carver's life.

Because what had happened straight after the signing was as strange as anything she'd encountered so far.

CHAPTER 2

"**M**AKE ME A sandwich and put my dick in your mouth!"
The angry guy stabbed his finger at Linda, his speech over. She pictured a severed penis between two slices of bread. Not quite what he meant, but it would amount to the same thing. Maybe she'd sketch it later, then again maybe she wouldn't.

Linda shuddered at the thought. His body odor hung in the air like an angry fug, a scented echo of his vicious, incoherent words. He turned on his heel and left the store.

Tall and lean, with a long, rangy body, his graying beard looked almost as greasy as his hair, which he'd tied back in a ponytail. He wore army fatigues and a Captain America T-shirt. This gave him a simultaneous look of being a grizzled Vietnam veteran and a little boy dressing up as a soldier.

There'd been something broken, and probably medicated, in his gaze. His eyes moved rapidly, never fixing on one thing, and saliva congealed in the corners of his mouth. He'd come in late and skulked at the back by the door. The other customers had given him a wide berth, sensing something to be avoided in his manner.

There was a collective sigh of relief as he stalked out of the store, and several people laughed nervously.

Linda looked to the owner, Frank, making a good show of bravado. "He a regular customer?"

Frank shook his head. "First time I've seen him, and the last, I hope. He's certainly banned from now on."

There was more nervous laughter. Frank clapped his hands and addressed the people crammed into the front of the store. "Who wants a signed copy of *Doom Divine*?"

Linda tried to swallow, her throat was constricted and her mouth dry. She caught the lingering odor of the scary guy and her stomach turned. The confrontation had got to her, for sure.

Linda was no stranger to imposter syndrome. Public appearances always triggered it. There was the constant expectation that someone was going to challenge her right to be here. Tell her she wasn't a real artist and she didn't belong with the proper professionals.

So, when the shouty guy barged through the crowd and stabbed his finger at Linda, she was almost relieved. She'd been dreading this her whole career and finally it was happening. Most of what he'd said had been rambling and incoherent, but the gist of it, the fact that she shouldn't be allowed to be here, selling comics she'd written and drawn, had hit home.

His reasons for attacking her were childish and sexist. She knew that. She would normally be angered by anyone who claimed that women couldn't draw comics and should be kept out of the industry. If he'd said that about any of her colleagues, she would be livid. But he'd said them about her and she was ashamed to admit that a part of her agreed with him.

It was the part of her with low esteem and poor self-worth. It was the part she wrestled with every day as she sat down to draw. But, God help her, it was there.

The thing was, as a creator she never really believed her rave reviews, only her bad ones. She didn't just take them to heart, they were burned into her memory. She knew writers and artists who could quote stinking reviews, from two decades ago, word for word. Any unkind words, no matter how random or unfair, stuck with you.

It didn't help that Linda was having a hard time accepting her change of fortune. A therapist told her she had 'negative entitlement.' This basically meant Linda never believed she deserved the good things that happened to her. The last decade had seen her readership dwindle and, as that declined, so did interest from editors and publishers. It seemed that as she got older, less men checked her out and less readers picked up her work. She'd begun to think it was the natural order of things.

Her initial success had come so early in her career, she hadn't thought to question it. It had seemed natural. It was only when the industry contracted, and she found work hard to come by, that she realized how lucky she'd been.

It had gotten so hard, she was thinking of quitting comics and getting a regular job. If she was honest, the gig with McPherson and the FBI was a step in that direction.

Then Obsidian told her about the spike in *Doom Divine*'s sales. It hadn't seemed real. It felt like a reversal of fortune you'd find in a Dickens novel, yet here she was, living it. When her last royalty check came, Linda was able to pay her rent and clear her credit cards. She even had money left to treat herself.

Something wasn't right about the situation though. It wasn't anything she could put her finger on, but it wasn't just her imposter syndrome. It was a nagging doubt that she was being distracted, taken away from something she ought to be doing.

The acclaim and adulation were gratifying, but they didn't allay Linda's feeling that she was dancing on the rim of the void. That one wrong step could send her plunging over the edge. This feeling had only grown since she parted with McPherson and Richard.

Along with her sense of dislocation, and the creeping belief she'd had since childhood that she wasn't really the person everyone thought she was. That she wasn't just in the wrong body, but the wrong life, the wrong existence altogether.

All of this played through Linda's mind as she sat down to begin the signing. Her fingers shook and her palms were so wet she had trouble taking the lid off her Sharpie pen. She avoided eye contact with the line forming in front of the table.

The first customer was wearing an oversized, black T-shirt with the cover of the first issue of *Doom Divine* on it. Linda had to force herself to look up into the woman's face. She was in her early twenties and had long hair, dyed purple, green, and black. Her lipstick was black and her lips were drawn back in the biggest smile.

"Nice T-shirt." Linda's voice was quiet and came out as a croak. Her throat was still parched.

"Thanks, it's a custom special. My boyfriend made it specially for me. It was my birthday last week."

"Happy belated birthday, I think your boyfriend's a keeper."

"Definitely, we're both huge fans. We loved your work on *Phantom Lady* and couldn't believe we missed *Doom Divine* when it first came out. He's gutted not to be here, his work hours were changed at the last minute. He's *so* jealous that I get to meet you and he doesn't."

Linda smiled, and her stomach finally settled. "Well, I hope you'll *both* come see me, next time I'm in town."

"You bet." The young woman handed Linda the first collection of *Doom Divine*. She shifted from foot to foot like a schoolgirl handing in her report.

Linda scrawled a brief note and added a quick sketch. Her usual motif was a profile of Lord Fiara De Sange, the shape-shifting vampire, but for some reason, she drew the Li'l Ghost Girl.

She hadn't planned to, and it surprised her. As if the Li'l Ghost Girl had stepped out from a bush and waved. She hadn't told anyone about the character who was haunting her work. She wasn't certain she wanted to draw attention to her but, for some reason, Linda felt strangely comforted that she'd made an appearance.

The rest of the people in line were just as respectful and enthusiastic about Linda's work. She began to relax into the role of minor comics celebrity. The people in the store weren't a threat and they weren't judging her. They were bright, quirky individuals who were as into comics as Linda. In fact, they were into Linda's comics and they wanted to tell her, that's why they'd come.

When Linda was done signing everyone's book, a few customers asked if she could do them a sketch. Linda had been caught out with sketches before. Back when she was a big name, and there were big lines at her convention signings, she'd been happy to oblige with a quick sketch.

All too often, she'd see the same sketch for sale on a collector's site within twenty-four hours, for as much as a hundred bucks. As a comic artist, Linda was used to other people profiting more from her work than she did, but it hurt when so-called fans profited from work she gave away for free.

To get around this, when Linda sketched these days, she personalized each drawing, so their re-sale value would be negligible. The first sketch she did was for a guy called Mike. It took about ten minutes, with at least twelve people watching, as she chatted and sketched.

She drew Mike with his arm around the rakish Lord Fiara De Sange. He lost a good twenty pounds in the sketch and he praised Linda on the likeness she caught. She sketched two more people and then Anna, the young woman who was first in line, asked for one.

As Linda started drawing, her mind began to wander. She stopped chatting and was vaguely aware of her pen moving across the paper. She hardly noted she was using several sheets of paper.

Anna made a few appreciative noises as Linda drew. These

soon became gasps and giggles, and comments such as, "Another page? Oh my, this is getting epic."

Linda came back to herself after drawing the third page. She had the sensation that she'd stepped out of her body, to watch it from a distance, and had suddenly snapped back. She looked down at the hastily drawn pages on the table in front of her.

"Is it finished?" Anna asked.

Linda didn't answer, she was too absorbed by the pages. The first one showed the Li'l Ghost Girl in the comic store, standing in back of the crowd. She was only waist high and couldn't see Linda at the table. She turned away and walked to the door. On the second page, the Li'l Ghost Girl left the store and walked across the concourse looking at the customers in the mall. In the third and final page, the Li'l Ghost Girl stopped next to a coffee shop. She looked in the window then beckoned, agitated.

The final panel on the third page showed the Li'l Ghost Girl jumping up and down and pointing to something in the window of the coffee shop, as though it was something very important that Linda should see.

Anna was reading over Linda's shoulder. "I don't get it, is there something I'm missing?"

Linda stood up. "It's something I'm missing."

She walked around the crowd at the table and headed straight for the door.

CHAPTER 3

LINDA LEFT THE store without collecting her things. She remembered her purse though, it was hanging from her shoulder.

She crossed the concourse, trying to trace the Li'l Ghost Girl's route. She couldn't explain why it was so important, but she knew she had to look through the window of the coffee shop. She had to see what the Li'l Ghost Girl was pointing out.

The character hadn't appeared since Linda's doodles in the airport, when the Li'l Ghost Girl was definitely trying to tell her something. Linda hadn't paid her any heed then, but she sensed an urgency now.

Linda imagined the skepticism on Richard's and McPherson's faces if she were to tell them she was listening to one of her comic characters. They definitely wouldn't get it. Linda wasn't certain she got it herself. But there was more to this character than ink marks on a page.

The Li'l Ghost Girl had a life of her own, like an outside force, intervening in Linda's life. She had a fragile insistence that was hard to deny, like a small child tugging at your sleeve. Or a totem animal, in a dream, with some cryptic message.

Linda found the spot where the Li'l Ghost Girl had stood at the window of the coffee shop. It wasn't hard to locate. She could've sworn she'd never seen the store before, but she'd drawn it with perfect accuracy. She must have taken it in when she came to the comic store.

Linda gazed through the window and her stomach sank. Sitting at a table right by the window was the shouty guy who'd disrupted her signing. He hadn't noticed her, he was too busy tapping on his tablet. Why had the Li'l Ghost Girl wanted her to see this?

Maybe this wasn't such a great idea. In the store, Linda was protected by the people around her, but she was alone out here on the concourse. Sure, there were people milling about, but they weren't paying her any attention and this guy was a loose cannon, he could do anything. Linda glanced back at the comic store, but something held her where she was. She wanted to know what he was saying and why it was so important.

Linda reached into her purse and took out her reading glasses. The shouty guy's screen came into focus, she had a good view of it over his shoulder. He was messaging **A Bombinator**@abo_min_ations, the troll he mentioned when he was raving at her in the comic store.

Shouty guy's Twitter handle was **Charles S** @TakeItAllB*tch. He was bragging to the troll about what he'd just done. Portraying himself as some kind of political activist, a grizzled veteran in the gender wars. **A Bombinator** was lapping it up, egging the guy on and telling him he was some kind of hero.

Linda's trepidation melted. She set her jaw and narrowed her eyes. Her hands curled into fists and the veins in her temple throbbed. The nerve of this guy. Where the hell did he get off, pulling this kind of crap? She reached into her purse to grab her phone and take a photo of what he was typing.

Her phone wasn't there. She must have left it on the signing table.

She couldn't let him get away with this. There had to be something else she could use to record what he was saying. She found a ballpoint in the bottom of her purse next to Carver's notebook.

Linda had brought the notebook to show Frank. He was an expert in rare memorabilia and she was hoping he could evaluate it. It was a good idea to find out the notebook's worth and, to be honest, she was thinking of selling it. If Linda couldn't take a photo of what the guy was typing, she could at least write it down.

But then it got weird. **A Bombinator** claimed he'd stumbled on the original pages of *Tales That Draw You In*. Linda would have been skeptical if he hadn't bragged about ripping off the person he got them from. What a sleazeball.

Was it possible that an original set of pages still existed and somehow they'd fallen into this idiot's lap? Linda would have to pass this on to McPherson. This was too important to overlook.

The floor suddenly felt like it was at the wrong angle. The perspective in the mall was all stretched out of shape. Sounds were distant and echoing. Her body was a hollow shell and she didn't fit inside it. She was breathing too quickly and her hands shook.

The only thing that made any sense was the weight of the pen and the notebook in her hand. They were anchors that stopped her slipping away, losing her grip on reality. She put the pen to the paper and her shoulders relaxed, her breathing calmed, and the world around her fell back into place.

Linda wrote **A Bombinator**'s message down and sketched the little icon he used as a profile pic—a broadsword, with an SS insignia on the hilt, cleaving a bleeding heart. She also took down Charles's Twitter handle **Charles S** @TakeItAllB*tch. She was so intent on this she didn't notice Charles himself. Not until she finished sketching, looked up, and met his eyes.

He was staring straight at her. Linda had no idea when she'd been spotted. His eyebrows were knitted and his jaw was clenched. There was a slow-burning fuse behind his eyes, it was on the point of detonation.

An apprehensive chill spread through Linda's gut. She stuffed the notebook and pen into her purse. Charles was already on his feet, heading for the door.

Linda was a child again, caught spying and in sudden, terrible trouble. She cursed the weakness in her legs, too slow to take her away from the window and back to the safety of the comic store.

She picked up speed as she crossed the concourse, praying that Frank hadn't closed up for the day, wondering what excuse she'd give for her sudden disappearance. The crowds had dispersed and the mall was suddenly very empty.

The comic store was in sight but Linda was exposed and vulnerable as Charles reached the doorway of the coffee shop.

"You better run," he shouted after her. "Spying on me. You ever hear of the Fourth Amendment, or the right to privacy? It's in the constitution, why don't you try reading it, you feminazi?!"

Most of the customers had gone by the time Linda got back. She muttered her apologies to Frank. He wasn't pleased by her sudden departure. He wanted to know why she'd deserted the event before it was through.

Linda tried to explain what she'd done but found it impossible to express the complex series of impulses that led her to leave the store. She didn't really understand them herself.

Anna had left and taken the pages Linda drew, probably

assuming they were for her. Linda had nothing to back up her explanation. It would have been hard to tell Frank about the Li'l Ghost Girl haunting her art, even if she'd had the pages as proof. Without them, it would be impossible to talk about. She hadn't worked out, in her own mind, why she felt compelled to respond to a wraith who possessed her pen at the strangest times.

Linda didn't want to leave the store by herself. She was afraid Charles would be hanging around, waiting for her in the parking lot, determined to get her alone. Frank wasn't keen to walk her to her car, he had to lock up the store and set the alarm and he didn't close for another hour.

Luckily, Mike, the guy she'd drawn with Lord Fiara De Sange, was a gentleman and insisted on walking her to the parking lot.

Linda climbed behind her wheel and waved to him, to show she was okay. When she pulled out onto a busy intersection, she noticed her hands were shaking on the wheel.

In the past few months, she'd been shot at by armed militia and harassed by Federal agents. Yet, a run-in with a crazed loon in a comic shop had deeply rattled her. Linda didn't know it then, but there was worse to come.

Much worse.

CHAPTER 4

AFTER CHATTING TO WEEZIE, Linda sat at her drawing board and tried to sketch out a new page. By mid-afternoon she had to admit it wasn't going well, the page layout was wrong, and the action didn't flow. Her head wasn't in it, and neither was her heart.

Every time she put a line on the page, Linda felt judged, as though Charles and his friend **A Bombinator** were looking over her shoulder and shouting abuse. It was hard enough to overcome her self-doubt when she sat down to draw without having this to contend with. She put down her pencil and opened her laptop. She'd feel better once she'd blocked them on social media and gotten them out of her mind altogether.

Linda grabbed her purse and dug out Carver's notebook and pen. They felt comfortable and familiar in her hands, like two old friends. As though she'd owned them longer than a few months. How had she ever considered selling them? There was an uncomfortable weight in her chest that felt like guilt.

Getting rid of them had been part of distancing herself from Richard and McPherson. The madness, paranoia, and threat to her life had gotten to be too much and she needed space.

It had taken over her life for a few months and Linda had forgotten who she was. She still went cold when she thought about how she acted at the comic con, the way she talked to people she really cared about.

She had to keep reminding herself of this, keep going back to the shame she felt when she thought about her actions at the con. Because, if she was really honest with herself, a big part of her missed the thrill and excitement she'd felt at being part of the investigation. Having access to special information had made her feel important, and it had kept her darker feelings at bay, distracted her from her own problems. Problems that Paul's disappearance had brought into sharp relief.

Linda thought she'd put all that behind her now. Promised herself she was through with Richard, McPherson, and the disappearances. Through with investigating Carver's tragic life and the mystery surrounding his eventual fate.

But the phone call with Weezie had made her realize she was far from through. Linda missed the thrill of the investigation and the way it made her feel. Had the encounter with Charles affected her more deeply if it was triggering her like this? Was the stress making her fall back into bad habits? Her therapist had warned Linda about this. All the more reason to get Charles and his crony out of her life for good.

Linda opened the notebook and turned to the page where she'd jotted down the direct message. She searched social media for **A Bombinator**, intent on reporting and blocking him, but she couldn't find any account with that name. She tried searching for the icon she'd drawn, showing the broadsword cleaving a bleeding heart, but didn't have any luck there either.

This wasn't too strange, even though she'd seen Charles messaging **A Bombinator** only yesterday. He was a troll and they deactivated accounts all the time to avoid getting shut down. She told herself this was fine, but she was breathing a little too heavily and for a second the room seemed to list and tilt, like a ship lost at sea.

Linda did find Charles' account and discovered, to her surprise, that he was following her. Maybe he knew what happened to **A Bombinator**. For reasons she couldn't quite articulate, it was suddenly important to know where his account had gone. She followed Charles back so she could direct message him.

Linda began the message several times. She was nervous about chatting to him. She had to strike just the right tone so she didn't trigger him. It felt like tiptoeing through a minefield.

Linda Corrigan @LindaCherself

Hi,

We ran into each other at the signing I did yesterday. I'm not trying to pick a fight, picture me waving a white flag, I just wanted to ask you about your friend **A Bombinator**. His account seems to have disappeared. You mentioned, when we met, that you knew him, so I wonder if you know why his account was taken down.

Linda wasn't certain if he'd get back to her, but he must have been online when she messaged because he sent a reply within ten minutes:

Charles S @TakeItAllB*tch

Bitch, i don't know what ur smoking, but u must be tripping!!! I didn't go to no signing yesterday, i was back at my crib getting ripped. I wouldn't go nowhere near any signing u was at, ever!!!

That wasn't the response she was expecting. He was so keen to confront her yesterday, why was he pretending it didn't happen? Was he afraid she was going to press charges? She tried again:

Linda Corrigan @LindaCherself

I'm not trying to cause a scene, or make any accusations, but I met you yesterday. Don't you remember? You told me I was a "talentless libtard feminazi" and you mentioned your friend **A Bombinator**. Later, I spied you through a coffee shop window (sorry about that btw) and you weren't too pleased. I notice **A Bombinator** isn't on Twitter now. All I want to do is check if you know what happened to him? That's all. If you could help I'd be really grateful.

Charles didn't reply. Linda fretted. She went back to her drawing board, tried to get her layout to work, failed, and fretted some more. Two hours later a message came in.

Charles S @TakeItAllB*tch

Okay, i've had all i can take with the insults, the accusations and the fantasies! U libtards. Really piss me off u know! I told u i never went to no signing, i don't know no **A**

Bombinator and i never have. Why are u making all this up? Really, don't u have anything better to do with ur time than persecute honest, decent folk like me? I don't know what ur talking about.

If u get in touch with me 1 more time about this i will not only report and block ur ass, i will track u down, come to ur house, tear off ur head and shit down ur throat!! U got me????

Linda shut her laptop. She couldn't stop blinking. Her head spun and she was suddenly aware she was breathing too fast. She lifted her hands from her desk and backed away from it with her palms out, like she was surrendering.

Such hostility and aggression. She should be used to it. She wasn't a stranger to trolls and had caught her fair share of flack. Even still, it felt like she'd been slapped in the face.

Something didn't sit right. He'd been so keen to tell her he was on a mission yesterday. So full of self-importance and false righteousness. He openly flaunted his association with **A Bombinator** in front of a crowd of people. Now he was refusing to admit he'd even been to the signing.

There was surely a rational explanation to all this. **A Bombinator** had probably told Charles off for using his handle and shut down his account before he got reported, or worse. Then Charles had panicked when Linda contacted him and had gone on the offensive.

Linda wanted to believe that. But this all felt horribly familiar. A nagging doubt was plaguing her. A doubt about the nature of the reality she was living in. What if this was exactly like what had happened with Paul?

There was an easy way to fix this. She grabbed her phone and went through her contacts until she found the comic store. She called the landline but it went straight to voicemail, so Linda tried Frank's cell. He picked up on the third ring.

"Hey, Frank, it's Linda,"

There was a pause. "Is everything okay?"

"Yeah, everything's fine, I'm just, um . . . calling to apologize for bailing on you at the signing."

Frank sighed. "Why'd you take off?"

"I thought I saw something outside, someone actually, I had to go check it out."

"Who did you see?"

"It was the shouty guy, Charles, I found out his name is Charles."

"What shouty guy?"

"You know, the one who interrupted the signing at the start, who got up and called me a libtard, feminazi, and mentioned his troll buddy **A Bombinator**."

"When did this happen?"

"At the signing, you were there. You said the guy was banned from your store."

"Linda, I have no idea what you're talking about."

"Really?"

"No."

"You don't remember a guy getting up at the start and shouting at me?"

"No."

"Honestly?"

"Honestly. Linda, what is going on here?"

There was no point continuing with this conversation, and Linda knew it. Now it was her turn to sigh.

"Nothing's going on. Look, I'm sorry, I think I've gotten a little confused, so many comic stores in such a short space of time, I tend to get them mixed up. There was a guy at another signing I did recently, I found out his name is Charles, he got up and attacked me, verbally I mean, not physically. He really laid into me, and he mentioned this other guy who's been trolling me online, trying to make me feel I'm not safe anywhere. It just really got to me, is all."

"I had no idea. That's awful. You should have said something, that'll shake anyone up."

"I know, I know, I was trying to put it behind me, but it obviously got me worse than I thought. I've been under a lot of pressure recently and I think this just pushed me over the edge. I'm sorry that I got confused and I'm really sorry I bailed on you like that."

"Forget about it, no harm, no foul. Trust me, it's far from the worst thing that's happened at a signing. Why is it all the talented ones are crazy? Except you, of course."

"You're saying I'm not one of the talented ones?"

"I'm saying you're not crazy. Listen, I loved having you in my store and you know you're welcome back any time, right?"

"Thanks, Frank, I love your store and you're always such a decent guy. Any time you need me, I'm there, okay."

"Okay, Linda, you take care now."

"You, too."

Linda hung up. She massaged her temples with her fingers. It was happening all over again, wasn't it? She could call every person who attended that signing, if she had their numbers, and all of them would say the same thing—no one got up and shouted at her. She was the only one with that memory.

Even the guy who'd been so proud of himself refused to admit he was there. He'd been egged on by his internet buddy—**A Bombinator**—and he'd made a point of telling Linda about this. Now Linda couldn't find any trace of this guy he'd been chatting to online.

Did that mean he'd disappeared too, just like Paul? Disappeared so completely no one else could remember he even existed? If he had, that might explain why no one could remember Charles at the signing. If **A Bombinator** hadn't existed, he wouldn't have encouraged Charles, and if Charles hadn't been encouraged he wouldn't have gone.

Linda glanced over at the notebook and pen. Then it hit her. She'd copied down **A Bombinator's** name and sketched his logo in the notebook, just like she'd sketched a portrait of Paul. Was that why she remembered him when no one else did?

Were there any other similarities between Paul and **A Bombinator**?

A Bombinator bragged to Charles that he 'might just have gotten my hands on the only copy of *Tales that Draw You In*.' Paul mentioned that he 'might have a little something cooking on the Carver front,' and he was just about to 'pull off an interesting little deal.'

Did that deal involve a copy of the original art for *Tales that Draw You In*? Had Paul located the same copy that **A Bombinator** stumbled on? Was he in negotiations to publish it just prior to disappearing? If so, what was the connection between a mythic lost comic and the disappearance of two human beings?

Linda looked down at her hands. Only they weren't her hands. They looked like her hands but there was something wrong with them, they didn't belong to her. She could move them but they were someone else's.

She tasted bile at the back of her throat, but it wasn't her throat, nor was it her stomach that was so nauseous. Her office, her possessions, and her whole apartment were wrong, they looked right but something was missing from them. As though an essential part of their reality had been siphoned off, leaving them empty replicas, hollow copies of the real thing.

It was as if Linda had taken a step in the wrong direction and the whole world had moved on without her. She was the only person who realized how things had changed. No one else knew and no one else cared. She could point to the proof she had, she could shout it in their faces, but everyone would just think she was crazy.

No, not everyone, there *were* two other people who believed her, but she'd turned her back on them.

Linda let out a deep breath of despair and dropped her head onto her desk. She was never going to find her way back to the old world, or even be a part of this strange new one, until she'd worked out what had happened to Paul and this **A Bombinator** guy.

And she was never going to work out what happened to them without Richard and McPherson's help. She'd promised herself she was through with them and the investigation. She hated to go back on her promises but, for the sake of her sanity, she had to go back down the rabbit hole.

CHAPTER 5

LINDA PRESSED THE BUZZER. The sky was leaden and overcast. It had been raining since she caught the ferry from West Midtown.

The sky had been clear when she left her apartment so she hadn't brought an umbrella. She didn't know Jersey City. She'd waited twenty minutes to catch the Light Railway from Paulus Hook, to go two stops and walk three blocks in the pouring rain. It would have been quicker to walk the whole way.

McPherson hadn't taken Linda and Richard off the payroll or canceled their status as special investigators. But now they had a 'unique protected status,' meaning their association with the FBI was deniable. Other operatives would only be told about them on a 'need-to-know' basis. McPherson was still owed a few favors in the Bureau, which was how he was able to do this.

Linda found this clandestine approach baffling. It wasn't how she imagined the FBI worked. McPherson assured her the FBI didn't operate the way most people expected, and the things you saw on TV were convenient fictions meant to reassure the public.

McPherson had scheduled their first meeting at an office complex, on the edge of Exchange Place, Jersey City's business district. According to McPherson, the FBI had false-front financial offices all over the country.

Linda pressed the buzzer again. She hoped her knapsack was as waterproof as the manufacturer claimed.

Richard's voice came out of the intercom. "Hi, um, who is it?"

"It's Linda, of course. Can you let me in? I'm soaked."

"Sure, give me a moment, to find the right button. Okay, how about this?"

Linda pushed the door but it didn't give. "No, I'm still stuck in the rain."

"What? Oh, sorry, try it now."

The door buzzed and clicked, and Linda entered. The lobby hadn't been cleaned for months. The elevator took her to the seventh floor. Richard met her in the corridor. His face flushed when he saw her and he shifted from foot to foot, scratching at his elbow. He opened his arms as she approached and for one awful moment, she thought he was going to hug her. An affectionate smile and a pat on the arm held him at bay.

"It's, um, this way." He opened the door to the office suite and showed her into the conference room.

McPherson got up when Linda entered and pulled out a chair for her to sit, ever the gentleman. His manner was as solicitous as Richard's was awkward. Neither one of them knew how to act around her.

The conference room was small. There was a long glass table with eight chrome leather chairs, over a decade old. On the far wall was an interactive whiteboard, which may have been used for presentations once. Linda could briefly see the Hudson River from the large window, between the other high-rise offices.

McPherson took his seat. "You're looking well."

"Thanks, you too."

Richard grinned and rubbed the back of his neck. "It's so good to see you. I couldn't believe it when I heard we were back on the road. I've been doing a lot of digging, I've got so much to show you, including a bombshell or two."

McPherson raised his index finger. "In a moment, first I'd like to hear what Linda's got to say."

Linda cleared her throat. "Well, I thought I was done with all this. I *was* done with all this, but then it happened again."

Richard leaned forward. "What happened?"

Linda unzipped her knapsack and pulled out Carver's notebook. Thankfully, the rain hadn't gotten to it. She turned to the page where she'd copied down **A Bombinator**'s message to Charles and told them about the signing.

Richard stared at the pages of Carver's notebook. "That's weird."

"Tell me about it."

McPherson rubbed the bridge of his nose. "You think this is connected to Carver?"

"One of the last things Paul said to me was he might pull off a deal concerning Carver. He seemed quietly excited. I don't think it's too big a stretch to assume he located a copy of Carver's lost art. Not when that same art turns up, a few months later, in the hands of some asshole who's trying to rip someone off. Especially when said asshole disappears just as mysteriously."

"And you're sure he disappeared?"

"I couldn't find any trace of him."

"He hasn't just deactivated his account, or something?"

"I'm not a hundred percent sure. Maybe someone at Quantico could run a trace on the account, find out who owned it and if he still exists. I'm willing to bet they'll come up with nothing though, no account, no name, no history of it ever having existed."

Richard tapped Carver's notebook. "Outside of these pages."

"Exactly, if I hadn't written down his Twitter handle and drawn his logo, I doubt I'd remember him or his trolling either. It's the notebook that clinches it for me."

"So, you really think the art for *Tales that Draw You In* still exists?"

Richard was geeking out. It was like someone had told him they had proof Santa Claus and the Tooth Fairy were real.

"I think it's causing the disappearances we're investigating."

McPherson looked skeptical. "And it's causing them how, exactly?"

"I don't know."

Richard stroked his beard. "My best guess—it's the Shadows in the Cave."

"How do you figure?"

"It *has* to be, who else has the influence to make a person disappear and eradicate all trace of them?"

Linda sat back in her chair and stared up at the ceiling. "I don't know, it's just . . . it doesn't sound plausible to me."

Richard frowned. "Why not?"

"I saw a whole convention forget an important member of the industry in one afternoon. This guy was huge, practically everyone there would have read at least one comic with his name on it, but in less than twenty-four hours no one could remember he'd ever been alive. Not even his mom, who doted on him. How could any human agency pull that off?"

Richard shrugged. "Well, as I told you, we have the technology to selectively remove memories."

"How could they selectively remove memories from so many people in such a short space of time?"

"Maybe they put something in the air conditioning, some sort of gas that causes selective memory loss."

Linda shook her head. "Even if that was possible, why didn't it affect me?"

"Because you have the notebook."

"How would that stop me being brainwashed by an invisible gas?"

"Perhaps the antidote was embedded in its pages, so it didn't affect you after you touched it."

"Paul touched it, too, he gave it to me."

"And they made him disappear, so it doesn't matter whether the gas or the antidote affected him."

Linda shook her head and stared out of the window. "I'm sorry, Richard, I know you're trying and I don't want to pick a fight, it just doesn't sound plausible."

Richard tapped his pen on the table. "None of this sounds plausible. I'm trying to come up with the simplest, most direct explanation, you know—Occam's razor. If it wasn't the Shadows in the Cave, then who was it? Ghosts? Aliens? Atlanteans?"

"I don't know, but if the Shadows in the Cave are involved, then it's indirectly."

McPherson held up his hands to bring calm. "Okay, why don't we look at what we can comfortably surmise? Number one, the reason we know about these disappearances is because Linda and I wrote names down in books belonging to Carver, this means we remember them, when no one else does.

"Number two, we know that at least one victim got hold of the art for this book we keep hearing about—*Tales that . . .* " McPherson made circles in the air with his index finger.

"*Draw You In*," Richard finished.

McPherson nodded his thanks. "Another victim was a comic editor, who might have been about to buy the art, and the victim I investigated was a dealer in comic art. He was also about to do a deal before he disappeared, so it's not too much of a stretch to suppose that all three of these men came across a copy of this original art."

"Number three," Richard jumped in. "Just before *he* disappeared, Carver was involved in a government sponsored program to investigate psychic phenomenon. A program that was secretly backed by the Shadows in the Cave."

Linda held up her hand. "Wait a minute, do you know that for a fact?"

Richard took a battered leather briefcase from the floor and put it on the table. He looked like a junior executive about to give a presentation, aside from his Superman T-shirt.

"I have a very good source that can confirm it."

"You mean this government mole guy you found on the dark web?"

"Dierngewrit, that's right."

"I'm not sure I can pronounce that, even though I've heard you say it. Can we just call him DG for short?"

"Okay, if that helps."

"It does, and you're certain he's legit and not just some guy in his mom's basement who's larping?"

"Oh, he's legit, all right. In fact, it's thanks to his info on Operation Consciousness that I was able to track down this guy."

Richard took a black-and-white photo from the briefcase and placed it on the table. It was around thirty years old and showed a short, bespectacled man with close-cropped, thinning hair and piercing eyes. He was wearing a lab coat.

Linda picked the photo up. For a second, her senses sharpened and everything seemed hyper-real. She didn't think she'd seen this man before, but she also felt like she knew him, as though she was holding a family photo. "Who's this?"

"It's Doctor Roland Hepplewhite, the last surviving member of Operation Consciousness. He lives in an ashram in San Diego."

"Wait, you've found someone from the program who actually knew Carver?"

"Told you I had a bombshell to share."

McPherson steepled his fingers and sat forward. "Will he talk to us?"

"He's avoided my questions so far, but he's agreed to meet. He wants us to go to him."

Linda turned to McPherson. "Will the Bureau foot the travel bill?"

"It'll take a bit of wrangling, but I think I can arrange it."

Linda beamed at Richard. He deserved it. The tension in the room dissipated, like a knotted muscle relaxing.

"Looks like we have a new avenue for our investigation."

Richard put the photo back in his briefcase. Linda knew he was dying to share the rest of the contents with them, but instead he closed it, looking pensive.

"And you're sure you want to carry on with the investigation? I mean, don't get me wrong, I'm thrilled that you're back with us, but hasn't your career just taken off? I've been reading all these reviews in the comic press and you're tipped for big things. Won't this investigation get in the way of that?"

Linda smiled. She was genuinely touched that Richard would worry about that.

"I've been thinking about that myself, for the past few days. The sudden interest in my work surprised me more than anyone and I know I should be capitalizing on it. But to be honest, I haven't turned out a page I'm happy with since I left the investigation. I keep trying, I sit down at my drawing board every day but I just don't seem to be able to do it. My heart isn't in it and my mind's elsewhere. It's with this investigation.

"I don't think I'll be able to think straight or go back to my old life until I've found out why these people are disappearing and what it all has to do with Carver, this government program, and even the Shadows in the Cave. I know the investigation wasn't great for my mental health, or my wellbeing, I'm sure it's been rough on you guys too. But I took the red pill, you know, I can't unsee what I've seen and I can't go back. Not until we've fixed this."

McPherson nodded, sagely. "Couldn't have put it better myself."

Richard banged the table with his fist. "Amen to that."

CHAPTER 6

"**GOD, I HATE** this heat." Richard turned up the rental car's AC.

Linda shook her head. "You can take the boy out of the East Coast . . ."

"You're not taking the East Coast out of this boy. This is unseasonably hot, even for the west coast."

"Yeah, but it beats the rain on the East Coast."

"Nothing beats the air conditioning in my motel room. Speaking of which, when we're done at the ashram there's something I really want to show you both."

"Now I'm worried."

"No, this is important. You both have to come by my room this evening, okay?"

McPherson broke his silence without taking his eyes off the road. "Okay."

"Promise?"

"I said 'okay,' already."

They turned off the I-15, Linda was content to sit in the back, watching the hills and occasional oak tree roll by.

They took the San Pasqual Valley Road out of Escondido passing a Safari Park and a historic battlefield. Halfway to the town of Ramona, they turned off onto a two-lane black top and climbed a hill.

Richard pointed to the road. "The turning's coming up on the right."

McPherson glanced at the built-in Sat-Nav. He'd followed it the whole way, politely ignoring Richard's directions. A painted sign pointed to a dirt road. It said, 'Horizon View Ashram.' McPherson took the turning.

The dirt road led to a paved parking lot. Down at the far end of the lot were two Humvees and four white SUVs, with an orange lotus blossom stenciled on their hoods. McPherson parked alongside.

At the end of the parking lot was a well-tended path. There were yellow, hand-painted signs where the path forked. The sign on the left had the same lotus blossom and read 'Volunteers and Resident Guests.' It led to a group of dormitories, fashioned like log cabins. They reminded Linda of summer camp accommodations.

The sign on the right-hand path was larger: *Brotherhood of Self Actualization*, and beneath the lotus blossom: *Horizon View Ashram—Reception*. This led to a long A-frame barn behind some trees.

As they walked toward the barn, Linda voiced her reservations. "Is it me, or does this place have a strange vibe? Not a bad vibe, just a strange, flaky one. What's the 'Brotherhood of Self Actualization'?"

Richard looked around him. "It's a minor religion. Kind of a cross between Hindu and Christian beliefs. Adherents practice yoga in order to become one with Christ, Krishna, and God."

"Does it have many followers?"

"More than you think. It makes millions a year, with its publishing wing and whole-food business."

Linda shook her head. "And they worship Ganesh and Jesus at the same time?"

Richard chuckled. "Actually, they worship Swami Ghoshtananda, the guru who founded it, he came over from India in the thirties. They consider him a major religious figure, on par with Mohammed or the Buddha."

"So, he was some kind of saint, then?"

Richard smirked. "Well, that's what they'd like you to think. He preached celibacy, abstinence, and yoga to find communion with God. But for decades there's been rumors about a harem of young, female followers, even when he was in his eighties."

Linda pulled a face. "Eew, really?"

"Three illegitimate children have come forward in the last twenty years. The grandchildren are suing the Brotherhood for a slice of the action. They won the right to determine where their grandfather is buried. The Brotherhood want to move his remains to a special shrine at their headquarters, in Boston, so people can make pilgrimages. The grandchildren are using the body as a bargaining chip in the negotiations."

"It all comes back to money, doesn't it?"

"Don't tell that to the monks."

They arrived at the barn. It was two stories high and as long as a warehouse. Underneath the eaves, there was a stained-glass window in the gable. It showed a guru with long, flowing hair and beard, meditating in the lotus position. Below him was the ever-present lotus blossom.

A porch ran around the front and right-hand side of the barn. Beyond the barn, Linda saw a collection of single-story buildings, of the type you'd see on a college campus.

McPherson pointed to the barn. "Speaking of monks."

The main doors opened. Three monks stepped out to greet them. They closed the doors behind them and stood close to the barn, as if guarding the entrance.

All three monks had buzzcuts and wore loose orange robes. The monk on the right had wire-frame spectacles. The monk in the middle was Indian, he looked to be in his mid-fifties and was shorter than Linda. He wore a purple and gold sash over his orange robes, a sign of rank.

"I am Brother Paramahansa, and this is Brother Prem and Brother Das," the Indian monk said. "I'm afraid Brother Ishtananda, cannot see you today, or any other day."

"By Ishtananda, do you mean Doctor Roland Hepplewhite?" Richard asked.

Brother Paramahansa bowed slightly "That is no longer his given name, but yes."

McPherson's eyes narrowed. "Why can't he see us? We've come a long way."

"After much meditation, and careful counsel with his masters, Brother Ishtananda has come to realize it would not be in the best interests of his spiritual development, or the aims of the Brotherhood."

The main doors opened behind the monks and an Asian monk in his early twenties popped his head out. He glanced nervously at Linda and the others, and pulled it quickly back in. Brother Prem gave him a cursory glance and frowned.

McPherson was not to be put off.

"So let me get this straight. You're attempting to break an

appointment with a government agent, when you, and many of your brothers, are guests in this country, is that right?"

"That is correct." Brother Paramahansa nodded with as much dignity as he could muster. He was wary of McPherson undermining his authority in front of the other monks. "I'm not a naturalized citizen, but I am here legally."

McPherson held up his hands in a non-judgmental way. "Well, Brother Hepplewhite, or whatever you're calling him, *is* a US citizen and it's his constitutional right to decide whether he wants to see us or not." McPherson dropped his hands, and dropped the pitch of his voice, as he looked into the monk's eyes. "Just as it's within my rights, as a government agent, to recommend that ICE check the immigration status of everyone living and working at this ashram."

A vein throbbed on Brother Paramahansa's forehead, and tiny beads of sweat appeared. His face appeared calm, despite this. "I've told you, everyone is here legally. All our paperwork is in order."

McPherson took a deep breath, looked down at the ground and shook his head as he let it out. Then he looked up and stared right at Brother Paramahansa over the top of his glasses. "Well, you see, that's the thing about ICE, once they start digging they don't stop until they find something, and everybody's got something they want to keep hidden. Same goes for the IRS."

"The IRS?" Brother Paramahansa was having trouble keeping his voice calm. "What do we have to do with the IRS? We are a charitable organization."

"With a commercial publishing wing and a whole-food business on the side. Last thing you want is an audit over something as foolish as denying us an hour of someone's time."

Brother Paramahansa exchanged glances with Brother Prem and Brother Das. He held up a finger to McPherson, as though he was about to deliver a sermon, and thought better of it. "Just a minute."

The monks went back into the barn. McPherson turned, with a self-satisfied smirk, to Richard and Linda. Richard rubbed his hands together and shot him a conspiratorial grin. McPherson shook his head. Richard put his hands in his pockets and stifled the grin.

The door opened and Brother Das, the monk with the wireframe spectacles, came out. "Brother Ishtananda has decided to see you after all." He held the door open for them to enter.

Linda followed McPherson and Richard into the entrance hall. Three long trestle tables sat along the far wall, covered with purple cloth. They contained a display of books and pamphlets about the Brotherhood and the Science of Self Actualization, surrounded by garlands of plastic flowers.

Framed black-and-white photographs of Swami Goshtananda hung on the walls. His long hair and beard were immaculately groomed, sometimes he wore a white cotton robe, in others just a loincloth. He always smiled and his eyes were filled with the wisdom of age and learning. His body was that of a thirty- or forty-year-old man even when his hair and beard were white.

Linda glanced around. "You know what, guys? Why don't you go ahead? I think I'll hang back and take a look around."

Richard and McPherson eyed her with surprise. Brother Paramahansa held up his finger and wagged it.

"No, I cannot allow that. This is a 'male-only' retreat."

Linda put her hands on her hips and raised her eyebrows. "Excuse me?"

"This is a safe haven from the temptations of the material world. Men come here to distance themselves from worldly pleasures. We cannot allow you to roam about and remind them of their baser desires. You can speak to Brother Ishtananda in the Library, but that is all the access we'll permit."

"You'll permit? Are you for real?"

"This is a religious establishment, we're completely within our rights. The monks here have taken vows of celibacy and abstinence."

"Yeah, and we all know how celibacy turned out for you."

Brother Paramahansa took several measured breaths. Linda recognized it as a yoga technique. His was a practiced stoicism. He was trained to stay calm under duress. But he couldn't stop the exasperation from flickering across his face. He'd heard those accusations one too many times.

Richard looked bemused. "C'mon Linda, you don't want to miss this interview, we could finally get some answers."

Linda shrugged. "Okay, then, take me to Ishtananda."

The monks led them down a corridor and into a book-lined room with desks and leather couches. Something felt wrong. It wasn't the flaky vibe Linda got from the place, it was deeper than that. It was why she'd wanted to skip out on the interview. She couldn't put it into words, but her pulse quickened and her head pounded as they entered the library.

Sitting at one of the desks, dressed in an orange robe, was a man in his late sixties. He was around five-seven and bald apart from a well-trimmed scattering of gray hair around his temples. He put on a pair of spectacles as they entered and his piercing, blue eyes leaped out at them.

Seeing him was a visceral sensation, like a punch in the chest. Linda caught her breath, winded. She'd never seen this man before, he didn't look at all familiar. So why did she feel like she knew him?

The perception was so strong it seemed to be pushing her from the room, like a presentiment that told her to flee, to get out of the library and away from the whole ashram.

Richard turned to look at her. "Are you okay? You've gone kinda pale."

Linda was sweating heavily. She mopped her forehead with the back of her hand. "Yeah, I think it's just the heat."

But it wasn't the heat, it was Ishtananda. Linda knew she was being irrational, knew she had no reason to be afraid, but she was. Afraid of what Ishtananda was going to tell them and what it might mean to her, personally.

CHAPTER 7

BROTHER ISHTANANDA GLOWERED at the three of them as they fetched chairs and sat around his desk.

"I just want you to know that I'm giving this interview under protest. I don't appreciate your heavy-handed tactics."

Richard slumped in his chair. His shoulders fell and so did his face. "We weren't being heavy-handed. We had an appointment. You said there were things that we couldn't discuss by email, because they were too sensitive, but you'd reveal the truth if we came to see you in person."

"That's before you started threatening to deport my brothers in the ashram. These are gentle men of God, not criminals. You shouldn't be threatening them with ICE."

Ishtananda's eyes narrowed and his jaw tensed. Linda could hear him grinding his teeth. He wasn't as adept at controlling his feelings as the other monks.

Richard fumbled for something to say. His jaw worked but no words came. He looked to Linda to help him, but she had nothing to say either, her stomach was in a knot. There was bile at the back of her throat and her hands were curled into fists. It was the thought of what Ishtananda had to say. Why was she in such a state about interviewing him?

In the end, it was McPherson who came to their aid. "I'm sorry for being heavy-handed. You're right, I shouldn't have come on so strong. This case has gotten under my skin and at times I don't use my best judgment. We've had so many doors closed on us, we've reached a dead end, and you're probably the only lead we have left. When your brother monks tried to stonewall us, well, I just lost it. I was wrong, but please don't let that affect this interview. I think you have an important story to tell and I think it should go on the official record. Someone with the power to do something ought to listen to you, and I think I'm that person."

Ishtananda wagged his finger at McPherson. "That's all very well for you to say, but you're protected by your position. The worst that's going to happen to you is getting demoted or side-lined."

McPherson held out his hands as a sign of admission. "Already happened, I've been side-lined and demoted in all but name because of my interest in this case. There's something here they don't want us to know. The same people who came after you have finished my career. Why let them get away with this? The truth needs to be in the public arena. We need to set the official record straight by making sure it includes your side of the story."

Richard cleared his throat. "Operation Consciousness has touched me too. It changed my life at the earliest age and I've never gotten over that. I grew up without a father, I lost so much before I even realized what had been done to me. I still don't know the truth. You could help with that. You have answers I probably don't even know I need. You've seen the things I blog about. You know I'm not a government goon and neither is Agent McPherson. He's one of the good guys. This is too big not to come out. We need some real juice for that to happen. We need to use government channels or nothing will change. They'll just deny everything and get away with it, once again."

Ishtananda shook his head and ran his right hand over the top of his forehead. "You didn't go through what I did. You weren't there, and they didn't try and destroy you, like they destroyed my career. I thought it might help to talk about it, but I'm not so sure."

Richard and McPherson didn't know what else to say. They'd made their pitch.

Ishtananda took a deep breath and tilted his head back. "I've done a lot of healing since I came to the ashram. I've built a new life and become a new person. This community, and the teachings of Ghoshtananda, mean everything to me. I don't want to harm them by discussing my former life, I don't want them to be discredited too. I don't want to put anyone in danger."

Richard looked to Linda for help. Panic rose in his face as he saw the whole interview going south. He was relying on her emotional intelligence. He wanted her to coax Ishtananda into cooperating, but she couldn't do it. She just froze. Her pulse quickened, her palms grew damp, and she couldn't think of a single thing to say.

McPherson appeared to have best read their situation. "Look, you've every reason to be cautious. With what you know, you're very probably in danger, and so are your brothers. You know the only way to guarantee your safety?"

Ishtananda's face turned white. He looked over his shoulder at Brother Paramahansa, hovering in the doorway, who appeared equally as grave, and then he turned back to McPherson.

"No."

"To go on the public record. That way, if anything happens to you, or the Brotherhood, suspicion will be thrown back on the people who want you out of the way. They've spent decades in the shadows, maybe longer. They know how to be discreet and they don't do anything to draw attention to themselves. If they know you've spoken to the FBI, they know questions will be asked if anything happens to you. Everything you say will be part of the official investigation and that leaves them wide open to scrutiny. You know as well as I do, that's the last thing they want. If we can find you, so can they. This is the best way to protect yourselves."

Ishtananda screwed up his eyes and massaged his temples. He let his head drop, took a ragged breath, and turned once more to Brother Paramahansa. The older brother closed his eyes, put his palms together and slowed his breathing. His lips moved as if in silent prayer. Finally, he opened his eyes and nodded.

Ishtananda looked relieved but still fearful. "Okay, I'll tell you what I know. But I want a full transcript of everything I say."

"That can be arranged."

He made eye contact with Paramahansa one last time. The older monk smiled and left them alone in the library.

Richard shifted in his chair, leaned forward, and began recording on his tablet. "Let's ease our way into this, and start with how you started working with Anton Le Corbusier?"

Ishtananda tilted his head back. He gazed over their heads, as if he were watching a playback of his memories in the air above them. "Well, the simple answer is I became his assistant after finishing a PhD in Biology, at Stanford. But, if I'm honest, it all began when I was twelve years old. During the summer I spent at my aunt's house.

"My parents were going through a messy divorce. My dad had split on us and stopped paying the mortgage. This meant my mom and I had nowhere to live. She was drinking a lot at the time and wasn't coping with the situation.

"It was decided that I should go live with my aunt, Sara. She was ten years younger than my mom and they didn't get along. My mom thought she was a flake. This was the early seventies, head shops were everywhere and Sara was a flower child, or an unwashed hippy, if you listened to my mom.

"I thought differently. Sara was fun. She wasn't much older than me and we liked the same bands and the same TV programs. She was cool. She let me eat what I wanted and go to bed when I felt like it. She was into 'following her bliss' and letting her 'freak flag fly,' so she didn't want to 'bring me down' by 'getting heavy' about nutrition or mealtimes.

"She liked to wear kaftans with bead necklaces and lots of bracelets. She had a birthmark on her right arm in the shape of the island of Madagascar. She told me that was because in a previous life she had lived there and she'd been a female shaman. She said she was still able to send her soul out, in her sleep, to walk its shores at night. One day she'd visit it for real and walk the beaches she knew so well from her dreams.

"I wasn't so young that I didn't take this with a healthy dose of skepticism. I was a precocious kid, prone to being a smart aleck. I told her if she ever got bored of Madagascar, she should come visit me. We could finally catch a late-night movie without her dozing off, cos she'd already be dreaming.

"She was like, 'You know what, I might just visit you some night. Would you be scared?' I was like, 'Not if you held my hand.'

"One night, she'd gone to bed early and I'd dozed off in the middle of a monster movie marathon. I dragged myself upstairs and fell on the bed without brushing my teeth or getting into pajamas.

"A few hours later, just before dawn, she shook me awake. I was groggy and didn't want to get up. It was a Sunday morning and I didn't have to be anywhere. I wanted to crawl out of my clothes and under the covers. She was insistent though. She hustled me out of bed and down the stairs before I realized what was happening.

"I asked her where we were going and she said to the neighbor's house. Then she took my hand and pulled me into the backyard. I was too old to be led by the hand. I was almost old enough to hold hands on dates. My aunt was only a decade older, and don't think I hadn't noticed how attractive she was.

"I can picture the walk across that yard as clearly as if it was happening now. The memory's never left me. Sara's birthmark was a deep crimson in the fading moonlight. The bracelets on her wrist jangled as she squeezed my hand and moved briskly next door.

"Her neighbor never locked her back door. People didn't back in those days. There were still safe neighborhoods. We let ourselves into the back kitchen. Sara told me to wait there while she went upstairs to fetch the neighbor.

"I still had no idea what was happening, or why we had to go to the neighbor's so early in the morning. The longer I waited in that kitchen, the less sense it made. I was confused and I began to panic. I couldn't tell what was taking my aunt so long, or why the house was silent.

"Finally, I left the kitchen and walked to the foot of their stairs. That's when the neighbor appeared. She was a middle-aged woman in a nightgown and bed jacket. Her hair was up in a net. She nearly jumped out of her bed jacket when she saw me.

"She shouted, 'Roland, what are you doing here at this time in the morning?'

"I began to get worried. 'Didn't my Aunt Sara come up and talk to you?'

"She blinked and shook her head. 'There's nobody up here 'cept my husband. I was having the strangest dream. I was at the beach on a tropical island and someone called my name. Then I woke up and, in a flash, I knew I had to come downstairs. You nearly frightened me to death standing there.'

"I was getting scared myself. 'Where's my aunt?'

"The neighbor padded down the stairs. 'Honey, she's most likely asleep in her bed next door, as you should be. I think we've both had a strange dream.'

"I didn't believe her. Something was wrong. I was close to tears. I ran up those stairs and pushed the neighbor to one side. I burst into all four bedrooms calling out my Aunt Sara's name, desperate to find her. I woke the neighbor's husband and he swore at me.

"Eventually, the neighbor got me to calm down. She took me downstairs and gave me a glass of milk. She wasn't pleased with the intrusion and marched me back to my aunt's place. The first thing I remember, when leaving her house, was how light it was for dawn. But it was only light on one side of the sky—the west side of the sky, which wasn't right for a sunrise.

"Then we saw the flames coming from the top floor of my aunt's house.

"The neighbor stood dead still. Her mouth hanging open. I began to look around for my aunt. It was more important than ever for me to know where she was. Maybe she hadn't gone up the stairs and I'd just thought that's where she was going. Perhaps she left the neighbor's house by the front door. She could be across the street or over at another neighbor's.

"Seeing how agitated I was, the neighbor made me wait in her yard while she went to phone for a fire truck. I guess she didn't want me tearing through her house again. The firefighters came in good time, and they got the fire under control even if they weren't able to save the house.

"The lights and noise of it woke the whole street. People stumbled from their porches in pajamas to see the flames being put out. I ran from neighbor to neighbor, asking everyone and anyone if they'd seen my Aunt Sara. Nobody knew where she was.

"When the flames were extinguished, the firefighters went into the house. I wanted to go in after them to see if any of my clothes, or books, or my catcher's mitt had survived. But the fire platoon chief held me back because it was too dangerous.

"Twenty minutes later, his men carried out a body on a stretcher. It was covered but I bolted toward it, desperate to pull away the cover and prove it wasn't my aunt. That she would come walking down that street at any moment. It took two of them to hold me back. I kept screaming, 'That's not my aunt! That's not my aunt!'

"A kindly firefighter put his hand on my shoulder. 'I'm sorry, son. She's gone. It was smoke inhalation. She didn't suffer. It happened in her sleep. She never woke up or knew what was happening.'

"I didn't believe him. 'No!' I screamed. 'No, she was just here. She woke *me* up. She got me out of bed. She took me next door. That's not her. It can't be her.' But it was. The coroner confirmed it, from her dental records, the next day.

"After several hours, I calmed down and gave them my mom's phone number. She came to get me the next day. I told everyone who'd listen how my aunt had gotten me out of bed and taken me next door. But no one believed me. The firefighters didn't believe me, neither did my mom or the therapist she hired.

"They tried to be kind, explaining to me that my aunt had never woken up. That she died in her sleep so she couldn't have left the house. My mom told me it had all been a dream. I'd been confused and walked next door, and thank God I did. My therapist said it had been a waking dream, like a fugue state, brought on by the trauma of the situation. It was my brain's way of dealing with the guilt of surviving when my aunt didn't.

"I was a rational child at heart, but I've never believed any of their explanations for what I saw and felt that night. Try as I might, and I have tried, I've never been able to shake the suspicion that I wasn't the one dreaming that night, when my aunt took hold of my hand, just like I'd asked her, and led me to safety.

"It was this suspicion that shaped the rest of my life."

CHAPTER 8

"**W**ow."

Linda thought of her own encounters with Li'l Ghost Girl. "So that experience turned you into a parapsychologist?"

Ishtananda shook his head. "Not at first. For a while, it pushed me in the opposite direction. I didn't understand what had happened and that scared me. I fled from the incident into the arms of science. That had provable hypotheses and empirical facts. I became an ardent rational-materialist.

"I graduated high school two years early and won a scholarship to Stanford. But the nagging doubt that there were things science couldn't explain wouldn't go away. Science couldn't account for what had happened to me.

"I was finishing up my PhD, when Le Corbusier came to lecture at Stanford. He wasn't known for parapsychology at that point. He'd published a few papers on the subject, in fringe journals, but he was still a well-regarded cellular biologist. I was thinking of working in this area so I went to one of his lectures on Polar Auxin transport. It was an inspiration. I approached him afterward and bombarded him with questions."

Ishtananda laughed, alive with the enthusiasm of his youth. Richard sat forward in his chair, caught up in the moment.

"How did he respond?"

"He took it well. He was pleased I was interested in his work. He encouraged me to read his papers. After that, I started going to all his lectures. He got used to seeing my face in the audience and answering my questions. We started to meet up for drinks on campus. Our conversations were very wide-ranging. No hypothesis was off limits, nothing was unthinkable, and that's how we got onto parapsychology."

Linda's brow furrowed and she tilted her head. "Okay, this may be a dumb question."

"There are no dumb questions."

"Is parapsychology considered a science?"

"It uses scientific methods and processes to interrogate disputed phenomena, so yes, it is a science. But that view is not shared by everyone, as we were about to find out."

"Did you tell Le Corbusier about your experience as a boy?"

"Eventually. I was afraid to at first. Becoming his friend was one of the most significant things that had happened to me. I was two years younger than my peers which made me socially awkward, I didn't have a wide circle of friends. I couldn't believe he'd taken an interest in me, he was such a fascinating man, with so many interests, from Eastern mysticism to old jazz 78s."

"78s?"

"Records, they used to be all the rage, before Spotify."

Linda blushed. "Sorry, I did know that."

"So, after several conversations about unexplained phenomena, I told him of my own experience and the impact it had on my life."

"How did he respond?"

"I didn't know it, but he had been secretly sounding me out for a project he was about to start work on. A benefactor, with a lot of money and even more influence, had left the college a major bequest. In return for this tax-free gift, the college had to undertake a scientific investigation into the existence of telepathy and other psychic human abilities. Because of my personal experience, he thought I would be perfect for the position of research assistant.

"I don't know if you guys can appreciate how big a deal that was to me. I was just finishing my PhD on a bursary, I'd come to Stanford on a full scholarship. I was flat broke and looking for any academic jobs I could find. The most I'd hoped for was teaching a few classes at a community college to people who were probably my own age. And here was Le Corbusier offering me a prestigious position on a Stanford research project. I knew that parapsychology was a contentious field, but I figured it would be a stepping stone to other research. I was soon to learn how wrong I was.

"It became apparent the Dean and faculty saw Le Corbusier as a safe pair of hands. I think they honestly believed he was going to take six months to thoroughly disprove the existence of psychic phenomena, and then they could pocket their little dividend. But

Le Corbusier had other ideas. He was already developing his grand theorem of 'Multi-Modal Consciousness.'"

Richard held up a hand, as though he was in class. "Wait, I've read about this online. It's linked to Rupert Sheldrake's theory of Morphic Resonance isn't it?"

Ishtananda looked a little pained, moving his head from side to side as he searched for the right words. "There's a lot of crossover. Le Corbusier did correspond with Sheldrake for a while, to compare notes."

Linda couldn't keep the confusion from her face. "Pretend for a minute that I have no clue what you're talking about and explain this resonance and multi-modal thing to me."

Ishtananda took a deep breath. "Morphic Resonance is a theory that Rupert Sheldrake came up with. He suggests every living organism is surrounded by a field of energy, both within and outside, like a magnetic field. Collectively, these fields comprise a shared consciousness. You've heard of Jung's collective consciousness, right?"

"Right."

"Well, this is similar, like a holding field or the cloud on your computer. Only it contains perceptual and behavioral information, like memories, thoughts, and the way people do things."

"Could you give me an example of that?"

"Playground rhymes, ever wondered how they spread so fast?"

"Word of mouth?" Linda said.

"You'd think so, but for these rhymes to spread by word of mouth, would take decades. But children all over the country just wake up one morning knowing them, without knowing how. If you train a rat to run a maze in London, then rats, from the same genus, in Sydney, or Moscow, can also run that maze without ever being taught. No one knows why."

"And you think that's morphic resonance?"

"Ever had the feeling you're being watched? You turn round and see someone staring at you. Across a crowded room, a busy plaza, or even the building opposite. Where does the feeling come from? How do we know we're being watched?"

"That's a lot of different things you've covered there."

"And they're all explained by morphic resonance. Le Corbusier took it a lot further. He suggested these morphic fields were like amniotic fluid for the evolution of consciousness."

Linda shook her head. "Okay, you're losing me again. Is this your multi-modal thing?"

"Multi-modal consciousness, yes. Le Corbusier always used the analogy of a unicellular being. Once upon a time, all life on earth was unicellular, like amoebas. Then, over time, we saw the development of multicellular lifeforms. It happened slowly at first, but over millions of years we ended up with the killer whale and the human being. Le Corbusier's hypothesis was that consciousness was going to do the same thing. Individual consciousnesses were eventually going to evolve into multi-modal consciousnesses. Superhuman, god-like consciousnesses, made of many singular consciousnesses. Morphic resonance was the medium through which this was going to happen. He even predicted the revolution in information technology. He saw the internet as a way of priming ourselves for this development."

Richard tugged at his beard. "So, the internet is like one giant consciousness, made up of lots of individual consciousness, almost like cells?"

"Exactly."

McPherson drummed his fingers on the table, a little impatiently. "What did the faculty think of his theories?"

"They hated them. But not as much as the results we were bringing in."

"So, you proved the existence of psychic phenomena?"

"We certainly thought so. Five experiments, under laboratory conditions, and the results were impressive. We had a success rate of seventy percent. Our data was conclusive, and peer-reviewed. But the faculty dismissed our findings as 'data bias' or 'confirmation bias.' They brought up every kind of bias, except for the most obvious bias staring them in the face, their *own* bias. Our data couldn't be right because psychic phenomena didn't exist, and because psychic phenomena didn't exist our data wasn't right. It was a closed argument from a set of closed minds.

"We were accused of quackery, fakery, and practicing 'pseudo-science.' The faculty were frightened of our results and frightened of becoming a laughing stock. They wanted to shut us down and spend the bequest elsewhere. Then Carver turned up, and the entire game changed."

CHAPTER 9

LINDA FELT A node of anxiety building in her gut. She began to get out of her seat until McPherson caught her eye and shook his head. She sat back down. Why did she feel this way? What was going on?

"How did Carver get involved with your program?" Richard asked.

"One of the grad students assisting with our experiments went along to his gatherings. It was the very early eighties, the new age movement was starting up and there were lots of gurus crawling out of the woodwork. Rachel, that was the student's name, heard about Carver from her friends. She was obviously taken with what she saw because she started petitioning to get him onto the program.

"Le Corbusier was reluctant. We'd had bad experiences with 'professional psychics,' and he wasn't keen on repeating them. Rachel was relentless though. She insisted he was the real thing, so Le Corbusier caved and agreed to meet. He was blown away when he did."

"So, Carver really did have psychic abilities? We've heard stories, from people we interviewed. Some claimed he could do strange stuff. But you're saying he displayed psychic powers under laboratory conditions?"

"Did he ever. He was a marvel. He breezed through every test we conducted, a hundred percent success rate. No one had seen anything like it. The results were incontrovertible. Our findings were peer-reviewed. We lent Carver out to research teams at several universities and they got identical results to us, even when they changed the parameters of the experiments to try and catch Carver out, which technically speaking was bad science. It didn't matter though, he still scored off the scale and they still got the same results."

"How come we know so little about this? Surely word would have gotten out and the media would have gotten hold of this. It should have changed the world of science forever."

Ishtananda sat up in his seat and jabbed a finger at Richard. "That was our problem, right there. It *should* have changed the world of science forever, but science didn't want to change, not in the way our research suggested. What we were suggesting was heretical. So, they shut down our program altogether, repressed our findings, and lied about the peer reviews. They charged us with fraud, and revoked Le Corbusier's tenure, saying we'd faked all our results and the peer reviews proved this. Even though every review, and every replicated experiment, had supported our findings. *They* falsified the records and accused *us* of fraud. It's beyond belief.

"They couldn't repress our findings altogether. We'd drawn significant attention from an important body—the US government. When Stanford closed us down, the government offered us full funding plus new premises, and they made Stanford hand over our research. We were elated. It felt like vindication, and the official recognition we deserved. What we didn't know, was it was simply the beginning of worse problems."

Richard looked incredulous. "How could things get worse than you've just described?"

"Carver started acting up. I think he wanted to be the next Uri Geller. He knew he was talented, and I'm sure he felt cheated out of the acclaim he deserved. He enjoyed the attention from an elite institution like Stanford. Everyone was dazzled by his talent, his weird charm, and his learning. For a high school dropout who drew funny books and peddled voodoo, he was widely read."

"So, what went wrong?"

"Things didn't pan out the way he hoped. No one wrote newspaper articles or invited him on TV. He could do all these marvelous things but the universities suppressed the evidence. I guess he probably felt it was the same old, same old. I mean, from what I can gather, this had been happening to him his whole life. Whenever he displayed his talents, people either didn't understand him, or thought he was too good to be true."

"What were Carver's talents?"

Ishtananda took a deep breath and steepled his fingers. "They were quite unique. He scored highly on the telepathic spectrum, and he displayed a tendency for precognition. But he had other abilities. As you might imagine, they revolved around his art."

"Can you be more specific?"

"If Carver drew someone's portrait, this gave him the ability to draw whatever they were seeing. It started with Zener cards."

"Those symbol cards with circles and stars and stuff?"

"Yes, they were standard tools in parapsychology. But we soon moved to other things, fruit, jewelry, even complex technical equipment he'd never seen before. At first we'd do it with the test subject behind a screen, then in the next room. Finally, we tried a different building and even a different city. Every time he got it right, and there were never any disparities. It wasn't just objects either, he could sketch the room from the test subject's perspective. It was uncanny, but it wasn't his strangest ability."

"You mean he had stranger abilities?"

"Much stranger. After we left Stanford, Carver kept pushing us to do other tests. He claimed he could draw the interior of people's minds. He would get test subjects to think of a memory and draw what they recalled as a collage of images. He could do the same with dreams. He'd unearth memories of shame or fear, traumas the subject was hoping to forget, secrets they didn't want revealed. It was the stuff of horror stories. Subjects were starting to get traumatized by what he was pulling from their minds. Especially when he started to draw their futures."

Linda had been sitting with her legs crossed, frowning at most of what Ishtananda was saying, captivated in spite of herself. She uncrossed her legs, becoming more engaged.

"Carver could draw people's futures?"

Ishtananda cleared his throat and an evasive expression crossed his face. "Well, that's a lot harder to substantiate than his other claims. We amassed some interesting evidence, but that line of our inquiry was shut down. You see, Le Corbusier had always believed fields of morphic resonance were four, or even five-dimensional in structure, as the fourth dimension is time, this would explain the human capacity for precognition. This wasn't a view his colleagues shared, not even Sheldrake."

"You said that line of inquiry was shut down," Richard said. "*Who* shut it down?"

"Our new sponsors—the US government. It wasn't of any use to the branch of government that was bankrolling us."

"You mean military intelligence?"

"You're going to think us naive, but it was the early eighties. The Cold War was on and we were up against an evil empire. I thought we were the good guys, that we stood for truth, justice, and the American way. All that stuff we read in superhero comics as kids. We knew the Russians were trying to weaponize ESP and I thought we could help defend our country."

Richard sat up in his seat. He was finding it hard to hide his excitement. "And they were interested in Carver's abilities?"

"You can see why. Think of how effective he'd have been in the field. They could have given him the photo of a Russian nuclear scientist and got him to draw whatever they were working on, blueprints, prototypes, the works."

"How did Carver feel about this?"

"He hated it. The minute he found the military was funding us, he wanted to quit. I think they got to him though, threatened him or something. He was different after we started working for the government, more truculent, less cooperative. Le Corbusier promised nothing would change, it would be exactly like it was before, and for a little while it was.

"Then things started to get really scary."

Linda found her palms were clammy. She had a strange feeling of foreboding as she leaned forward and asked: "How scary?"

"Very scary. We came into work one day to find armed soldiers checking our IDs. I was marched to a room where guys with buzz cuts and dark suits made me sign an NDA and a new contract at gunpoint."

"Seriously, they pulled a gun on you?"

Ishtananda looked a little embarrassed. "Well, no, but the room was full of armed guys and it was pretty intimidating. They weren't the sort of people you said 'no' to."

"Then what happened?"

"They told me we were relocating, but they wouldn't say where. Our labs and offices were being packed up by military personnel. Two armed soldiers drove me home and gave me an hour to pack my things. They stood there sneering while I rushed around my apartment trying to pack a suitcase. They even tried to stop me bringing a framed photo of my boyfriend. I shared the apartment with him at that point. I picked up the phone to tell him what was happening and they cut me off. Then they pulled the phone out of the wall. He left work to come say goodbye and they refused to let him into my apartment. It was private property but they commandeered it.

"I was in pieces when I got back to the lab. I was herded onto a troop carrier and driven for over twenty-four hours straight without a single stop. They gave us one bottle of water for the whole journey and a single meal of basic rations, which wasn't vegetarian, so I couldn't eat it. We had to sleep where we sat and pee in a mess can in front of our colleagues. No one would tell us where we were going or what was going to happen. I still have nightmares about that journey."

Richard sat up straight in his seat. He was tapping the table with his index finger and trying hard to control his excitement. "Where did the troop carrier take you, eventually, I mean?"

"To a secret compound in the middle of the Chihuahua Desert."

"About eighty miles south of Albuquerque?"

"Something like that, I'm not sure of the exact distance, but Albuquerque was the nearest city."

Richard raised hands in the air as if giving praise to God at a Bible meeting. His face was just as beatific and elated as his body language. "Operation Consciousness, I knew it, I knew it. That's what you were involved in, wasn't it? That's what we're talking about?"

"No one ever called it that, not to us. And it's not what we called our work. I only heard that name later when I'd gotten out."

Richard leaned over the table towards Ishtananda. His eyes had a wild quality and flecks of spit fell from his lips. "Did you ever meet a man called Donald Ford? He would have been in his early forties, around six foot high, a little thick around the middle. He was employed to monitor the psychological effects of the program. Looked like me, only without the beard or the Batman T-shirt."

Ishtananda shrank back in his chair, his arms crossed protectively. "I didn't meet any contractors. There were other personnel, but they were always in the shadows, we weren't allowed to interact with them."

McPherson put his hand on Richard's shoulder. "Take a breath."

Richard nodded, dropped his head, and breathed deeply. He took off his glasses, rubbed his eyes with a knuckle, then held up his hand. "I'm good."

McPherson turned to Ishtananda. His voice was soft and calming. "You'll have to excuse my colleague. This case has personal significance to him and he's a little invested."

Richard looked up. "I'm pretty sure my father died as a consequence of working at that compound. I've spent my life trying to prove it and to find out what really happened to him. I'm sorry if I got a bit carried away."

Ishtananda uncrossed his arms. There was compassion in his eyes and voice, but he was still guarded. "I understand. I'm sorry I can't tell you more about him. We might have met briefly, I don't know. I tried to put so much of what happened from my mind. It was a dark time for me. For all of us, your father wasn't the only one to lose his life there."

There was a moment's silence while everyone shifted uneasily in their seats. Then McPherson said, "Why don't we wind things back a bit? You say the compound was in the desert?" "It was hopelessly remote and so hot. Nothing grew there, no trees, no bushes, no wildlife. There were no roads, just a dirt track. There was barbed wire all around the twelve-foot fences and the only way on or off the compound was by jeep. We weren't allowed to drive them, only military personnel were."

Linda rubbed her chin. "Did anyone try and leave? I mean, you were free to go, right?"

"In theory we were free to go, but we didn't have any vehicles."

"Could you have walked?"

"We would have died of hunger or thirst before we got anywhere. There were armed guards at every exit and in the corridors of our sleeping quarters, which were like cells. They even had a nightly curfew."

"For real?"

Ishtananda nodded, a grave expression on his face.

Richard put his palms together, as if he were about to pray, trying not to get over excited. "So, were Carver and your colleagues the only people you interacted with?"

"No, there were other researchers at the compound. Some of them Canadian, some from Europe. We were discouraged from speaking about our backgrounds but all of them had been coerced into working there. There were also five other test subjects. A young Asian guy called Hyun Chul Lee, an Indian woman called Meera Kaur and a French woman called Valerie, I can't remember her surname. The other two guys were from the States. I think one of them was called Bob, or Bobby."

He held up his hands hopelessly, unable to recall more.

Linda put her elbow on the table and rested her chin on her palm. "Were the other test subjects as powerful as Carver?"

"In their own ways. Valerie was a remarkable Remote Viewer. Meera had exceptional telepathic abilities and was highly precognitive. But we didn't always understand the things she predicted. Chul Lee was another matter altogether. We never found a term for his talents, but it seemed he could influence matter, at an atomic level."

Richard squinted and wrinkled his nose. "Give me an example?"

"Well, he could touch certain objects and make them appear elsewhere in the compound."

"He teleported stuff?"

"It seemed to me he was getting the material world to absorb the object and spit it out somewhere else. He could alter the structure of physical objects by touching them too, turn things inside out that didn't actually have an inside. It's hard to explain, you'd have to see it and even then you'd have a hard time believing it. I didn't deal with the others, so I can't tell you about them."

"And you never had any contact with the people running the compound?"

"Not directly, they'd send up daily memos, outlining the work they wanted us to do, occasionally they addressed us through a one-way speaker system. They were observing our work from behind two-way mirrors, which happened quite a lot. Mostly the soldiers just barked orders at us."

"What work did . . . " Linda's voice was hoarse. She cleared her throat and started again. "What work did they want you to do?"

"They were interested in Le Corbusier's theories of Multi-Modal Consciousness. They wanted us to meld the minds of all six test subjects to create a being of pure consciousness, the next stage in evolutionary consciousness."

"Did you manage to do it?"

"Ultimately, I can't say. We did manage to create a telepathic bond between all six subjects. We were able to prove they were all sharing each other's thoughts and sensory perceptions, but only for a limited time. Sometimes for an hour, sometimes for a few seconds. We might have done better if they hadn't insisted on such bizarre working methods."

"You mean the two-way mirrors and the speakers?"

"Those didn't help, but I'm talking about the totally unscientific practices they had us engage in."

"Like what?"

"They had us incorporate magical symbols into our work and even demanded we perform rituals. They wanted us to conduct experiments at certain times of the day or month, all based on the positions of the continental shelves, or the movement of the Earth's strata. There was even talk, and this is really going to sound crazy, but there was even talk of them using other beings in their experiments."

"For real?"

"Oh yeah."

"You mean like aliens?"

"I don't know if they were aliens. I mean, I didn't see any of this. I just heard rumors of large insect-like creatures that were part real and part imaginary, and only half existed. They were used after we left."

Richard looked unconvinced. He made eye contact with Linda and McPherson. Linda could tell they were all thinking the same thing. That Ishtananda's mental health must have been affected by the stress.

Richard pressed on. "How did this help counter Soviet psychic espionage?"

"Your guess is as good as mine. By this point Le Corbusier and the other members of our team were starting to push back against the conditions being imposed. We began refusing to cooperate."

"What happened?"

"They confined us to our quarters, put guards on our door, and restricted us to one meal a day. When we still wouldn't play ball they marched us into a jeep with only the clothes we were dressed in and drove us to Albuquerque. They gave us a month's severance pay and told us to say nothing of what we'd been doing. We'd be in big trouble if we did. A few months later the whole project fell apart."

"What happened?"

"I don't have the full details. They cut off our access to the project, but we were able to make discreet inquiries from the few connections we still had. It seems they brought in some hi-tech equipment to supercharge the subjects' psychic bond. It was supposed to unite their minds into a powerful thoughtform, a sort of gestalt-consciousness. But it seems the experiment backfired."

Linda felt a subtle dread pooling in the pit of her stomach, but she didn't know why. "Backfired, how?"

"Two of the subjects died of a brain aneurysm. Valerie fell into a coma and never woke. I visited her in hospital in Albuquerque. Of the other three, two were in a permanent vegetative state and Carver simply disappeared."

"Disappeared?"

"For all intents and purposes. They never found him. They spent a lot of time and resources looking for him. Like I said, the compound was in the middle of nowhere. You couldn't survive a trek through the desert on foot, and all the exits were guarded. But somehow Carver slipped through the net or winked out of existence. Either way, they couldn't find any trace of him."

"So, that's it? That's all anyone knows about Carver's fate? He just disappears after an experiment goes wrong?"

"That's all *I* know. Someone might know more, but they haven't told anyone I've ever met."

"How many people did you ask?"

"I asked a lot of people. That was my problem. I thought I'd been discreet but I got a visit from some really frightening people. Men in black suits who warned me to leave off."

Linda made a pained face. "I've encountered some of them too. So, they scared you off."

"They did. Then the IRS audited me. That took the last of my savings, and I only narrowly avoided jail. I couldn't get an academic job anywhere in the country. One former colleague told me I was unofficially blacklisted. No one would even hire me as a janitor. To deal with the stress, I started meditating and doing yoga and that led me to the teachings of Swami Ghoshtananda and the Brotherhood of Self Actualization. The woman who ran my classes suggested I sign up for a two-year residency with one of the Brotherhood's communities in Nevada. I applied for that and was accepted. A couple years after that I began to train as a monk, and that led me here."

Ishtananda held his hands together, palms touching as if in prayer, and bowed, as though he'd just recited a litany. He raised his head and his eyes darted between the three of them, somewhat nervously.

"I'm happy here. Happier than I've been in a long time. I don't worry about academic politics, or my career, and I finally get some answers. Which is more than I got from parapsychology."

Linda tilted her head to one side. "Did you finally get the answer to what happened to your aunt?"

Ishtananda smiled a tight, humorless smile. "I know to ask the right questions, and to accept the answers I'm given." He took a deep breath and continued. "As you can see, I've taken a big risk confiding in you. What happened back then nearly broke me, physically, mentally, and spiritually, and I would dearly like to put it behind me.

"I hope you find what happened to Carver and I hope it helps you solve your case. But, please, be careful with the information I've given you. Don't let it come back to haunt me or damage our ashram."

McPherson's voice was sober. "We'll do our best."

Everyone got to their feet and began to collect their things. Before he turned off his tablet, Richard held up his index finger.

"Just one more thing." He sounded like Colombo. "Have you ever heard of an organization called the Shadows in the Cave?"

Ishtananda looked genuinely nonplussed. "Should I have?"

"They may be behind Operation Consciousness."

McPherson gripped the back of his chair. "We don't actually know that, it's just one of many leads we're following."

"But it's the best lead we've got."

"And it's also proprietary information."

Ishtananda went pale. He stood up and began to look nervously from McPherson to Richard. "I don't need to know this. I've already forgotten the name. Don't tell me anything else."

"That's all right, there's no need for concern. My colleague spoke intemperately."

Before Ishtananda could reply, Brother Paramahansa appeared with two other monks who escorted them to the parking lot.

McPherson started the car in silence. Richard looked awkward and penitent. "Sorry about mentioning the Shadows in the Cave."

McPherson just grunted and pulled out of the lot.

Richard turned to Linda in the back seat. "You okay? You

didn't seem yourself in there. You were kinda agitated the whole time."

Linda shook her head. "I'm fine, I . . . I'm just a bit frustrated we've hit another brick wall. We looked so close to solving the mystery and it's just thrown up another mystery. I guess I'm not great company today either."

"Okay."

Richard turned round and Linda stared out of the window. What she'd learned today had left her uneasy, and not just because it left unanswered questions. She thought the unease would lessen the further they got from the ashram, but it only increased.

She didn't know where the foreboding came from. It had the feel of a memory as much as a presentiment. But Linda knew they'd started down a road to disaster and there was nothing she could do to get off it.

CHAPTER 10

THE DRIVE BACK to the motel was mostly silent. Linda was still trying to shake her unease. McPherson seemed lost in thought but also strangely expectant. Richard made several attempts to engage them, but when they didn't reply he slumped in his seat and pulled out his phone.

After an hour, Linda suddenly said, "It's over then, isn't it? I mean, we barely got started again and now it's over."

Richard looked genuinely distraught. "Not necessarily."

McPherson drummed his fingers on the wheel. "It's my experience, in a case like this, that new leads often appear when you least expect it and when you think you've exhausted all other avenues."

Linda bit a hangnail on her thumb. "Do they, though?"

McPherson shrugged. "I found you two, didn't I? Just when I thought the case was stone cold."

Richard nodded. "It was colder than a corpse in deep freeze."

Linda shook her head. "Great analogy there."

"Well, it was, and look how far we've come."

"Only to hit another brick wall. Hepplewhite, or Ishtananda, or whatever you want to call him, was our last lead. All he could tell us was Carver disappeared. Why is he so elusive? Every time we get close to Carver he up and disappears on us. Where do we go from here?"

"There's still DG."

"Your deep state informant?"

"Yes."

"Are you sure he's for real, and not some right-wing nut who's roleplaying online?"

"Why does he have to be right-wing?"

"Most of them usually are."

"There are left-wing nuts too, you know."

"Okay, maybe he's a liberal nut who thinks you're a right-wing nut and he wants to wind us all up."

"The information he's given me so far has been impeccable. I don't think he's a nut and I don't think politics comes into this. I think he wants to lead us to the truth. Besides, he promised he'll be in touch."

"I'll believe that when I see it."

Richard turned and leaned over the back seat. "Are you sure you're all right? You've been, I don't know, snippy all day."

Linda bit her lip. "I'm sorry, I *have* been snippy. And you've been great at getting in touch with all these leads for us. I think I'm just disappointed that we didn't learn more about Carver, and that whole place gave me the creeps."

"I can understand that. But we did learn a lot about Operation Consciousness."

McPherson harrumphed. "You also gave away a lot."

Richard hung his head, abashed. "Sorry about that."

They pulled into the motel's parking lot.

"That's weird," Linda said.

There were no lights on anywhere in the motel or the parking lot. The sign was dead and all the streetlights in the near vicinity were out. There was darkness wherever they looked.

Linda got out of the car and looked around. "Did this just happen?"

McPherson also got out. "No, it was like this when I pulled in. You only noticed when I turned our lights off."

Linda wasn't used to so little light or noise in the middle of a city. Her mouth went dry and the hair rose along her arms and the back of her neck. This was all wrong.

The flashlight on Richard's phone came on and he held it up. "Use your cells."

Linda put her flashlight on and noticed her cell was nearly out of charge. McPherson pulled a penlight out of his pocket. Was it standard FBI issue, or was he prepared for every situation, like a Boy Scout?

Their rooms were next to each other on the end of the L-shaped layout, furthest from the manager's office. They stumbled across the darkened parking lot and stepped onto the porch.

Richard's key card wouldn't work on his lock. "I think the power's out."

"You don't say."

"How are we going to get into our rooms?"

Linda put down her bag and took hold of his door handle. "There's always a way."

She jiggled the handle a few times till she felt it move the way she wanted, then the tumblers clicked into place and the door opened.

Richard was impressed. "How in the hell did you do that?"

Linda smiled. "I've always had a strange knack with locks."

Linda helped McPherson with his door then unlocked her own. It was eerily quiet in her room. She cast her beam about the space. Her suitcase wasn't on the bed where she'd left it. Richard's knapsack was at the foot of her bed.

What was it doing there? Had Richard put it there? Why would he do that and not tell her? Where was her suitcase? She couldn't see it on the floor so she opened the tiny closet. Her suitcase wasn't there but McPherson's spare suit was hanging there and his shoes were below it. Who had put them there and what had happened to her things?

Linda checked the drawers in the tiny dresser. She found Richard's underwear and his T-shirts but none of her things. She saw her hand shake in the beam of the flashlight.

She headed to the tiny bathroom and found all her toiletries lined up on the sink and in the shower. She hadn't left any of them in the bathroom. She hadn't even unpacked when they'd arrived that morning. She'd just unzipped her suitcase and changed her top.

What was happening here? Who had done this?

There was a knock at her door. Linda whirled round and shone her beam at the door. Then her body stopped moving. It simply shut down and refused to listen when her mind told her to get the door.

There was another knock, louder, more insistent. Linda felt her chest rise and fall. Her head swam and she realized she hadn't been breathing for the last minute. She took control of her limbs again and went to answer the door.

It was Richard. He was gripping her panties and spare bra in his fist. "I, um, someone left these in my room."

She snatched them off him, her fear turning to anger. "I could have collected them myself."

"Yeah, um, sorry. My knapsack is missing."

Linda turned her phone flashlight on it. "It's right here. Did you do this? Did you come into my room?"

"What? No. I didn't. There wasn't even time to unpack when we got here. I just dropped my stuff and we left."

McPherson appeared behind Richard. "Someone's been in our rooms. My clothes and luggage are missing. They've put some of your things in my closet and bathroom."

Richard was relieved to be off the hook. "Yeah, we found the same thing. Who do you think has done this?"

"Someone who wants our attention."

Linda had a sudden flashback to the men in black who cornered her in the diner. Were they behind this? She felt sick. She didn't want to be in her room any longer. It had been violated. Someone had gone through her things and scattered them between the three rooms, silently judging and mocking her.

Linda stepped out onto the porch. Glad to be out of her darkened, threatening room. The three of them were an oasis of light in a pitch-black space.

There was a porch light, with a protective wire grill, outside each of the rooms. The light outside Linda's, directly overhead, snapped on. Linda's eyes had gotten used to the gloom and the sudden brightness hurt them.

They all squinted and held their hands over their eyes to shield them. The light only stayed on for five seconds, then it blinked off and the light outside Richard's room snapped on. That stayed lit for another five seconds and then the light outside McPherson's room came to life.

The lights outside each of the rooms came on for five seconds then went out in sequence. Traveling all the way along the L-shaped layout until the final light outside reception was illuminated. It didn't go out after five seconds, instead, it started to wink on and off like a slow strobe.

In spite of herself, Linda gripped Richard's arm. "What the hell is happening?"

McPherson pointed to reception. "I think we're supposed to go in there."

Linda shook her head. "No way! I'm getting in the car. I want to get out of here."

"This could be important, wait there a moment."

McPherson went into his room.

Richard placed his arm around Linda. "He's right, you know. It's okay, you're safe, I'm with you."

Linda gently took Richard's arm from her shoulder. "I'm good, I just want you all to know this isn't a good idea."

McPherson emerged a moment later with a shoulder holster under his jacket and beckoned for them to follow. "Stay by me."

The light outside reception continued to wink on and off as they approached. Linda kept close to the others. McPherson put his right hand in his holster and removed his weapon, pushing the door open with his left.

The reception lobby was unnervingly dark. Normally it was bright. Now there wasn't any light from the street. The whole space felt close and oppressive, as if the darkness were pressing in on them. Their flashlight beams seemed to pick out only tiny details without dispelling the blackness.

Linda felt a sharp pain in her shin and tumbled forward. She hit Richard's shoulder blade with her face, dropped to the floor, and lost her cell. She saw its beam skitter across the ground. She'd tripped over one of the chairs. Her shin and hip were bruised, her pride more so.

Richard retrieved her cell and helped Linda to her feet. "You okay?"

Linda rubbed her hip. "Yeah, there's nothing here. I think we should grab our stuff and go."

McPherson wagged his finger. "Not yet, we have to find out why they wanted us to come here."

A sudden screech made them all jump. It was followed by a series of whines, boings, and clicks. Linda recognized the sound, but she hadn't heard it in decades. It was a dial-up modem. Who the hell had a dial-up modem these days?

The sound came from behind the desk.

An eerie, green glow lit up the station. It pulsed on and off. McPherson motioned them to walk around the desk. The noise of the modem stopped, but the computer screen had come to life and a pixelated, green cursor was flashing, replicating the monitor screen of an ancient PC from back in the eighties.

The cursor moved across the screen leaving a series of pixelated words in its wake:

I told you I'd be in touch!

Richard gasped. "Oh my God, it's him."

Linda peered at the screen. "Him? Who?"

"DG, he said he'd contact me and he's true to his word!"

"He's a bit of a drama queen, don't you think? Couldn't he have just sent a text?"

McPherson shook his head. "Texts can be intercepted. This is more secure. He's hacked the motel's system using an encrypted line. The blackout is just a false flag, to draw attention. To pull this off takes someone with serious influence."

The words on the screen disappeared. The cursor flashed then started typing again:

Pay close attention! I will tell you this only once.

Richard shone his flashlight at the desk. He reached out a hand and began searching the surface, knocking things to the floor before he finally stumbled on a pen and a pad of paper. The screen cleared and the cursor began to type once more:

Let Baal contend with him
Who routs the Midianite.
And sends old John and Sam
To bless the traveler's sight.

Richard scribbled it down as quickly as he could, holding his flashlight over the pad with one hand and scrawling with the other. Then the screen went dead.

Richard was still writing. "Shit, did you get that last line."

Linda recalled it as best she could. "To, um, bless the . . . traveler's sight."

"Was that sight as in seeing or site as in website?"

"Seeing sight, I think."

Then the power came on. The strip lights flickered to life, the coffee machine started with a whirr, a click, and a series of thuds, and the computer pinged and rebooted itself. The brightness stung Linda's eyes. She squinted to stop from being dazzled.

A door banged behind them. "What the hell are you doing in here?" a voice said.

Linda turned to see a short, Latinx man with a purple shirt pointing a shotgun at them. The gold and black tag on his chest said 'MANAGER.' He spotted the weapon in McPherson's hand.

"Drop it, man, right now. I mean it, I will blow you away. I will drop you where you stand!"

Sweat broke out on his forehead. A vein throbbed in his neck. Linda saw his finger tighten on the trigger.

Is this how I'm going to die? she thought.

CHAPTER 11

MCPHERSON HELD UP his hands with his gun pointing toward the ceiling and stood very still. He spoke in a calm and measured voice. "Sir, I'm an agent of the FBI."

"I don't care who you are. I will you shoot you dead."

"Sir, killing or wounding a federal agent is a criminal offense that brings a mandatory sentence of twenty-five to life. My associates have seen me identifying myself, so you can't claim exculpatory ignorance, and they will testify against you to that effect."

"I'll shoot all of you if any of you move."

"Then you'd be arrested as soon as the police arrive and charged with multiple homicide. That's a capital crime and you'd definitely get the death sentence. I see the security cameras have come back online. They will have captured me identifying myself as a federal agent. That's all the evidence the police would need to convict you. You could try running, but there'd be nowhere on God's green earth that you could hide after a crime like that."

The manager was beginning to falter in the face of McPherson's calm and indefatigable logic. His hands shook, his finger relaxed on the trigger, and he lowered the shotgun slightly.

McPherson lowered his own weapon. "Okay, I'm going to slowly put my gun on the desk then I'm going to reach inside my jacket and show you my ID."

The manager raised his shotgun again. "Don't you move. Don't you move an inch, I mean it."

"What's your name, sir?"

"What's that?"

"Your name, sir, what is it?"

"It's Luis, what's it to you?"

"Okay, Luis, I can't put my weapon down and I can't show you my ID, to prove who I am, unless I move. Don't you want me to put my weapon down?"

"Of course I do."

"Good, so I'm putting my weapon on the desk and then I'm going to put my ID on the desk and step back so you can take a good look at it. You've still got the drop on me."

"Damn right, I have."

McPherson did what he said he would and stepped away from the desk. Luis walked slowly up, stared at the ID, then at McPherson, then the ID again. As soon as he realized McPherson was on the level his whole manner changed. The angry belligerence was replaced with compliance and contrition.

"Oh, jeez, I'm sorry, I didn't know. I thought you guys were breaking into the place. The lights went out, so I went to check the fuse box and I took the shotgun for protection, cos y'know, you can't be too careful on this job. I thought you were intruders. I was really freaked out. Otherwise, I'd never have pointed this at you."

He held up the shotgun which veered dangerously in their direction. All three of them took a nervous step backward.

McPherson held out his hand. "Maybe you should let me have that."

"Yeah, of course, sorry."

Luis handed the shotgun to McPherson. "So, are you guys investigating the motel? Is this like a terrorist attack or something?"

McPherson broke the shotgun open and took out the shells, then retrieved his badge and gun. "We're guests. We booked in this morning with one of your colleagues."

"Oh, right, you're the three in the end rooms."

"That's right, there was a light flickering outside reception, so we came to check it out. I drew my gun because, as you say, you can't be too careful on this job."

"A light was flickering here, what's that about?"

"Beats me, maybe the backup generator kicked in."

"We don't have a backup generator, not one I know of."

"Well, you got me, then. Listen, we have to get back to our rooms. It's been a long day and, with all this excitement, we're beat."

"Oh, hey, sure, you guys have a great night. Let me know if there's anything you need and sorry about y'know, pointing a shotgun at you."

"That's okay. You came good in the end."

They filed out of reception and headed back to their rooms. The lights in the rest of the motel and on the streets outside had also come back on.

Richard looked as bewildered as Linda felt, but she could tell he was also a little excited. "So, what do you think it means?"

McPherson held a finger up to his lips. "Wait till we're back in the room. However, it's fair to say I think we've just hit an important new development."

CHAPTER 12

LINDA WALKED STRAIGHT through the door of her room, turned and fell backward onto her bed. Just let her body drop like a bag of old bones. Her adrenaline was ebbing and her muscles were sore and tired.

Richard followed her into the room, still clutching the pad he'd written on. "Should we be like, going through our stuff and swapping all our possessions back?"

Linda groaned and put a pillow over her face. "What are you even doing in here? I just want to sleep."

"McPherson told us to meet in here, didn't you get the memo?"

"There was a memo?"

"It's a turn of phrase."

"I know what it is."

"Well, he *is* sorta like our boss. So, y'know, here I am."

Linda took the pillow away and sat up, regretfully. "Why do we have to meet now? It's been a long day and I'm dog tired."

Richard stared at her, incredulous. "Did you not see what just happened?"

"Yes, I saw, I was there, remember, and I nearly got killed by the guy on the desk. But I've gotten alarmingly used to people pointing guns at me over the last few months, so forgive me if it just leaves me exhausted."

"I'm not talking about that, I'm talking about DG, he reached out. He got in touch."

Linda rubbed her eyes and stretched. "Okay, I realize that's a big deal. Sorry I'm not as pumped as you, I've just had a bit too much excitement today. What are we going to do about his cryptic message?"

"We're going to crack it." McPherson strode into Linda's room. "It's a puzzle, we're going to crack it and follow the lead."

"C'mon in, why don't you? Make yourself at home. It's not like it's late or anything."

McPherson ignored her. Richard was staring hard at the pad. "I don't think it's a code, where we have to substitute words or letters or anything. Like Linda said, it's a cryptic clue."

McPherson pursed his lips and nodded. "Any ideas what it means?"

Richard pulled out his phone. "Let me try the Wi-Fi again, I can't connect to it in my room." He tapped in the code, stared at his screen, grimaced, then relaxed.

"So, let's go over the verse line by line."

Richard squinted at the notepad. "Let Baal contend with him . . . I'll Google it, can't hurt to check." He ran his finger across his phone screen.

"Wait, here's something, apparently there was an ancient Hebrew prophet and military leader called Jerubbaal or Yeruba'al. Nineteenth-century Biblical scholars translated this as 'let Baal contend.'"

McPherson scratched his ear. "That sounds promising."

Richard went back to his phone. "There's more, he led the Israelite tribe of Manasseh and won a major victory over the Midianites. Seems he led a troop of only three hundred men against a much larger army and won despite the overwhelming odds. Kinda like the Spartans and the Persians."

Linda got off the bed and filled the kettle. "Well that explains the second line about routing 'the Midianite.' Anyone want a coffee, as we're not going to get much sleep?"

McPherson shook his head. "No thanks."

Richard looked up from his screen. "I'm good."

"So how does the rest of it go, again?"

"And sends old John and Sam
To bless the traveler's sight."

"Who are John and Sam?"

Richard scratched his beard. "Your guess is as good as mine. But I may have found something that could help us find out."

"What's that?"

"Jerubbaal is also known as Jerubbesheth and Gideon."

"As in the Bibles?"

"Exactly and . . . wait, give me a second," Richard tapped his phone screen. "Yes, Gideons International got its start in 1898 when two traveling salesmen, John H. Nicholson and Samuel E. Hill, met in the Central Hotel in Boscobel, Wisconsin.”

“Right, that's who 'old John and Sam' are. So, do you think they 'bless the traveler's sight' with the good book?”

“You mean, leaving Bibles in hotel rooms?”

“It makes sense of that line.”

McPherson pointed at Linda. “You're right, it does. So, this DG wants us to find a Gideon Bible, right?”

Linda took a sip of coffee, pulled a face at how bad it tasted and went to her nightstand. “Well that shouldn't be too hard.” She opened the drawer, took out the Bible and held it up. “What now?”

Richard gestured in the air with his finger. “Open it up, flick through the pages, see if you find anything.”

Linda riffled through the pages and shook the Bible to see if anything fell out of the pages. Then she shrugged. “Nothing.”

Richard frowned. “Nothing? But we worked out the clue. There has to be something, we worked it out.”

Linda raised her index finger as it came to her. “Because this isn't the only Bible. Whoever was messing with us went through our rooms and moved all our things around. That wasn't just random, they were telling us something.”

“What?”

“To search each other's rooms. We have two other Bibles.”

“But how would they know whose room we'd meet up in?”

Linda threw up her hands in exasperation. “Just go get the other Bibles already.”

McPherson indicated the door to Richard. “You grab yours. I'll get mine.”

A few minutes later, McPherson returned with his Gideon Bible, flicking through the pages as he came through the door.

Linda peered over his shoulder. “Anything?”

McPherson pointed to a word on the page that had been underlined in ball-point pen. “Just random words like this, all of them underlined.”

“Do they mean anything?”

“I can't tell yet.”

Richard burst into the room, his face lit up with excitement. “You guys, look at this.”

He opened up the Bible to reveal that a square compartment had been cut out of the pages. Inside the compartment were two die-cast metal statues about two inches high. One was a miniature hammer, the other a chisel.

Richard lifted out the hammer with his fingers and held it up. "What do you think this means?"

Linda pointed to McPherson's Bible. "Maybe the answer's in here. There are lots of random words underlined on different pages."

"So, you think if we wrote them all down in order, from the earliest page to the last . . ."

" . . . then we might have another message, exactly."

Richard grabbed the notepad again. "Okay, read me out the first word."

McPherson flicked to the front and scanned the pages. "It's in the introduction—*You'll*, as in 'you will.'"

Richard jotted it down. "Okay, the next one."

They carried on like this for nearly half an hour until they had fifteen words. Richard chewed on his pen. "Okay, the first clue was a four-line verse with an A/B rhyming scheme, written in iambic trimeter."

Linda raised her eyebrows. "Written in what now?"

"Iambic trimeter, each line has three metric feet. Didn't you learn this in high school English class?"

"Must've been too busy doodling. That's how I spent most of high school."

Richard wrote out the words as a four-line poem and showed it to them:

You'll find the absent lights
That troubles troglodyte.
Where crimson scholars rub
The lying tripartite.

Linda rubbed the bridge of her nose with her fingers. "Just as cryptic as the last one. I s'pose a simple 'come meet under the bridge at midnight' was too much to ask."

McPherson took the notepad from Richard. "It seems to be a clue in two parts. The first two lines contain the word *find*, so it's fair to say they're telling us what we're looking for, and the next two lines start with the word *where*, telling us the location of our search."

Richard hovered at McPherson's elbow, examining the pad. "Then we're looking for *absent lights*, does that mean they're missing or they're not there?"

Linda bit her bottom lip. "I don't think we're looking for missing lights, unless you count the trick your friend just pulled with the motel lights a moment ago. So what's the absence of light?"

"Darkness, but this is plural, it's more than one darkness."

"Like a shadow?"

Richard threw his hand up. "Obviously, and a *troglodyte* is cave dweller, maybe one of the cave dwellers from Plato's allegory of the cave."

"The clue's telling us where we'll find the Shadows in the Cave. Are they for real then?"

"Yes, they're very much for real, that's what I've been telling you, and this proves it."

McPherson looked up from the pad. "Then who are the *crimson scholars*?"

Richard's thumbs were busy on his phone. "I'm getting too many conflicting hits from googling *crimson scholars.*"

Linda tapped his arm to get his attention. "Try adding the word 'college,' that might narrow it down."

"Okay, I think you're on to something. The intercollegiate athletic teams of Harvard are known as Harvard Crimson and Harvard's main campus newspaper is the *Harvard Crimson.*"

"We're going to Harvard then. Stands to reason a shady cabal that secretly runs the world would base itself in the world's most elite institution."

McPherson tapped the pad. "Harvard's a big place though. It's got three campuses and covers hundreds of acres. We could spend weeks searching it."

Richard took the pad back and underlined the last line. "We need to identify the *lying tripartite.*"

Linda drained the last of her coffee. "Could that be an anti-Catholic thing? I know Harvard was founded by Puritans and only allowed WASPs to study there until, like, the twentieth century."

Richard handed the pad to her and picked up his phone. "I'm not getting anything conclusive from that."

McPherson pointed out the third line on the pad to them. "It says *rub* the *lying tripartite.* What do students or professors rub at Harvard?"

Linda thought about her lecherous college tutors, but bit her lip.

A moment later Richard looked up from his phone screen with a smile.

"It says that students like to rub the statue of John Harvard, the college's first benefactor, who lent his name to the university. But the statue's inscription calls him the founder of Harvard, which isn't true and it gives the date as 1636. Harvard wasn't founded until 1638 and the statue isn't a likeness of John Harvard. No one knows what John Harvard looks like, so the sculptor, Daniel Chester French, just used a random good-looking student as his model."

"And all this is relevant because . . . ?"

"The students call it 'the statue of three lies.' In other words—*the lying tripartite.*"

"And where is this dishonest statue?"

"It's in Harvard Yard, totally accessible to the public."

Linda climbed off her bed and rubbed Richard's arm affectionately. "Holy Harvard, Bat Boy, I think you've cracked this cryptic conundrum."

Richard grinned and turned to McPherson. "So I guess we're going to Boston. Do you think the Bureau will spring for that?"

McPherson knitted his brows, looking pensive. "I'm certainly running up the air-miles on this case, sooner or later someone further up the chain is going to start asking questions. Until then, the heck with it. If this is as big as I suspect it is, they're not going to be able to ignore what we uncover and that will justify all the expenses. I'll arrange the flights first thing tomorrow. It's a five-and-a-half-hour flight, so we'll probably leave after lunch. Is that good with all of you?"

Linda nodded. Richard picked up his Gideon Bible. "What about these little statues, the hammer and chisel? We don't know how they fit into all this yet."

Linda lifted the miniature chisel out of the Bible. "Do they fit in, or are they supposed to distract us?"

McPherson took the chisel from Linda and dropped it back in the Bible. "We don't know what's pertinent and what's not just yet. My guess is they were left here for a reason. We should take them with us and find out how they fit in when we get to Harvard. Anyone disagree?"

Linda shrugged and sat back down on the bed. The coffee hadn't done the trick. She'd perked up for a minute, but she was bone weary again.

McPherson patted Richard on the back, a fatherly gesture that was not lost on Richard. "Remember before when I said you needed to release the better man inside of you? Well you certainly did that today. Great work, the both of you."

Richard beamed, but his shoulders drooped almost instantly and his head bent forward. "Thanks, listen, guys, it really has been a long day and I'm pooped all of a sudden. Think I'm gonna go hit the hay."

"I guess it is late at that."

Linda fell back onto the bed. "Could one of you knock the light out as you leave?"

Richard yawned. "Sure, night."

But Linda was already asleep.

CHAPTER 13

BROTHER ISHTANANDA COULD not empty his mind. His thoughts were as cluttered as the floor of a freshman dorm. He was sitting in the Chapel of Tranquillity, a single-story log cabin that smelled faintly of the resins in the wood. There was a simple altar at the far end, beneath a stained-glass window.

The window had four panels, an orange lotus blossom symbolizing the Brotherhood of Self Actualization, Christ as the shepherd, Lord Krishna speaking to Arjuna in his chariot, and a diagram of an atom.

Taken together, the panels were meant to represent the teachings of Christ, the teachings of Krishna, and the teachings of science, all of which the Master—Goshtananda had combined to create the doctrine of Self Actualization.

Ishtananda had been trying and failing to meditate for the past half hour. He'd risen at dawn, unable to sleep, and come to the Chapel. He blamed the FBI agents. Something about them wasn't right. Only one seemed legitimately FBI. The other two were like people you'd meet in an alternative bookstore.

The one who contacted him, and asked most of the questions, described himself as a special advisor. Maybe the woman was a special advisor too. She certainly seemed jumpy.

Or maybe the FBI had changed its recruitment strategy. Things had certainly changed since he became a monk. What with smartphones, broadband, and social media. All perfect distractions from inner peace.

Inner peace was eluding Ishtananda at the moment. It seemed the longer he studied and practiced Raja Yoga, the longer the road to self-perfection grew. But hadn't the Master taught that "the journey to self-perfection was a goal in itself" and "the longer your journey, the greater the lesson you are being taught"?

The Master's teachings were always a solace, no matter how troubled Ishtananda was. He concentrated on the meditation techniques the Master had taught. Techniques that had been developed over millennia by countless Brahmins and brought to perfection by Goshtananda himself.

He began with his breathing—five long, deep breaths, then ten short, quick ones. He opened up the halls of his mind to the universal rays of enlightenment and basked in their warmth and brightness.

When his mind and body felt lighter and emptier, he repeated the mantra his Master had bequeathed.

"I am the Father. The Father is me. God and I are one."

Ishtananda pictured himself in the lotus position, floating above his brain. Its folds of grey matter stretched beneath him like an intricate maze. He reached out his arm, in his mind's eye, and spoke the words his Master had taught him.

"Father, Thou art within me, I beg Thy power to cauterize my brain. To quell the anxieties, wipe away agitation, and open neural pathways to success."

Ishtananda pictured a burst of pure flame leaping from his fingers to burn a pathway in his brain. The flames extended from his fingers, parting the lobes of his brain, to reveal the sacral consciousness that sat beneath his mind.

At the center of his brain, in the heart of this sacred consciousness, was a closed lotus blossom. Ishtananda concentrated on opening each of the petals to reveal the divinity within. This was God at the core of his being.

As the last of the petals unfolded, Ishtananda could see a figure, obscured by the blinding light that spilled from the center of the lotus. He had never gotten this far in his meditation before. After all these years he was about to meet the Godhead that lay at the very crux of his being.

In his trance state, deep within his mind's recesses, Ishtananda moved closer to the figure in the lotus, to his destiny as a seeker after the truth. As he approached he was struck by the smell of burning. He had never experienced this while meditating.

The burning smell was evocative and undercut with another scent. It was perfume, the sweet, musky fragrance of patchouli. It was familiar, but he wasn't sure why.

Then the figure stepped from the lotus and it all came back. He knew where and when he'd smelled that perfume.

The figure walked right up and looked him in the eye. The vision had taken on a life of its own.

He hadn't looked into those eyes for a long time, not since he was a little boy. This wasn't the divine being at the apex of his existence, it was someone he'd lost long ago.

It was his aunt. She opened her mouth and began to speak. Her words weren't in sync with her lips. They seemed to be coming from a great distance, so he couldn't catch them at first, but they rose in volume.

When he finally heard them, they were a scream, filled with imperative.

"Get out! Get out now! Run, get as far away as you can!"

Ishtananda snapped out of his trance, as if someone had put a hand to his chest and pushed. He fell backward, his legs uncrossed, and the back of his head hit the floor.

As he stared at the wooden ceiling, he was aware that the burning smell and the scent of patchouli still filled his nostrils. The two aromas conjured a distant memory. This was exactly what he smelled the night his aunt roused him from his bed and sent him next door.

Ishtananda got to his feet. That's when he noticed his legs were shaking. Sweat ran in cool rivulets between his shoulder blades, pooling in the small of his back. His heart beat faster and his chest was tight.

This was not the calm and elation he felt when he finished meditating. The vision of his aunt had been vivid, but he hadn't realized how unsettling. Another problem caused by the FBI. Hadn't he been persecuted enough?

Ishtananda took control of his breathing and forced himself to take deep, even breaths. The vision of his aunt would be something to discuss in group meditation tonight. He would seek the counsel of his brother monks.

In the meantime, he decided he would go and help the monks on kitchen duty prepare breakfast. His name wasn't on the rota, but his help would be welcomed and he enjoyed the work.

As he stepped out of the chapel, the scent of burning and patchouli faded. It was replaced by something Ishtananda hadn't smelled in a long time, the aroma of freshly cooked meat. He'd been a vegetarian before joining the Brotherhood and hadn't really missed meat, except for the odd craving for Polish sausage. So, the smell that assailed him was not pleasant.

He had no idea where the scent was coming from or why it should be here in the ashram. He tilted his head back and sniffed to determine the source. He took a step forward, and his bare foot landed on something warm and soft that gave beneath his weight.

Ishtananda pulled his foot back in revulsion. Someone had left what looked like a large, thin rectangle of belly pork on the wooden porch. A pool of dark blood spilled out where he'd trodden on it.

Ishtananda did not understand what it was doing on the porch of the chapel. Who would do such a spiteful and thoughtless thing? Who would be so provocative as to leave a piece of meat lying around in a community of vegetarians? Had someone broken into the ashram to taunt them?

Despite his distaste, Ishtananda bent down for a closer look at the thin strip of meat. Someone had scored a set of markings into the surface of the meat. There was also some ink on it.

The ink was in the shape of a simple dove of peace. It dawned on Ishtananda where he'd seen the dove before. You don't live and work closely with a brotherhood of monks without becoming intimately acquainted with their identifying features, particularly birthmarks and tattoos.

That was Brother Vandanetta's tattoo.

This wasn't a piece of meat. It was . . . It was . . .

It was human skin.

The situation became completely unreal. Why was there a slab of Brother Vandanetta's skin lying on the porch here? Was Brother Vandanetta hurt? What had happened to him?

Ishtananda kept staring at the skin, trying to make sense of it. Trying to find some reason for its existence. It became apparent that the scorings were not random knife marks, but careful, considered strokes.

They were, in fact, drawings.

Clumsy but intricate drawings, each one inside one of three square frames like a . . .

Like a comic strip.

The frames were comic panels. The first panel showed a darkened corner, but it was a corner Ishtananda recognized, a corner in the ashram's kitchen. A face peered out of the shadows. A face Ishtananda also recognized. One that had a deep, personal meaning to him.

He'd once done an exercise while training as a monk. The

instructor had asked the initiates to personify their rage and destructiveness so they could recognize and overcome this facet of their personality.

The face Ishtananda pictured came from a drawing Carver had shown him. In the shadows of a darkened alley were two bloodshot eyes, sharp teeth twisted into a predatory grin, and a hand, gripping a blood-drenched meat cleaver.

Ishtananda wasn't certain he'd ever overcome his rage and destructiveness, but he had recognized it. It was the face of Carver's character—the Hatchet Man.

A face he now saw leering up at him from a comic panel carved into a strip of his brother's skin.

The second panel showed Brother Vandanetta and Brother Krishnamutti coming into the kitchen, laughing and chatting as they prepared to make breakfast.

The third and final panel showed a figure step out from the shadows and raise the meat cleaver, completely unseen by the monks.

Ishtananda smelled the aroma of freshly cooked meat again. A chill numbness crept over him.

His aunt had told him to get as far away from here as he could. She'd come into his vision to warn him. After all these years, she was still trying to save him. If he left, he might be safe, but his brother monks were in danger. He was no longer a twelve-year-old boy. He was a grown man with responsibilities to his community.

He wasn't sure if the crude drawings on Brother Vandanetta's skin were meant to goad or frighten him. Whatever his aunt's warnings, if there was a chance his brothers were still alive he couldn't leave them. He had to help. He needed to go to the kitchen.

Ishtananda walked around the bleeding chunk of human skin and made his way to the kitchen. He noted, almost subliminally, how calm and implacable he was. He let go of fear, panic, and his disgust at what had been done to the body of his brother monk. He didn't even register the grassy dew on his bare feet. He had one driving aim—to get to the kitchen and help his fellow monks.

The dining hall was a long, white, single-story building with a terracotta roof. At its rear was the professionally equipped kitchen.

The doors of the building were propped open, as if in invitation. Someone was expecting him. Ishtananda thought about the fear in his aunt's eyes, and the imperative in her voice. He thought about that night, five decades ago, and what would have happened if he'd just ignored her, rolled over and gone back to sleep. Would he ever have woken again?

He looked back through the open doors. Had his aunt really just visited him in his vision? Was she actually trying to warn him? Or was it all some delusion, a psychotic break triggered by the stress of the FBI visit?

He needed answers. His whole life had been a search for answers. He was a seeker after the truth, however unacceptable that truth was. The only answers he was going to get, the only truth he was going to find, lay in that kitchen.

He entered the dining hall.

Ishtananda's back was clammy with sweat. The cotton of his robe was plastered to it. He tried and failed several times to control his breathing. It came too fast, fueled by the same rage and fear that made his legs shake.

He walked still further into the dining hall.

The greasy aroma of cooked meat hung strong in the air. Something he'd never smelled in the dining hall before. There was a bitter undertone that told of fat and juices rendered to charcoal. Something was burning and it coated the back of his throat as he breathed.

Chairs and tables were pushed to the side, leaving the center of the hall empty. Something lay in the middle of the floor. Ishtananda went to look at it. It was another rectangular strip of human skin with a three-panel comic strip carved into it.

Ishtananda felt as though he was watching himself from a distance as he knelt to get a better look. He almost wanted to tap himself on the shoulder and say *that's not a very good idea.* He looked all the same and, while he was no expert, he thought he recognized the style of the drawings. Someone was making a clumsy attempt to copy Carver's style.

The first panel depicted a close-up of Brother Vandanetta's head. The top of his skull was missing and a hand was reaching in to remove his brain. The meat cleaver, which had taken off the top of his skull, was also in the frame.

The second panel focused on Brother Krishnamutti's chest. His ribcage had been cracked open and the skin pulled back to reveal the cavity beneath. Hands were reaching inside to cut out his heart with the meat cleaver.

The last panel showed a torso split from sternum to crotch. The intestines of the unlucky victim were being tugged out.

This whole situation seemed unreal. A few minutes ago, he was meditating in the chapel. Now he was staring at an atrocity that would not look out of place in a concentration camp.

Was Carver behind this? Had he come out of hiding all these years later? He'd be an old man in his late eighties, if he was still alive. He wouldn't have the strength to do such a thing. So who was doing this, and why were they copying Carver's drawing style?

Ishtananda noted his breath again. It was ragged, nearing hysteria, as if he was about to scream or burst into tears. A natural reaction to such brutality. But a reaction he wasn't going to indulge. His rage kept it at bay.

He was shaking again, but it wasn't from fear. His whole body vibrated with righteous indignation. How dare anyone act in this manner. How dare they do this to his brethren? He didn't care if it meant his death or destruction. Ishtananda was going to confront this evil. To stare it in the eye and condemn it.

The smell of burning meat grew stronger. He could see smoke coming from the door of the kitchen.

He got to his feet. However much he might want to flee, however much he could imagine his aunt taking his hand to pull him to safety, Ishtananda knew nothing was going to keep him from the kitchen.

The smoke alarm went off as he pushed open the door. The smell of burning meat was undercut with another odor, like a voided bowel or an open sewer.

Ishtananda was numb as he stepped into the kitchen. Lost to his compassion, a stranger to his humanity. All that remained was his anger.

On the floor, in front of the grill, were the bodies of Brother Vandanetta and Brother Krishnamutti. They were naked, lying on their sides in a pool of blood and feces. The top of Brother Vandanetta's head had been removed and his skull was empty. Ishtananda could see the red, matted interior of his brain pan. His back had been flayed.

Brother Krishnamutti's chest had been opened, stray ribs stuck out at random angles. His stomach wall had been sliced clean through, ragged flaps falling into the empty cavity.

The meat on the grill sizzled and popped. Ishtananda saw a

brain, a heart, and what might have been a human liver, in amongst the endless loops of intestine. Blood and other fluids leaked onto the grill.

The smell of excrement was stronger as he approached the grill. The organs were burned black on the bottom and raw on top, still wet and glistening.

At the very front of the grill was a final chunk of skin, sizzling like prime steak. Ishtananda stood over the grill. The heat was blistering and the smell was unbearable. Nevertheless, he made himself read the three comic panels carved on the skin.

The first panel showed a crude caricature of Ishtananda himself, he looked livid as he approached the pantry.

The second panel showed the interior of the pantry. In the shadows were a pair of bloodshot eyes, an evil grin, and a hand holding a meat cleaver. Ishtananda was shouting.

The final panel showed the meat cleaver buried in Brother Ishtananda's head.

Ishtananda smiled and nodded, as though he'd finally received an answer to one of his many questions. He walked over to the pantry and threw open the door.

It was dark and in the shadows of one corner, he saw a pair of manic, bloodshot eyeballs and below them a set of impossibly large teeth, grinning back at him. The light from the kitchen caught the blade of a meat cleaver.

Here, in front of him, was his rage and self-destruction made flesh. As though Ishtananda's darkest feelings had stepped from his psyche to confront him. A momentary pang of guilt gripped him. As if he'd unleashed this personal demon and set it on his brothers. Then his rage returned, colder and harder than ever.

"Why?" he screamed at the figure in the pantry, feeling the tendons knot in his neck. "Why? Why? Why? How could you do something like this?"

The meat cleaver moved slowly up into the air. But it fell rapidly. Ishtananda's final and definitive answer.

Ishtananda heard a loud *thunk*! His jaws came together hard enough to chip several teeth. He felt something warm and viscous run down the front of his face.

He took a step backward as a white-hot pain shot through the top of his head. His legs went into spasms and collapsed under him.

He hit the floor, and blood filled his eyes, so he closed them. Sparks danced behind his eyelids and the pain reached an insufferable crescendo of agony.

He wanted to stand and flee. To get away from the terrible thing in the pantry. But his body kept twitching and jerking and wouldn't obey him.

He tasted something cold and cloying on his tongue, like frozen peanut butter and ashes. Then he couldn't taste anything. Or hear anything. Or see or feel a single thing.

***

For a long time, there was only darkness.

Then his sense of smell returned. A distant odor of burning and patchouli reached him. He had no form, but he followed it.

The odor grew stronger and with it the memory of who he once was. He stopped moving and his sense of hearing came back.

Footsteps approached from a great distance. Far away in time as well as space. He strained to hear and after a while they grew louder.

As they moved closer, he was aware of a colored, shimmering haze. It was formless to begin with, but eventually it coalesced into the image of his aunt. She was dressed just as she had been on that fateful night when he had last seen her.

He too had put on a form. He was his twelve-year-old self, his eyes cloudy from sleep.

"I thought it might be you," he said.

His aunt reached out and stroked his cheek. "Who else would have come?"

"Will I . . . ?" He swallowed and took a deep breath. "Will I finally get some answers now?"

"Eventually," she said. "But only when you start asking the right questions."

CHAPTER 14

THEY CAUGHT A cab from the terminal outside Logan Airport. They didn't have to wait long, but Boston in March was much colder than California.

Linda had not packed for a cold New England spring. She hadn't known they'd be going to Boston and her flimsy overcoat was no match for the chill winds. She hugged herself for warmth and blew on her hands, wishing for a pair of woolen gloves.

Linda noted that taxis in Boston were much like those in New York, only white with a green stripe across the rear. The driver didn't say a word the whole journey.

The sky was gray and overcast when they climbed out at Peabody Street. The driver dropped them right by the campus. McPherson gave him a five-dollar tip.

They entered via the Johnston Gate, its black wrought iron surmounted by two redbrick pillars with plaques on them. They were built in the Colonial Revival style favored by so many nineteenth and twentieth-century campus buildings. Years of drawing Gothic buildings had made Linda attentive to architecture.

The trees along the walkways had bare branches and there were far fewer students or tourists than Linda expected. Even still, the grounds and buildings all basked in that dream-like privilege only found on Ivy League campuses.

Richard read the directions on his phone and led them to University Hall, a low-rise, white granite building located in Harvard Yard. Outside its long, west façade, Linda saw the bronze statue of John Harvard.

It sat on a six-foot, pink marble plinth in a cobblestone enclosure right in front of the hall. The bronze statue showed a young clergyman, dressed in seventeenth-century garb with an open book in his lap. It seemed to Linda that he had just looked up from the book and was mulling over something he'd read.

As the other two took in the statue, Linda glanced around the lawns and buildings of the yard. "Now what happens? Is someone going to approach us like in a spy movie? Do you think we're being watched?"

Richard took his glasses off and cleaned them with the tail of his shirt. "We're always being watched. There are 15.3 security cameras for every hundred people living in this country alone. If you carry a cell phone, they can track your every movement and listen to what you're saying at any time."

"I know all that. Mr. Paranoia. I meant are *they* watching us, right now, the Shadows in the Cave?"

McPherson turned away from the statue. "I'd say it's highly probable. With the trouble they've taken to get us here, I'd imagine they'd want to make sure we're where they want us."

"Are they going to make themselves known, do you think?"

"My guess is we have to earn that, and I don't think we're there yet."

"How do we earn it?"

Richard stepped onto the cobblestones and started to walk around the statue in an anti-clockwise direction. He stopped to examine the Emmanuel College seal on the southern side of the plinth, then carried on around to the northern side and took in the Harvard College seal.

Linda joined him. "What are you looking for?"

"I don't know yet, but so far every communication with DG has been about conundrums and cryptic clues. I'm guessing this statue is just another big puzzle."

"Is this where the hammer and chisel come in?"

"Could be, this is a statue, after all, and that's what sculptors use."

"Sculptors usually use them on stone, not bronze, so should we be looking at the plinth rather than the statue."

"Unless that's a double bluff."

"How do you mean?"

"Well, the statue's made of bronze and so are the hammer and chisel."

"I see what you mean."

Linda and Richard circled the statue in opposite directions.

Linda searched the plinth for any sign of a clue and Richard searched the statue, because he was taller and could see more of it.

"I think I've found something," Richard said on his third time around. He was standing on the northern side of the statue pointing at two bronze books, sitting on top of each other by the back leg of John Harvard's chair.

Linda joined him. "I saw those books. What's so special about them?"

Richard pointed at the bottom book, which was longer and thinner. "Check out the spine."

"Oh yeah." Linda saw what appeared, at first, to be a keyhole in the spine of the book. It was around two inches high and when she inspected it more closely she saw it wasn't a keyhole, but a hole shaped exactly like the two-inch bronze hammer.

"Has this always been here?"

Richard shrugged. "I don't know. I shouldn't think so, but if it hasn't it means the Shadows in the Cave have vandalized a national treasure and gotten away with it."

"What do we do next?"

McPherson came and stood behind them. "That hole's the same shape as the hammer, right?"

"Yeah."

"So, have you tried slotting the hammer into it?"

Richard pulled the Gideon Bible from his backpack. "I will now."

He opened the Bible, took the hammer, and reached up to the statue. Stretching out his arm, he was able to line up the hammer with the hole. He fumbled his first attempt at getting it in and the hammer slipped from his fingers and tumbled to the ground.

"Damn, this is harder than it looks."

Linda retrieved the hammer and handed it to him. "Here you go."

"Thanks." He tried a second time and, with a bit of care and patience, he was able to slot the hammer into the hole. There was a solid clunk as the hammer fitted into place, as if Richard had just activated some mechanism.

Sounds of whirring and clicking came from inside the two bronze books. They reminded Linda of the noises a vending machine makes. This was followed by two audible clicks as if catches were being released.

The spine of the thicker, top book opened up and fell forward as if it was on a hinge, revealing a dark interior. From inside this interior a rectangular gray box appeared, like an old VHS tape being ejected from a player. The box was the same size as a videotape.

Richard reached up and took it. The spine of the book snapped back into place and the hammer was ejected from the hole in the bottom book. Linda picked the miniature hammer up. When she glanced back, the bottom book no longer appeared to have a hammer-shaped hole in its spine.

Linda blinked. "That's weird."

Richard was examining the box. "What is?"

"The hole just disappeared, the one you put the hammer in."

Richard looked over at the books. "That *is* weird."

McPherson tapped the box in Richard's hands. "Strange as that is, this is what we should be concentrating on."

"You're right."

Linda examined the box for the first time. It appeared to be coated entirely in Teflon. There were no markings on it, but there was a metal disc set in the center of one of the sides. Something was engraved on the disc.

"What's this marking?" Linda said.

Richard looked closer. "It appears to be a set of balance scales."

"Oh yeah, like the old-fashioned kind Lady Justice holds."

"Do you think we're supposed to weigh something with it?"

"Like what?"

"I'm not sure." Richard ran his finger along the bottom of the box. "I think there's something else inscribed on the bottom."

Richard turned the box over and pointed at some letters. He took off his glasses and peered at them, his nose almost touching the box. Then he handed it to Linda. "Can you make this out?"

Linda squinted at the letters. "I think it's Latin. It says: 'Vos adepto unum ire.' Does anyone know what that means?"

McPherson spoke up. "Roughly translated it means 'you get one go.'"

"Didn't figure you for a classicist."

"I pick things up along the way."

Richard looked perturbed. "I think we're supposed to weigh something on this disc, but we only get one turn, so it better be the right thing."

Linda rubbed her chin in thought. "It has to be one of the miniatures from the Bible, the hammer or the chisel."

"We already used the hammer, so maybe it's the chisel."

"Unless it's a double bluff and the chisel is a red herring."

Richard bit the inside of his cheek. "Or unless they weigh exactly the same."

"There's no way of telling that without weighing them and there are no other scales to hand. Do we just flip a coin?"

"Or maybe we try and think like our clue-master. Like you said, a chisel is used on granite, which the plinth is made of, but so is the hammer. However, the hammer is also used in a forge where they would have smelted the bronze for the statue."

McPherson crossed his arms. "And if we get this wrong, the trail ends here."

"So, our whole hunt rests on getting this right."

Linda clicked her fingers. "It has to be the chisel, because that's associated with the plinth, and the statue rests on the plinth, just as our hunt for the Shadows rests on getting this right."

Richard took the tiny chisel and held it over the scales. "Okay, here goes, moment of truth."

He placed the miniature bronze chisel on top of the metal disc. The box hummed and the disc turned one hundred and eighty degrees. A tiny crack appeared, just below the top of the box, revealing a lid for the first time, which sprung open, sending the chisel clattering across the cobblestones.

Linda, Richard and McPherson all craned their necks to see what was in the box. It contained two ornate, copper canisters, each one about three and a half inches long, held to the inside of the box with metal catches. Below each was a small plaque containing one word. The plaque on the left said: PAINT. The plaque on the right said URINE. Above the canisters was a slightly larger plaque which read: CHOOSE ONE FOR GOOD LUCK.

Linda peered at the contents of the box. "Oh great, more choices."

Richard wrinkled his nose. "I suppose we only get one go at this too."

McPherson patted the plinth. "Which one of them has the biggest connection to the statue?"

Richard looked up and to the right, staring off into space. He pursed his lips as if he was trying to recall something.

"In 1890 the statue was daubed with red paint by drunken students. They got away with it that time, but in 1984 a group of students were apprehended by the police trying to paint the whole statue crimson. The police joked that they caught them red-handed."

Linda stepped back and took in the statue, especially the toe of its left boot, which was shiny and much lighter than the rest of the statue. "That doesn't sound all that lucky to me. Aren't the students supposed to rub his foot for good luck?"

McPherson snorted dismissively. "That was made up about thirty years ago by guides showing tourists around."

Richard clicked his fingers. "Yes, but it's become another tradition for students to pour urine on the foot knowing that tourists are going to touch it."

Linda pulled a face. "Eww! I guess the paint's not lucky, because if you get that on your hands, you get caught by the police. But if you rub the toe you might get good luck, but you also get stinky fingers. So it has to be the urine, right?"

Richard stared into the box. "Can't fault your logic there. Shall we take the canister on the right?"

"Go for it."

Richard reached into the box. He took hold of the canister on the right and pulled it away from the metal catches holding it in place. There was a soft clunk as Richard lifted the canister free, and a hidden compartment opened inside the box.

Clear liquid poured out of the compartment, filling the inside of the box. The plaques and the remaining canister began to fizz and melt as the liquid engulfed them. A fierce smell like burning hair wafted from the box.

Richard threw the box at the ground in front of him. "Oh my God, acid!"

The box hit the ground and some of the acid splashed out onto the cobblestones. It hissed and smoked where it landed, melting holes in the stones. McPherson put a hand on Linda and Richard's shoulders and guided them backward out of the range of the acid.

When the acid stopped sizzling, Linda stepped tentatively forward and looked in the box. It was empty and blackened. "Well, I hope we made the right choice, because we can't swap it for the other canister now."

Richard removed the lid of the canister and took out a small vial of yellow liquid that was encircled by a scroll of paper. He unrolled the scroll and showed it to McPherson and Linda. It contained a verse:

A chemist's credit cuts
Strip budgets to the bone
Where tiny green then dug
Now inches to the throne.

Linda sighed. "Okay, I'm going to need coffee before I even attempt to get my head around that."

CHAPTER 15

AFTER DUMPING THE blackened box in the trash, Linda accompanied Richard and McPherson to a coffeehouse in the campus center. A glass and concrete building whose brutalist architecture and glazed pavilions seemed out of place with the rest of the campus.

Preppy, disinterested students sat at the tables all around them, doing little to hide their passive disdain. Patently disgruntled that this space in their exclusive college was open to the general public.

Linda's coffee was watery and acidic, but her bagel was fine. No one talked, as the three of them ate and slurped coffee, which suited Linda fine. It gave her a chance to catch a breath and reflect on this strange new turn the investigation had taken.

As interesting as this unexpected diversion was, Linda couldn't shake the feeling they were being purposefully distracted. This strange scavenger hunt felt like they were geocaching on some FBI team-building exercise. She wasn't convinced it would bring more information about Carver or what was causing the disappearances.

Richard, on the other hand, was completely invested. He was convinced the answers lay with the Shadows in the Cave and he was desperate to find out what happened to his father. When it came to the intellectual puzzles, he was totally in his element.

What Linda couldn't work out was why McPherson was so engaged. DG had gone out of his way to intimidate them with his power and influence. He'd taken over the electric grid in California and shut down an entire block to get their attention. He'd used secret mechanisms in public monuments as drop points for his clues. Was McPherson simply impressed by how much juice the guy had?

From what he'd said, McPherson had spent his whole career in the FBI. He painted himself as a maverick, but he had a strong conservative streak and he seemed to respect chains of command. He had a healthy respect for his superiors and DG had shown himself to have power and influence. Was that why he'd caught McPherson's interest?

Or maybe they were all caught up in the thrill of the chase. Linda couldn't deny it was exhilarating solving the clues and finding the next location. DG had contacted them just when their investigation had hit a brick wall. Did he know they couldn't go any further? Did they have any other choice than to follow his lead? Linda supposed not.

She wiped her fingers and picked up the scroll from the table. Reading the clue once again.

A chemist's credit cuts
Strip budgets to the bone
Where tiny green then dug
Now inches to the throne.

"Anyone have any ideas who the chemist is, and why his credit got cut?"

Richard was still on his phone. "There's thousands of famous chemists who went to Harvard, including Nobel Laureates like Martin Chalfie and Donald J. Cram."

"If they're winning the Nobel Prize, I'm guessing they got a lot of credit, so it's probably not them."

McPherson slurped his coffee. "Maybe the word 'credit' doesn't mean what we think it does."

Richard looked up from his phone. "You mean like believing something is true, or a debt or something?"

"Possibly."

Richard took to his phone again. "I tried the debt angle, but I'm mainly getting stories about Charles Lieber, who your guys arrested for lying about a lab he was paid hundreds of thousands to set up in China."

"My guys?"

"The FBI."

McPherson nodded and drained his cup.

Richard tapped the table with excitement. "I think I might have something else. There's a historical case of a Harvard chemistry professor murdering his creditor in 1849."

Linda leaned over to look at Richard's phone. "That sounds promising."

"On the thirtieth of November, John White Webster is said to have killed his creditor, George Parkman. Webster was living beyond his means and had taken out loans with several other people, using the same collection of old dinosaur bones as security."

"Dinosaur bones?"

"That's what it says here, I guess they were worth a bit of money.

"Anyway, this really annoyed Parkman and he kept hounding Webster to pay off his debt. Parkman came to his rooms, Webster snapped and hit him with his walking stick which killed him. So Webster took the body into the dissecting lab, next to his own rooms in the basement of the Medical College, and dismembered his body."

"That explains the second line about stripping 'budgets to the bone' too. But who or what is 'tiny green?'"

Richard scratched his beard. "I'm not sure."

Linda pulled out her own phone and began googling John White Webster as well. A few minutes later she tapped Richard on the arm. "Do you think 'tiny green' might be a code word, substituting pseudonyms for an actual name?"

"It's possible, why do you ask?"

"Another word for 'tiny' would be 'little', right? And 'green' might be a pseudonym for 'field', as in 'village green.'"

"Wait, wasn't there a janitor at the Medical College, called Littlefield?"

"Yes, Ephraim Littlefield, he hated Webster and suspected he'd murdered Parkman after Parkman went missing and the police started looking for him. So, he dug through a wall in the basement to Webster's privy, where he found a bunch of body parts that the police later identified as Parkman's. 'Throne' is old slang for toilet."

"So, you think we should look in a toilet in the basement of the Medical College next?"

"I think it's our best shot."

McPherson pushed back his chair and stood. "I think we should flag down another taxi."

Richard waved this away. "With this traffic, it'll be cheaper and quicker to get an Uber. I'll order it now."

Linda got up from the table and put the scroll in her pocket. Despite her previous reservations, she found she was quite excited to get to the basement of the Medical College. What, she wondered, would she find in the place where a dogged janitor once found the dismembered body of George Parkman?

CHAPTER 16

"**YOU SURE WE** don't need to clear the building?" The orderly had a tiny sheen of sweat on his upper lip. He was a tall, stooped guy with a receding hairline and acne scars on his cheek. His face was flushed with a combination of excitement and concern at having the FBI in his workplace.

McPherson scanned the sub-basement corridor. "As I said before, no one's in any danger. Are any of these doors locked?"

"I don't think so, we mainly use this floor for storage. If you need to get in somewhere I can probably find the key."

"Thanks, we can take it from here."

The orderly seemed reluctant to go back to his duties. "It's not any problem, just ask at reception and they'll call me."

McPherson waved him away without looking. "Okay, noted."

Linda smiled sympathetically at the orderly as he turned and slunk back upstairs. They hadn't told him why they were there, but ever since McPherson showed him his badge, the orderly had been eager to help, maybe hoping for a break from the drudgery of his daily routine.

Linda did not share his eagerness. The excitement she'd felt when they'd left the Campus and headed to the Medical School had now fizzled. When they got to Longwood Avenue and began making their way around the current medical school they discovered they were in the wrong place and the wrong part of town.

After fruitlessly questioning various members of the administration, they learned the Medical School had only been in place since 1906. It had moved twice since 1849. First to Copley Square and then to its present location. The old Medical College had been torn down long ago and nothing remained of the building. Finally, someone produced an old map of Boston. From that, they were able to work out the latitude and longitude of the old Medical College and find the new building that stood in its place. They even had a good idea where George Parkman's remains had been found.

One final Uber ride had dropped them outside a redbrick building on the corner of North Grove Street and Cambridge Street, part of the Massachusetts General Hospital complex. Among other things, this building housed the Pediatric Asthma Program. Once inside the building, they began another round of conversations where McPherson showed his badge and explained what they were looking for, only to be passed on to another overworked administrator who didn't really have time to help them.

Eventually the orderly had taken them down to the sub-basement. By this point, Linda was bored and disengaged.

Richard was staring at an app on his phone that allowed him to pinpoint longitude and latitude. He pointed down the corridor. "It's this way."

Linda and McPherson followed him to the end of the corridor and around a corner. Richard stopped in front of a scuffed, wooden door. He tried the handle and it opened inward.

Beyond the door was a long, low-ceilinged room with a network of pipes, clanking and hissing overhead. McPherson found the light switch and a dim bulb came on. It did little to disperse the gloom.

The floor of the room was littered with discarded boxes. There was a large boiler in the corner, sitting on concrete blocks. The temperature was warmer and the air felt close and stifling.

Linda turned to Richard. "Where now?"

Richard frowned. "I haven't got any signal."

He walked out into the corridor and back the way he came. Linda heard his footsteps recede and then return. He came back into the room still frowning.

"Any luck?"

He pursed his lips in frustration. "I can't get any signal at all."

McPherson looked around the room. "I guess we'll have to do the rest with instinct and observation."

They began to comb the room, kicking aside boxes and peering into corners filled with dust and cobwebs. Linda walked around the side of the boiler and discovered a set of steps by the far wall.

"Hey guys, I think I've found something."

The steps went down into darkness. Linda clicked her phone's flashlight on. She shone the beam down the steps and saw that they led to an old wooden door.

On the middle step sat a large, gray rat. It was busy preening itself but when the light hit it, the rat turned to regard Linda with a startled look. It remained frozen in place for a couple seconds but then its nerve broke and it charged up the steps.

It ran over Linda's foot and she leapt back, nearly dropping her phone. She kicked out at the creature but missed. It twitched its pink, hairless tail and put on an extra burst of speed, just as Richard joined her.

The rat bolted straight at Richard but swerved at the last minute. Richard threw up his hands and shrieked, a shrill high-pitched cry that scared Linda more than the rat. He put a hand to his chest and panted. Finally, he swallowed and looked over at Linda. "God, I hate rats, hate 'em. You okay?"

Linda nodded. The rat had disappeared but McPherson stood right behind them, rolling his eyes and shaking his head in slow disapproval. "You find anything, other than a scared rodent?"

Linda pointed down the steps. "There's another door down here."

McPherson led the way down the steps and tried the door. It opened inward with a creak of rusted hinges. Damp, stale air wafted from the tiny room, no bigger than a broom closet.

Linda shone her beam into the space and saw an ancient, porcelain toilet, the kind that had its water tank mounted high above it on the wall with a chain hanging down. Linda scoured the cramped space with her beam to make certain there were no more rats. The floor was covered with dust and rubble, but no rats.

"What now?" she asked.

Richard leaned forward and looked around the tiny room. "We could try pulling that chain."

"Don't let me stop you."

"Oh, so it has to be me now?"

"Well, I'm not pulling it."

McPherson tutted, stepped past them both, and took hold of the chain. He gave it an experimental tug but nothing happened, so he pulled harder. The chain lowered and there was a sound like cogs and gears turning from inside the water tank.

This was followed by a creaking noise and the front of the water tank lowered itself like a drawbridge. A long skeletal arm emerged from inside the tank and reached out toward them.

Richard gripped Linda's shoulder and they both gasped. Linda lowered her flashlight beam then brought it back. "Is that real?"

McPherson rolled his eyes. "I think it's animatronic."

The skeletal arm opened its bony fist, and sitting in the center of its palm was another box, identical to the one they had found in the statue.

CHAPTER 17

L INDA REACHED OUT a tentative hand to retrieve the box. She half expected the skeletal fingers to close as soon as she touched it.

There was a silver disk on the top of the Teflon-coated box, with a set of scales engraved on it. Linda turned it over in her hands. "I guess we have to weigh that vial of pee."

Richard tapped the box with his index finger. "Do we weigh it in the vial or pour it on the box do you think?"

"Eww, we weigh it in the vial. I'm not holding it while you pour pee all over it."

"You're probably right, but it's always worth exploring options."

"Not that option."

"I think the scale triggers a release that opens the box. It's obviously set to very precise parameters, I think that's why they made us choose between the hammer and the chisel and the two vials."

"So, they're not trying to mess with our heads?"

"Well, that too."

"What if we've made the wrong choice, what happens then?"

"I don't know, I guess the box won't open, or it'll self-destruct."

Linda held the box out at arm's length. "It won't blow up, will it?"

Richard shook his head. "Probably just do that acid thing it did last time, only everything in it will be destroyed."

Linda cleared a space in the dust and rubble on the floor with her foot, then she placed the box in it. "I think we need to put it on a level surface so it can weigh the vial properly and it doesn't roll off, or anything."

Richard knelt next to the box and held the vial of urine over it. "Well, here goes nothing, I guess."

Given how big his fingers were, Richard placed the vial onto the box's silver disc with remarkable delicacy. Then he stood quickly and stepped back, as though the box genuinely was going to self-destruct.

The box hummed like the other had and the disc turned one hundred and eighty degrees again. Linda heard Richard breathe an audible sigh of relief as a tiny crack appeared, just below the top of the box, revealing its lid. Then it sprung open and the vial of pee went skittering into a forgotten corner.

McPherson bent forward to inspect the contents of the box and so did Linda. Inside were two pieces of old, yellowing bone held in place with metal catches and another copper canister. Below each piece of bone was a one-word plaque reading PHALANX and MANDIBLE. Above the bones was a larger plaque which read: IDENTIFY THE IDENTIFIER.

Linda wrinkled her nose. "Okay, I am not touching either of those bones."

McPherson raised his eyebrows. "Didn't figure you for squeamish."

"I'm not squeamish, I just don't want to lose the end of my fingers to any acid."

Richard rubbed his beard thoughtfully. "The acid isn't released until we take one of the bones, or at least it wasn't last time. I think the ends of your fingers are safe. We should really be worrying about which bone to pick."

Linda frowned at Richard. "If you make any puns about having 'a bone to pick with me,' I will put both your hands in that acid."

"Actually, that never crossed my mind, but it would've been kinda funny. What sort of bones do you think they are?"

"Probably human, given this is the exact spot where Ephraim Littlefield found George Parkman's bones. A phalanx is a finger bone and a mandible is a jaw."

Both Richard and McPherson seemed to be surprised that Linda knew that. She looked put out. "What, I'm an artist, we study anatomy, I know these things."

Richard looked abashed. "I'm just impressed, is all. We've identified what the bones are, but which one is the identifier?"

"Could it be the bone they used to identify the murder victim?"

"Of course, didn't they identify him from his teeth? Or to be more specific a section of his jaw?"

"I skimmed that bit but I think you're right."

Linda nodded at the box. "Well, go on then."

Richard's hand hovered over the bones, then he withdrew it. "Does it sound lame to say I'm kinda nervous? Y'know, with the acid and everything and what if we're wrong?"

McPherson sighed, shook his head, and then bent over the box. He lifted out the canister and handed it to Richard.

"Here, hold this."

Then he took hold of the jawbone and pulled it free. There was a soft clunk and another compartment opened inside the box. The finger bone hissed, fizzled, and dissolved into a mess of foam and acrid odors.

McPherson took the canister from Richard, opened it, and pulled out a small scroll of paper. "Time to find out where we're going next."

Linda groaned. The reaction caught her by surprise, but her feet were sore, her calves were aching and it felt like the energy was suddenly draining from every cell in her body. Her eyes started to brim as she held up her hands to McPherson and Richard.

"Can we . . . can we just hang tight on the next clue? We had a long flight, followed by a long day, we've covered half of Boston on this crazy scavenger hunt and all I want to do is grab some food, take a bath, and get some sleep. Can't this wait till tomorrow?"

McPherson breathed out heavily, his brows furrowed. "I don't think it works that way. Whoever's set this up wants us to keep at this. If we quit now we lose this whole lead and we may never get it back. And this lead is the only one we have."

Richard looked like a birthday boy who's just been told he's not getting cake. "I thought you were into this. We're so close, this is really important. It could open up the whole case for us."

Linda put a hand to her forehead and closed her eyes. She knew they were right but she wanted to scream and stamp her foot. "Aren't you guys just a *little* tired of being toyed with? How do we even know this grand puppet master is who we think he is?"

McPherson made a low noise in his throat to show his displeasure. "Well, we won't find that out by dropping out now, will we?"

Richard looked at her imploringly. "This is how we find what happened to Carver in that compound. How you finally get an answer about what happened to your friend."

"You mean it's how you get an answer to what happened to your dad in that compound."

Richard blinked, a little stung by Linda's words, and she regretted her abrupt tone. Then the imploring look returned to his face and he rallied himself.

"Well, of course that's what I want to find out. I've never tried to hide that. Just as McPherson doesn't hide that he's working this case to exonerate himself with the Bureau so he can get his career back. We've all got skin in this game, we're all personally invested. That's why we've got to see this through."

Linda knew he was right. She'd put her career on hold for this, just as it was starting to take off again. She had to hold her tiredness at bay, dig deep, and push through. "Fine, okay, let's finish this. But can we please get out of this crappy toilet?"

CHAPTER 18

THEY CLIMBED THE steps back to the boiler room, picked their way past the discarded boxes of supplies and stepped out into the corridor. McPherson unrolled the small scroll and held it out for them all to see. It read:

> A bibliophile is sunk
> His mother clears his shelves.
> And where his memory blooms
> You may just find yourselves.

"A bibliophile is a book lover, right?" Linda said.

Richard tapped his chin in the way he always did when he was thinking. "Yes, it is, but I wonder what it means by sunk? I still can't get any signal down here, can we leave the basement?"

They left the basement by a back staircase and found an empty corridor. Richard smiled as his phone finally found a signal. "Okay, I'm not really getting anything for 'sinking bibliophile Boston,' or any variation on that."

Linda rubbed her eyes and glowered at McPherson, still annoyed he'd forced her to continue doing this. "How come you never contribute when we're puzzling this stuff out?"

McPherson's eyes narrowed slightly. "I do when it's appropriate, besides this is the stuff I pay you two for."

Linda couldn't argue with that. "Do you think 'sunk' is literal or metaphorical, as in finished, or over?"

Richard shrugged. "Could be both or either, let me check."

"Maybe 'his mother' is also important, was she throwing out his books after he died?"

"Or maybe donating them, that gives me an idea." Richard

stabbed at the phone screen with his thumbs, then punched the air. "Yes! Harry Elkins Widener was a businessman and book collector, and guess which famous ship's maiden voyage he was on?"

"Not the Titanic?"

Richard pointed at Linda to show she was correct.

"He was born to a wealthy Philadelphia family and started collecting books at an early age. After he died, his mother built the Widener Library for his old college and donated his collection, which even included an original Guttenberg Bible."

"Did she plant any blossoming trees in his memory, like cherries or something?"

"Don't know, why?"

"I was thinking about the line 'where his memory blooms.'"

"Can't find anything about planting trees, but there's a portrait of Harry in the Memorial Rooms, it's by the French painter Gabriel Ferrier, and a fresh vase of flowers is placed in front of it every week. And get this, the room might be haunted by his mother, Eleanor's ghost."

Linda couldn't keep the skepticism out of her voice. "Is that right?"

"It's what they say. Apparently the portrait of her darling Henry was taken down for renovations sometime in the early two-thousands and the admin staff at the library were attacked by their own library."

"What do you mean—attacked?"

"Plaster started raining down on top of them, they couldn't work at their desks. Then they put the portrait back and the vase of flowers and they never had that problem again. Some members of staff claimed it was his mother's doing, from beyond the grave."

"And no one thought to blame the construction crew who were doing the renovations? No, they just went straight for his poor mother's ghost."

"When you put it like that . . . "

Linda bit her thumb and looked up at the ceiling. "If it is the Memorial Room with his portrait and the flowers, that would explain the words: 'blooms' and 'memory.'"

"What do you think the last line is saying?"

"If the clue is sending us to the Memorial Rooms in the Widener Library, then I guess that's where we'd find ourselves."

"Maybe, what if it has deeper meanings though?"

"Deeper meanings?"

"Yeah, it's a cryptic clue after all. What if this goes back to what we were saying just a moment ago, about how we're all personally invested in this case now? DG obviously knows this, or he wouldn't have contacted us, or set this trail of clues up. If there are real answers at the end of this trail, maybe we'll unlock more than mysteries, maybe we'll unlock ourselves."

Linda smiled. In spite of her weariness, she liked the sound of that. A sudden pang of affection rose in her chest. Despite her snarkiness, Richard was doing his best to keep her focused and on-side, even though that was probably McPherson's job and not his.

He had made this last clue fun for her, no matter her fatigue. Despite the bluff, geeky way he presented himself, he could be surprisingly caring and perceptive. Maybe he had a point about finding themselves. Hadn't she thought the *same* thing just before she joined the case? That in her search for Carver and the answer to Paul's disappearance she might just stumble upon herself.

Linda squeezed Richard's shoulder affectionately, and he jumped in surprise and then blushed. "We better book that Uber before the library closes."

"It's open till ten this evening. I was hoping we could grab a bite to eat on the way."

Linda's stomach came alive at the mention of food. She turned to McPherson. "Can we do that? I'm famished."

McPherson looked more resigned to the food break than agreeable. "We can get something to go but we have to finish it before we get there."

As they headed to the main exit, the orderly who'd shown them the basement appeared out of a side corridor and joined them. "You guys find what you wanted down there?"

McPherson barely acknowledged him with his eyes. "Yes. Thank you, you've done your country a great service."

The guy was not going to be put off so easily. "So listen, I know you can't give me any specifics, but what kind of case are you guys working, major crime, fraud, terrorism?"

"It's a sensitive matter, I'm not at liberty to say anything at the moment."

The orderly stepped right in front of them as they reached the exit. He looked brazen, but also a little abashed at the same time.

"Okay, I'm going to come right out and say this. I'm wasted in this job, y'know? I'm not reaching my potential and I've been thinking for a while that I should join the Bureau. Maybe not as an agent, I could be one of those special advisers you use, on y'know medical matters and stuff. I haven't applied yet but when I do, could you put in a good word for me? Tell them how big a help I was on this case, that kinda thing. Do you think you could do that?"

The orderly looked down at his feet self-consciously, his momentary courage giving way to self-doubt, so he didn't see McPherson rolling his eyes: "Son, I'm afraid the Bureau just doesn't work that way. There's a strict screening process, applicants aren't given the nod because an agent puts in a good word. Not that a word from me would do you the least bit of good with recruitment. You do an important job here, you help save lives, trust me, there's few people in the FBI who can say that."

The orderly looked up briefly and smiled an apology, stepping out of their way, then he dropped his head and spoke to his feet. "Sure, yeah, okay, I get that, doesn't hurt to ask, though." He threw up his hands in a resigned gesture. "Hey, how else am I gonna learn, am I right?"

Linda tried to catch his eye to smile at him or say something reassuring, but he was already turning away, sloping back to the side corridor. He didn't look up to see them leave.

Out on North Grove Street, Linda felt bad for bitching and moaning in the basement. The orderly they'd just brushed off would love nothing more than to throw off his job and join them on this Harvard hunt. Linda was getting paid to do this. She had no right to complain.

So why the sudden sinking feeling in her stomach? What did she fear they were going to find at the library?

CHAPTER 19

THEY RETURNED TO Harvard Yard as it was getting dark. Lights shone in the windows of the surrounding buildings and the streetlights cast twisted shadows through the branches of the trees.

The Widener Library loomed up ahead of them. A huge rectangular building of Harvard brick and limestone traceries. The grand steps that led up to it seemed like they should be on the Senate Building in Washington, as did the grand colonnade of Corinthian columns that fronted it.

Once inside the building, McPherson showed his ID to the staff and they sent for someone in admin from the north wing. A buttoned-up woman in a green cardigan with her hair in a bun greeted them a few minutes later. She introduced herself as Meg and looked every bit the Harvard librarian.

Unlike the hospital orderly, Meg had no interest in their business with the library. Instead, she prattled merrily about the building and its collections as though she was giving a tour to visiting dignitaries. She told them the library housed over three and a half million books in more than a hundred different languages, with one of the world's most comprehensive collections of humanities and social sciences. It had over fifty-seven miles of shelves with five miles of aisles over ten levels.

They followed along behind her, their footsteps clattering and echoing in the great spaces of the library. Richard looked genuinely interested in what Meg was saying, McPherson nodded politely and Linda craned her neck to take in the huge stacks and high ceilings.

The Memorial Rooms were in the center of the library. The grand marble entrance was flanked by two murals that Meg informed them were painted by John Singer Sargent to memorialize the dead of World War One.

Meg led them into the rooms, which were finished in English Oak paneling and were filled with display cases and ornate, glass-fronted bookshelves. Many of the cases were roped off and there were signs everywhere saying: 'Room Alarmed' and 'No Photographs.' The rooms smelled of wood polish and old books.

They stopped by a marble fireplace above which was a portrait of a youthful Harry Elkins Widener. To the left of the fireplace was a desk with a vase of red carnations on it.

"In memory of Mr. Widener," Meg told them. "The family still pays for the flowers. It used to be roses, but they changed to carnations a while ago because they wilt less."

McPherson thanked her for her assistance and asked if the rooms could be closed to the public for the next hour or so.

Meg nodded obligingly. "I'll speak to security, they'll put someone outside the entrance." And with that, she left them to it.

Richard looked around at the shelves and display cases and whistled. "What I wouldn't give for a place like this to store my comics."

Linda chuckled. "You and me both."

"So, where do we start?"

Linda walked over to the desk on the left. "I think it's pretty obviously the flowers, isn't it?"

She reached out to pick up the vase and Richard placed a hand on her arm to stop her. "Careful, this whole place is alarmed."

"And we're the FBI, what are they going to do, arrest us for crimes against foliage?"

The vase seemed to be stuck fast to the antique desktop, but Linda couldn't see what was holding it in place. She tugged again and thought she felt it move slightly. It didn't come away from the desk but she was sure it rotated just a fraction.

Richard was still hovering at her elbow. "What's the matter, is it heavy?"

"No, it won't come away from the desk."

"Do you want me to try?"

Linda gave it an experimental twist, it seemed to move anti-clockwise but not clockwise. In fact, it would freeze up if you tried to move it in that direction. "No, wait, let me try something."

Linda saw her reflection in the glass of the bookcase behind the desk. She also saw that there was a mirrored surface painted onto the other side of the vase. She turned the vase around on the desk in an anti-clockwise direction until the mirrored surface was facing her. As soon as it was, she heard a 'click' and the vase refused to move any further.

Richard looked puzzled. "What did you do?"

"You remember the last line of the clue?"

"You just might find yourselves, yeah, what about it?"

Linda pointed at the mirrored surface. "I spotted this on the back of the vase and moved it round until we see, or rather find, ourselves in it."

"Nice thinking."

The fireplace began to rattle and make a series of noises like tumblers turning in a slot machine. Then a bell clanged inside the chimney, a trapdoor opened at the top of the fireplace, and a Teflon-coated box tumbled into the grate.

McPherson bent and turned the box over so the silver disk was on the top. "Best to leave it in the fireplace so we don't get acid on any of these rare books."

Richard squatted down to stare into the fireplace. "Good call."

"Do you still have the bone?"

Richard ransacked his pockets. "It's here somewhere. Wait . . . no, oh, here it is."

He leaned into the fireplace and placed the mandible on the scales. "Here's where we find out if we chose right."

Once again, the box hummed and the disk turned one hundred and eighty degrees. The lid sprung open and jettisoned the bone.

Richard shuffled his feet in a rhythmless approximation of a happy dance. "Yay, we chose right."

Linda glanced at McPherson, who was doing his best to hide his embarrassment.

Linda bent to look over Richard's shoulder. Inside the box, held in place by yet more metal catches, were an avocado-shaped rock with a mottled texture like snake skin and a silver pendant in the shape of an upside down, lowercase letter 'y.' There was only one plaque inside this box. It read: 'CHOOSE THE CALCULUS.'

"What do you think, Professor?"

Richard pointed at the pendant. "That's the Greek letter lambda."

"And that means . . . ?"

"Lambda is the set of logical axioms in the axiomatic method of deduction in first-order predicate calculus."

Linda stared at him. She wasn't certain she even blinked.

Richard reddened. "What?"

"Was that even English?"

"Sorry, I guess you never attended Math Camp as a kid."

"Ya think?"

Richard cleared his throat. "It's a . . . um, sign used in calculus."

"And what's this?"

"A rock, or something, I guess."

"What's its purpose?"

Richard shrugged. "Breaking glass."

Linda gave him another disapproving stare. Richard looked aggrieved. "Have you seen the number of windows and display cases in here?"

"You think they want us to commit a heist?"

"There's no canister, so maybe the next clue is hidden in one of the rare books."

"Or, hopefully, we've come to the end of the hunt."

"That's more likely."

"So, it's probably the pendant then?"

Richard reached for the box. "Only one way to find out."

Linda put her hand on his wrist to stop him. "Wait, this feels, I dunno, too easy."

"You think calculus is easy?"

"I wouldn't know calculus if it bit me on the ass. But there's something off about this."

Linda looked to McPherson standing over them. "What do you think?"

McPherson thought for a moment then pointed at the box. "We need to identify the rock before discounting it."

"It's some kind of mineral, by the looks of it."

Richard was hunched over his phone, his thumbs flying over the screen. "Nothing for 'rocks and calculus' or other variations on that, but when I searched for 'minerals and calculus' I found there are rocks that form in the human body when a foreign object's lodged there. And, get this, they're called calculi, though I've no idea why. One of the most famous ones is owned by Harvard. It was removed from a Civil War veteran in 1871, after he was shot in the sacrum at the Battle of Gettysburg and survived. The calculus formed around the bullet."

Linda prodded the rock. "Do you think this is the actual calculus?"

"Probably, or one just like it."

"So, we have a calculus and a symbol used in calculus. I guess you could say we're caught between a rock and a hard sum."

"You've been planning that line since I told you about calculus, haven't you?"

"Let's say I was honing it."

McPherson put his hands on their shoulders and moved them both to one side. Then he knelt in front of the fireplace. "The little plaque says to 'choose the calculus,' so I vote we choose the rock."

"Do we get a say?" Linda said.

"When you start paying me to advise *you*. I've listened to your advice and I'm making an executive decision."

McPherson took hold of the rock and pulled it from its catches in the box. Linda heard the soft clunk of the hidden compartment opening. She watched as the acid swirled round the pendant and it diminished by the second. The smell of its dissolution was particularly bitter and she had to put a hand over her face.

"There was no canister, so was that the last of the clues?" Linda said.

McPherson weighed the rock in the palm of his hand. "Yes, I believe it was."

"So, what happens now?"

There was a low creaking from between the bookshelves. A section of the wood paneling slid to one side to reveal a hidden passageway.

Linda saw the barrel of a thirty-eight appear from the passageway, but she couldn't make out the person holding it.

"Now, you come with me," a voice said from the shadows.

CHAPTER 20

EVERYONE FROZE, Linda and Richard on their haunches in front of the fireplace, McPherson standing to their side. Linda looked up at McPherson, he motioned for them to get to their feet.

McPherson squared his shoulders. "I take it you're this Dierngewrit fellow?"

"Call me DG, isn't that your little sobriquet? And I'm going to insist you follow me."

Linda felt her legs shake. No matter how many times she had a gun pointed at her, she never got used to it. "Come with you? In there?"

"There's ample room for us all. Step inside, turn to your left and then your immediate right. Remember, I'll be right behind you and I'm armed."

Richard had his hands up, he clenched and unclenched them in agitation. "There's no need for the gun, we want to come with you. We want to talk. We've flown across ten states to be here."

"I'll decide what's necessary and what's not. Now, we don't have much time. A bored and curious security guard is going to come through that door at any moment and I don't want him to learn about this passage or any others in the library."

The pistol disappeared into the shadows but Linda could make out its shape along with the figure holding it. She and Richard looked to McPherson again. He nodded and gestured for them to go ahead.

Richard went first. He moved with a loping mixture of trepidation and eagerness as he stepped into the passageway and glanced round, blinking in the dim light. "Are there other passages like this one? Are they all over the library or do they go further?"

Their captor said nothing, simply prodded Richard in the back with the barrel of his pistol so he stumbled forward. Linda followed him into the passage. It smelled of old oak, stale air, and dust. She didn't suffer from claustrophobia, but the passage was cramped and there were three of them in there, one of whom was still holding a gun.

She was breathing too quickly and she felt sick and lightheaded. The shadows seemed to darken and the walls of the passage felt like they were encroaching on her, squeezed from outside.

McPherson stepped in behind Linda so the gun would be on him. This simple protective gesture helped her gain control of her breathing. Her eyes adjusted to the dark and her panic ebbed.

They turned left and right as instructed and began walking down the passageway. DG clicked a flashlight on, so they could see a few steps ahead. It also meant that if they stole a glance behind them, they'd be dazzled by the flashlight's beam.

As Linda's fear subsided, it was replaced by an anger born of tiredness and resentment. She was fairly sure this DG guy wasn't going to shoot them, after going to such lengths to get them to a library in Harvard. She was done with being moved around like a pawn on a chessboard, and she couldn't stop herself from baiting him.

"So how come you can't just drop us a line like normal folk? You know, 'Hey you wanna hear about the Shadows in the Cave? Hit me up sometime, we'll do coffee.' Why all this cloak and dagger stuff?"

DG had a deep and cultured voice, jaded and amused at the same time. "For one thing, Ms. Corrigan, I am nothing like 'normal folk.' People in my position are constantly under observation, from the moment we wake until the moment we fall asleep, someone is watching everything we do."

"And that makes you different from any influencer, how exactly?"

"The people watching me will do a lot worse than gossip on Tattle Life. I have to be careful what channels of communication I use and I can't just invite people over for coffee and a cozy chat about the shadow government. I need to be more discreet in my extra-curricular communications."

"Right, because nothing says 'discreet' quite like sending the FBI all over Boston asking questions."

"Touché, Ms. Corrigan."

"Seriously though, why couldn't we just meet you in an underground parking lot, like Deep Throat?"

"Because you are not Woodward and Bernstein and I am not revealing prosaic truths about a corrupt politician. Have you heard of the Mysteries of Eleusis?"

"Is it anything like *Murder She Wrote*?"

"No, it's an ancient rite that took place in the Greek town of Eleusis, north of Athens, as early as the Mycenaean period, but even then it was considered impossibly old and its origins were shrouded in mystery. The ceremonies were considered so holy that no one who took part could breathe a word of them, because they contained truths that predated mankind itself."

Richard gasped. "The Faith That Came Before Man, the Qu'rrm Saddic Heresy."

"Very good, Mr. Ford. There were three stages to the Mysteries."

Richard stopped suddenly and Linda bumped into him. He turned and put a hand on her shoulder. "Sorry, there are steps here, what should I do."

"Perfect timing. You should descend, Mr. Ford. The first stage of the Mysteries was the Descent into the Chthonic world of the Mystery. The second stage was the Search, initiates would have to walk a maze in Minoan Crete or visit certain stations in Nineveh and Eleusis. They would do this to prepare themselves to receive the revelation. Some truths must be hard won and they must be hunted down, because without the hunt you can't receive them."

"That's what you were doing, sending us on a search for the truth?"

"Sending you on a search to prepare you for the truth, a search around the secret stations of Harvard, each of which has darker history than anyone suspects."

The passage at the bottom of the stairs was made of stone, it ended abruptly at a glass security door with a keypad. "Don't turn around, keep looking straight ahead, and type 457812 into the keypad."

Richard did as he was told and the glass door opened onto a concrete corridor around ten feet high and ten feet wide that seemed to stretch for miles. Large metal pipes ran along the ceiling and the walls along with power lines and other colored cables. The temperature was subtropical, it had to be at least ninety or a hundred degrees.

Linda, though not dressed for the cold Boston, still began to shed layers, it was so hot. "Where exactly are we?"

DG still held the flashlight, even though the corridor was fully lighted. "It's known as the Tunnel, but it's actually a series of tunnels that run beneath the Business School, the Yard, the Houses, and the Law School. It's where steam, power, and other utilities are carried all over the university. It was built between 1914 and 1927. Not many people know it's down here, but it did harbor a Nazi spy during the war."

Richard was looking around him, craning his neck, his face lit up with fascination. DG shone the flashlight into his eyes. "Eyes front and keep walking due south."

"Sorry, I was just taking it all in. How much further do we have to go?"

"Until I tell you to stop."

They walked in silence for a while, in the sweltering heat of the tunnel, their footsteps clattering down the endless corridor. Occasionally they passed locked doors and crossed junctions with other corridors.

Linda could smell the sweat in her armpits, and her throat was parched. She was about to ask if there was anything to drink when DG told them to stop. "Open that door to your left."

Richard obliged and they followed him into a darkened room that was even hotter than the corridor. DG shut the door behind them, and now the only illumination came from his flashlight. There were four large, square tanks in the room. Three of them had pipes running in and out of them. The fourth sat in the far corner. DG directed them towards it.

The tank was about seven feet high and just as deep. DG stayed in the shadows but reached up to one of the corners and released a catch of some sort. There was a loud clank and then a screech as a panel slid to one side revealing the darkened interior of the tank.

DG shone the torch into the interior. "Step inside."

Linda felt her breathing quicken again, and her legs shook. She didn't like the idea of being in the tank. "What's inside?"

"You'll have to step in to find out."

Richard could see she was nervous. He put a reassuring hand on her arm and took her elbow. "It's okay, I'll be right there with you."

She let herself be led inside. The space became very cramped when McPherson joined them. DG remained in the doorway and shone his beam at the far wall of the tank.

The outline of a man had been painted on this wall in yellow paint. Inside the outline were four small apertures, each roughly oval. One aperture was positioned inside the head, another by the heart, a third just above the legs and the final one in the left knee of the outline.

Linda squinted in the dim light. "What's this supposed to be?"

DG let his flashlight beam play across the figure. "This is your final test."

Richard looked nervously at the outline on the wall. "What do we have to do?"

"There are four apertures in front of you, each in a different part of the figure's anatomy. You have to place the object you chose in the library into the aperture that is closest to where it was originally removed from the donor's body. If you get it right, everything will be revealed to you."

"And if we get it wrong?"

"I'll close this door and in an hour or so the Tunnel's crew and repair staff will come and let you out, but all your hard work today will have been for nothing."

"No pressure then."

"Do you still have the rock thing?" Richard asked McPherson.

McPherson reached into the pocket of his jacket. "The calculus? Here it is."

Richard took the calculus. "It's heavier than it looks."

Linda felt confined by the small space and wanted this part over as soon as possible. "Do you remember where they removed it from?"

"If I recall it was his sacrum. Do you know where that is?"

Linda held out her hand. "Give it here."

"Okay, but you're sure you know where it is? I mean I don't want us to blow it at the last minute."

"Trust me, I don't want to spend any longer inside this tank than I have to. I'm an artist, I've studied anatomy for years, I know where the sacrum is."

McPherson sounded just the tiniest bit skeptical. "Do you mind if I ask where it is, before you go putting that stone anywhere?"

"It's the triangular bone at the back of the pelvis that sits between the hips. It's made up of fused vertebrae and it ends in the coccyx. Do I get a gold star, professor?"

"Hopefully, you get us out of here."

Linda bent forward and dropped the calculus into the aperture just above the legs. She straightened up and . . .

. . . nothing happened.

Richard shifted from foot to foot. "It hasn't worked. You got the wrong hole."

"Hold on, it hasn't finished."

There was a sudden rattling noise behind the wall, like a cascade of pebbles. Then, with a wrenching crack, a section of the wall began to detach itself and swing inward like a door. On the other side of this door was a carved stone tunnel.

DG stepped into the tank, still holding the gun and the flashlight. "What more of an invitation do you want? This is what everything has been leading up to."

Linda stepped through the stone doorway into the carved tunnel beyond. The first thing that hit her was the cold. The Tunnel had been heated by the steam in the pipes but now she was surrounded by cool, damp rock. She put on the layers she'd shed and pulled her light summer jacket around her but it gave little warmth.

Linda stumbled a few steps into the tunnel and waited for Richard, McPherson, and DG to join her. It was dark and she needed the flashlight to see by. She pulled out her phone to use the flashlight as the others caught up.

DG informed her: "That won't be necessary."

"Was this tunnel also built in 1914?"

"No, this network of tunnels is much, much older. We've been here a very long time."

"How long?"

"You might say they built the college around us. Did you learn nothing from the search? You saw the benefactor, from our ranks, who gave his name to this college. You saw how we deal with those who try and expose us."

Richard cleared his throat. "Would that be George Parkman or John Webster?"

"One was a declared enemy, the other a useful stooge. You also saw how we lionize those who guard our secret truths and hidden texts."

"You mean Widener?"

"We built a temple to the written word in his name. We've taken you round the stations of our hidden power and now it's time to ascend."

Linda felt the slope of the tunnel growing steeper. "If we're going to ascend, why is this tunnel going down?"

"Have you no appreciation for metaphor, Ms. Corrigan? This ascent is not physical, so it can only be made from the depths of the earth."

As DG said this, the tunnel Linda was following took a sharp turn to the left. She followed it round the corner as the tunnel fell steeply down and narrowed. Then she stopped abruptly and Richard, stumbling forward in the dim light, walked right into her.

She put out her hands to stop herself pitching forward and righted herself just in time. The tunnel ended without warning, replaced by the sheer drop of a long, deep shaft.

The shaft was wide enough that Linda couldn't see the opposite side. All she could make out was a set of stone steps cut into the shaft's wall. They descended in a spiral that snaked down into darkness.

McPherson and DG had also come to a halt. DG spoke up from the narrow tunnel. "Keep going, Ms. Corrigan, this shaft is the reason Harvard was built where it was. This is where your answers lie. This is the revelation for which we've been preparing you."

CHAPTER 21

FOR A MOMENT, Linda simply froze. The cavernous gulf of the shaft was too wide and too deep. Her legs wouldn't move and her brain refused to register what it was seeing.

She felt a gentle hand on her shoulder, it was Richard. "Are you . . . are you okay?"

Linda swallowed, but her throat was so dry it hurt. Her voice was hoarse. "No, I don't think I can do it. I need to go back."

"I don't think that's an option. He's got a gun on us."

"We could rush him. He's not going to shoot us, he went to all this trouble to get us down here."

"He wouldn't need to shoot us, he could just push us over the edge."

Linda felt the strength drain from her legs, afraid they would go out from under her. "Don't say that."

"Like you said, he went to all this trouble to get us down here, I don't think he's going to let us go back."

McPherson called from behind Richard. "Is there a problem, what's holding us up?"

Linda's throat was too dry to reply in more than a whisper. "I can't go, you'll have to go on without me."

DG would brook no dissent. "That's not an option, Ms. Corrigan, you have to see this through."

That did nothing to help her confidence. The great chasm yawned in front of her, its steep sides seeming to fall downward forever. Linda wanted to turn and bolt back up the tunnel like a fox run to ground.

McPherson came to her aid, his voice full of kindness and authority. "Turn to face the wall and put your palms flat against it. Look at the wall or look at your feet, but don't look over your shoulder. Take one step at a time, don't think about where you're going, just concentrate on each individual step. We'll take it at your pace, there's no rush."

DG was less sympathetic. "We do need to get there today."

Linda ignored him. She filled her lungs, let the breath out and moved from the tunnel onto the first stone step. She pressed herself against the jagged rock of the wall. It was cold and sucked the heat from her body, making her jaw shake and her teeth clatter.

Linda glanced down at her feet. Still clinging to the wall, she shuffled sideways toward the next step. The step was only a few feet long but it took forever to reach the edge.

Linda put her right foot out and let it dangle in mid-air as she lowered it onto the next step. The step wasn't there. She kept lowering her foot but the step wouldn't meet it.

Linda feared there was no step, that her foot would just keep falling until she lost her footing and toppled backward, plunging into the abyss behind her, falling forever. She dug her fingers into the wall and felt two of her nails break.

She was just about to pull her foot back when the toe of her sneaker hit something. Linda transferred her weight slowly and her right foot finally settled on the step. Still clinging to the wall, she moved her left foot down to meet the right.

She'd made it. One step down and only . . . how many more steps were there?

Linda glanced to her side and saw countless steps curving round the huge deep wall of the shaft, going endlessly downward and out of sight. That was a mistake.

She swung her head back and stared at the wall, feeling the heat leach out of her palms. The step beneath her began to sway and then the whole shaft started to spin. Linda's stomach lurched and her heart pounded against her ribs.

She heard a series of quick, high-pitched rasps and realized it was her own breath. There was shuffling to Linda's left and she ventured a look. Richard had left the tunnel and had moved to the first step next to her. McPherson was standing in the tunnel watching.

Richard had pressed himself right up against the wall too and was shuffling just as slowly along the step. The fact that he found it just as terrifying gave Linda some small comfort. It also filled her with compassion.

She understood his fear and she didn't want to make his ordeal any worse by holding him up. Linda shuffled like a crab to the edge of the step and put her foot down onto the next one. The distance between the steps didn't seem so great this time and she was able to get onto the next step without any drama.

Her legs were firmer, the step was solid beneath her feet, and the shaft stopped spinning. So long as she looked only at the wall in front of her and the step directly beneath, Linda was able to make her way slowly down the stone staircases with Richard, McPherson and DG following.

She caught a brief glimpse of McPherson and DG, descending as though it were a staircase in any building, totally unfazed by the sheer vertical drop directly to their right. McPherson seemed a little bored, while DG remained in the shadows.

Linda wasn't certain how long she kept going like this. She concentrated on every step, taking each one as they came. She kept her eyes away from the yawning void inches behind her and her thoughts away from plummeting into the endless drop that would claim her if she lost her footing.

Linda lost count of the steps she shuffled along. Her fingertips were raw where she'd dug them into the crags of the wall. The sound of their feet on the stone steps echoed all around her, reverberating down the shaft, reminding Linda that behind her, less than an inch from her heels, lay certain death, deep within the bowels of the earth.

Finally, Linda's feet found a ledge that ran around the curved wall of the shaft. It was wider than the steps, but no less precarious. Linda pressed herself to the wall as she inched along it. Beside her, Richard did the same.

Linda was pressing herself so hard against the uneven crags of the wall that she lost her balance when her arm hit empty air. She flailed and fell forward. The wall had disappeared. Something grabbed her arms, arresting her fall. She realized fingers were digging into her flesh.

The darkness was so deep Linda couldn't see who had hold of her. She'd stumbled through some sort of entrance and several figures had grabbed her. She was pulled deeper into what must be a cavern, the toes of her sneakers scraping the rock floor as she dangled in her captors' grip. A sack was placed over her head. It was made of a soft, smooth material like satin.

The hidden figures pinned her arms to her side, grabbed her

ankles and lifted her from the ground. Linda was carried into the cavern, but was so disoriented she had no idea how far or in what direction.

Her captors laid Linda down on a hard flat surface. Her hands were raised above her head and her legs were forced apart. Something cold and metal was clamped around her wrists and ankles. Only when she was incapable of breaking free was the sack removed from her head.

Linda found herself in a large cavern with a high, stalactite-covered ceiling. She was chained to what looked like a medieval torture device. It was a rectangular wooden platform with manacles at the top and bottom to hold her captive. Linda turned her head and saw Richard and McPherson chained to similar devices on either side of her. In front of them was an alabaster pedestal that looked like something from an ancient Greek temple.

Ten robed and hooded figures surrounded them, five of whom were holding burning torches. DG stood in the middle of the throng. He was tall, around six-five, and dressed in an expensive suit. He had dark hair, which was graying at the temples, and a long, haughty face.

DG opened his jacket, placed the thirty-eight in a shoulder holster, and signaled to the robed figures to bring him something. "This is where you finally get some answers. I can promise you two things—you aren't going to like them, and it will be a most unique experience."

CHAPTER 22

FOUR OF THE robed acolytes left the main cavern. Linda glanced at Richard and McPherson. Neither of them were fighting their bonds or speaking to their captors. They were just looking warily around at their surroundings.

Were they drugged, or just overwhelmed by the situation? Linda was a little overawed herself. She hadn't tested the manacles holding her in place, though they were biting into her ankles. Was she shallow for wishing she'd stuck more closely to her diet?

The four robed figures returned carrying a large, liquid-filled tank and placed it on the alabaster pedestal. The tank looked like an aquarium at first glance, but the liquid inside gave the impression it was constantly turning itself inside out through a spectrum of impossible angles. Holding the shape of the tank's interior, and countless others, all at the same time.

It hurt Linda's eyes to look at it. Or rather, it wasn't so much her eyes that hurt, as her optic nerves, struggling to process the images the liquid gave off. In addition to the liquid, the tank appeared to have several inhabitants.

The glass of the tank was marked with arcane symbols, written in gold leaf, forming nearly unthinkable shapes. Linda doubted she could replicate any of the symbols, even if she were drawing them with the tank right in front of her. All except for one, a lopsided diamond shape that seemed very familiar to her. Something about it reminded Linda of her early childhood, the part she'd all but forgotten.

DG placed his hands on the tank and leaned forward to address them. He looked like a zealous priest about to deliver a sermon.

He paused for a moment and his face broke into the most mercenary and self-satisfied smile Linda had ever seen. Most politicians could have taken lessons.

"What you'll never discover, no matter how much you dig, is just how long we've been around. They didn't just build this college around us or even this nation, they've built many civilizations. No one knows this. We make sure of that. Occasionally, when someone gets a little too inquisitive and that person is allied with an agency like the FBI, we take steps to silence them."

Richard became agitated, for the first time. "I don't understand, I . . . I reached out to you. You were on the forums, the ones only hardcore truth-seekers find. You opened up, you wanted me to know things."

"I baited the hook and I reeled you in, Mr. Ford. If your persistence and initiative were enough to get you that far, you might actually be a minor annoyance to us. So we're taking steps to rectify that."

There was a half-sob in Richard's voice. "You don't have to kill us."

"We're not going to kill you, Mr. Ford."

"You're not?"

"No, as I told you, we're going to give you the answers you're searching for."

There was a burst of light from inside the liquid of the tank. It was like a crackling electrical discharge and for a brief second it lit DG's face from below, giving his features a demonic aspect. He looked down at the tank's inhabitants with the kind of love a vivisectionist has for their rats.

DG trailed his fingers in the liquid of the tank, then held them over the surface. His fingers came out clean, but as he dangled them above the liquid several gelatinous drops leaped from the tank and coated his digits, as if they were dripping in reverse. The strange liquid played about his fingers, distorting whatever it coated, like inhuman discharge. Then it evaporated into a cloud of what Linda could only think of as anti-twinkles. Tiny pinpricks of darkness that seemed to steal light from the air rather than emit it.

DG considered this wistfully. "You should quite honestly consider this an honor. In the history of humanity, only a handful of human beings have ever seen these creatures. They would likely have been extinct before the Cretaceous period, had they not been cultivated and kept alive by beings that predate us by eons. These beings named them Scwyrms.

"The Scwyrms taught them so much. They exist at that very tipping point where matter becomes pure consciousness, where energy waves become purely notional but continue their existence on other planes of being. This is their larval state, before they transition into something near incomprehensible. We keep them like this artificially, prolonging their infant state for centuries, only occasionally allowing two of them to reach maturity and then mate. These little offspring are the result of the last union we allowed."

Richard was breathing heavily. Linda thought he was going to hyperventilate. "What are you going to do with them?"

"I'm going to introduce you to perhaps their most fascinating feature, you see these creatures can feed off human memory. They are capable of storing these memories at a cellular level, and also of transmitting them, if kept in suspended animation. Just as a horse fly will vomit up its meal if it finds something tastier and more nutritious, these creatures will dump their last memories, if they find something fresher."

He patted the tank. "At least one of the memories in here is nearly four hundred years old, so one of you is going to be transported way into the past."

DG turned from the tank and motioned for his acolytes to approach. Two of the robed figures stepped up and placed what looked like a lead-lined apron and gloves on him, then they placed a visor over his face.

DG dismissed them and directed his attention back to the tank. He reached inside and grasped one of the Scwyrms in his gloved hands. From the turbulence of the liquid in the tank, the thing seemed to fight him at first. Moving with what appeared to be a practiced grace and precision, DG soothed the occupants of the tank so that he could lift one out.

What emerged from the liquid was a creature about three feet in length. It looked like an oversized maggot with a head that resembled a jellyfish. Its body was pasty white and oozing some form of slime or mucus. It was crenelated and writhing in DG's hands. Its head had the bell-shaped hood of a jellyfish from which four frond-like arms protruded. The arms stretched out, like snake tongues, tasting the air around it.

DG held it out in front of him and moved away from the tank. The Scwyrm's fronds seemed to pick up Linda's scent and reach out to her, curling and uncurling as if to draw her to it. Linda strained against her manacles, trying to break free. She thrashed from side to side to avoid the creature, but she was held fast.

"Don't! Don't you dare," Linda demanded. But DG ignored her.

DG placed the Scwyrm gently on her chest. The length of its body covered her torso and the top of her legs. It was heavier than it looked and knocked the breath out of her, making breathing difficult because it was pressing hard on her chest. As she gasped for air, a distant part of Linda's mind noted one small blessing, it meant she caught less of the Scwyrm's hideous odor.

Its smell reminded her of her father, in his last days, as he lay in a hospital bed, surrendering to the cancer that dogged him for the last two years of his life. Of the stale sweat and putrescence that clung to a body given over to a slow death.

The odor of the Scwyrm was much stronger, as though it had taken every rotten thing Linda had ever smelled in her life, every dead dog and stagnant pool, and cooked it down to its absolute essence.

At first, the creature did very little as Linda tossed her head back and forth to get away from its scent and to knock it off her. Then her desperate, futile actions caught its attention.

The Scwyrm began waving its long, jellied arms over her chest and face as if it were tasting the air above Linda to identify her. Then it laid those cold, damp fronds on her face, like a blind person trying to get a picture of her features.

The creature's touch was icy, but also contained a tiny charge, like a battery. It sent uncomfortable sensations through Linda's skin, like a virulent itch she could do nothing to scratch.

She threw her head from side to side to shake it off but the creature pressed its arms more firmly to her face. Then it began to wrap them around the top of her head, covering the back of her head as well as the forehead and temples, like some dank, foul-smelling bandage.

There was nothing Linda could do to resist. When the fronds had wrapped themselves twice around her cranium, their muscles went taught and rigid. This caused Linda's head to snap backward, and the icy fronds held it in this position.

Once the Scwyrm had Linda's head in place, it lifted itself off her chest and folded itself over, bending in the middle so its tail, which had been lying by her crotch, was now dangling over her face.

The tail was bifurcated, split into two long, thin, maggot-like appendages. Each section of the tale ended in a puckered orifice that reminded Linda of a sphincter. The Scwyrm lowered its tail toward Linda's face until the split tail was resting on her mouth.

Linda clamped her lips shut to keep the cold slime it exuded from getting in her mouth. The two ends of its tail made their way toward her nostrils. The Scwyrm held her in place and there was nothing she could do to stop it.

The tails entered her nose and Linda panicked, fearing she would be smothered by this ancient thing. The tails crept further and further up her nasal cavities. Their scent was rank and they gave off the same charge that the arms of its head did, which was maddening in so intimate a space as her nostrils.

Linda was terrified she was going to suffocate from lack of oxygen, but the creature emitted gusts of fetid air from both of its orifices with such pressure, Linda felt her lungs forcibly inflate.

The long, thin tendrils from the creature's head descended on her face next. They lifted her eyelids and began to work their way around her eyeballs, pushing their way into her eye sockets. This was excruciating to begin with but the tendrils were so cold they numbed not only her eyes but the whole front of her face.

The tendrils wormed their way round the back of her eyeballs and wrapped themselves around her optic nerves. As they crept further down the bundle of nerve fibers, it dawned on Linda that they were making their way toward her brain.

The tails had advanced beyond her nasal cavity and up into her olfactory tract. With a sharp stab of white-hot pain, the tail broke through into her brainpan. Linda's whole head was engulfed in the most intense migraine she had ever suffered, its onset sudden and devastating.

At the same time the tendrils had reached her thalamus, giving her the worst brain-freeze she'd experienced in her life. That was when things got very confusing.

Linda was conscious of the creature attempting to interface with her brain, probing and exploring it. This brought a physical awareness of her brain as a functioning organ. Linda was rarely aware of her internal organs, unless they caused her some pain or discomfort. She had never felt her brain functioning as a physical sensation before and she didn't like it.

The Scwyrm was doing something to the chemical-electrical

signals of her frontal and temporal lobes. Rerouting and reprogramming them to its own purpose. The effect was not pleasant.

All five of Linda's senses began to malfunction. It felt like she was having a seizure. The soles of her feet were convinced they could smell her sneakers. The back of her neck could taste the fabric softener on her blouse. Her kidneys could hear her lower colon singing to them.

Then the pain and discomfort faded and her senses came back online. Only they weren't her senses, not anymore. It was as if someone had grafted another cerebral cortex onto her own. Every one of the things she was feeling were alien to her. For a second the shock was so great Linda felt violated. She was experiencing the sensations of another human being at a level of intimacy no one should ever know.

She was not herself. She was inside the memory of someone who'd lived a long time ago. The change was sudden and complete. One minute she was in a cavern under Harvard and the next she was in the seventeenth century. Like blinking and finding she was looking out of a different set of eyes at a land that had long passed. The creature was regurgitating an old memory directly into Linda's consciousness.

This meant it had found a memory of Linda's that it liked. And now it was going to feed on it.

CHAPTER 23

THE **TASTE OF** sour milk and coarse pipe tobacco was in Linda's mouth. It wasn't pleasant. She smelled beeswax, animal fat, and the urinous stench of human bodies that haven't bathed in months, most especially her own.

She could feel the rough wool, starched cotton, and pinched leather of her clothing. Her hemorrhoids itched madly. The small of her back ached and her scrotum, stretched with age, chafed against her undergarments.

She was a man. But which man? As the question formed in her mind, the answer followed in its wake. The whole matrix of this other life presented itself to her. A thousand fleeting recollections from which he'd constructed his sense of himself.

He was Angus McKay and he was seventy-two years old. He was gripped with the worst foreboding of his life. It came as a cold, heavy weight in his gut.

Angus had learned to trust his gut. It had kept him alive as a boy in the Highlands of Scotland and it had served him just as well in the New World. It had seen him across many oceans and it had made him a fortune.

His daughter, Mary, was calling him down from his room. She had news about her daughter, Fiona, Angus's eldest granddaughter. Angus didn't usually like to be disturbed before supper. The afternoon was his time for quiet rumination or taking a nap. But Mary was insistent he'd want to hear what Fiona had to say.

Angus was preparing himself to come down. Taking his time, and dwelling on the many matters that demanded his attention as an elder of the colony.

His granddaughter, Fiona, was headstrong, that was true enough. Her mother and father had trouble keeping Fiona on the path of righteousness. She did not always conduct herself as the granddaughter of a revered elder should. Of late, it seemed the only word she did heed was that of her grandfather.

Maybe it was her spirit, or her likeness to her grandmother, but Fiona had always been Angus's favourite. He didn't flaunt this fact. He did well by all his grandchildren, but the whole family knew. What only Fiona knew was that Angus had made her the main beneficiary in his will.

She had come of age for courting and tongues were wagging all about Charlestown. Her family was prominent in the colony, so everyone spoke of the young men Fiona rode out with. Angus kept a watchful eye on the situation but had decided to let her enjoy her youth and beauty before he found her a suitable husband. An indulgence he never granted his children.

As he laced his boots and rubbed the sleep from his eyes, Angus wondered if his foreboding came from some indiscretion his granddaughter had committed. Was there a prominent family with whom he had to have a word or a young scion who might benefit from a grand trip to Europe?

Angus ran the colony with a light touch, so his power and influence extended further than any of the colonists realized. He was a Shadowcaster, a prominent member of the Twelve Families. This was how the Families had taken charge since coming to these shores. It was how they'd ruled Europe for millennia.

They had prospered quickly in the New World. They possessed skills and knowledge unique to them. They'd carried it with them over the ocean, a treasure trove of forbidden lore that came from an age before time and a race that predated man.

As he readied himself to go downstairs, Angus considered this ancient knowledge. Some of it was recorded on scrolls unlike any that existed in the human world. With words woven, in a language no human mouth could pronounce, into the hide of animals extinct so long the scrolls were their only surviving remnant.

Other knowledge was hidden so ingeniously a person would train a whole lifetime just to read them. Knowledge written in microscopic script on the internal faces of a diamond's crystal lattice. Microscopic script that could only be read when the diamond was exposed to just the right light, at just the right angle, so it emitted rays that cast burning symbols on a wall.

Only the Shadowcasters, the elite of the Twelve Families, knew where this knowledge came from and who had recorded it. Beings who knew the Earth when the land was a single continent. Who created a time capsule for their essential selves, preserved in the form of a faith. A faith deemed heretical by the religions of every race that came after. That held the seeds of destruction and escape from the material world.

This knowledge brought the Twelve Families much favor. They knew how to tame the land, to produce healthy livestock and fruitful harvests, and they knew enough to let the other settlers prosper from their good fortune.

They found the funds to establish the Thirteen Colonies' first public school and helped the Great and General Court of the Massachusetts Bay Colony vote to establish a college. They never announced themselves, they achieved all this through proxies and anonymous funds. They'd learned over the centuries to remain—he smiled at his own pun—'in the shadows,' exerting their influence with an invisible hand.

This was why proxies like Captain John Hull, Mint Master of the Massachusetts Bay Colony, proved so useful when they dealt with the Massachusetts Legislature. Through him, they had introduced coinage marked with one of their sacred emblems—the Pine Tree. Sadly, the British monarch thought this an act of treason and demanded they scrap the coins or he'd void their charter.

In time, the colonies would have to be taken out of the King's hands so a new nation could be founded on this land. This matter was in hand and plans were afoot to throw off the yoke of the old world and create a new nation, secretly allied to the Shadowcasters' grand stratagem. A nation that might come to be the proudest and mightiest on the planet.

Angus stood before the looking glass, a forbidden item in a Puritan colony where they were seen as doorways to vanity and self-regard. He smoothed the wrinkles from his clothing with rough, callused palms. Turned to one side and then the other to make sure he was presentable. He could wear the shortcomings of his age in private, but in public, and before his family, he had to present as a powerful patriarch.

This was how his grandfather, and later his father, had hidden in plain sight. It was how he had learned to avoid the colony's suspicions and keep safe the secrets whose burden now fell upon his shoulders.

Angus's family had left Dunballan, a tiny village in the Highlands of Scotland, just north of the town of St. Leonards, when he was a wee bairn. An ideological rift had opened up between the original Twelve Families. A rift that had brewed for generations according to his grandmother.

The schism arose from their hidden faith, the Faith that Came Before Man, known by some as the Qu'rm Saddic Heresy. Seated as a child at his grandmother's feet, Angus had learned the secrets of the universe, as had every member of the Twelve Families.

He had been taught that the material world was a prison that held God captive. That when God had entered the universe he had split as a ray of light splits when it hits a prism. At first, God had split into Himself and His Twin, the Weorold Cyning. Then he had split further, becoming the pantheon of Gods, Goddesses, Orisha, Annunaki and other angels. Finally, God had put on the material form of all living things in the universe and in doing so had forgotten He was ever God.

This was the plan of the Weorold Cyning, who could never admit that he came second and was inferior to God, because he was simply a part of God. So he trapped his Brother in the material world and forced God to worship him as a "vain and jealous god". So that all living things would forget that they were really God experiencing Himself individually and would give over their power to the Weorold Cyning.

The schism that arose among the Twelve Families came when some of the families tried to argue that the Weorold Cyning was the equal of God. This mistake had arisen many times before, because the Weorold Cyning offered power to his followers, promising the secrets of creation and control of monsters. Up until now, the mistake had always been expunged from the Twelve Families, and their faith had remained pure.

But the rift had run too deep this time. Angus had just come of age when it tore the Twelve Families apart, pitting six families against six. Those in the Weorold Cyning's camp, led by the McLaughlin family, stayed in the Scottish Highland town of St. Leonards. Those who cleaved to the original faith fled with whatever records and scrolls they could salvage.

They traveled first to the Netherlands, where they hid among the Huguenots. Shadowcasters had been doing this since the dawn of humanity. In the ancient world they hid among the Gnostics, who in turn moved among the early Christians. In Mesopotamia, they had hidden among the worshippers of Inanna who mingled in the temples of Ningal, consort of the moon god Nanna.

While they were in the Netherlands, the six families who fled were joined by the McLaughlin family. They claimed to have mended their ways but they were not trusted. However, the McLaughlins were skilled diplomats and soon won everyone round. There was much rejoicing that they'd returned to the fold.

The McLaughlin family brought powerful knowledge with them. It was they who suggested the seven families join the English Puritans making their way to America to become part of the Massachusetts Colony.

Their time in the New World had changed the families. The McLaughlins weren't content to use their influence invisibly and beneficently, they hungered for power and turned once again to worship of the Weorold Cyning as God's equal. Of late, it had been all Angus could do to contain their malign influence, but he would stand firm and resolute against them.

Angus held the position of Philosopher among the Shadowcasters. He led the seven families to the New World and through them, he led the thirteen colonies. He controlled the knowledge the families had and the power it brought them. So long as he was alive he would use this power to check the McLaughlin family's schemes.

These were his thoughts as he readied himself to see Fiona and Mary. His joints creaked and his knees popped as he made his way downstairs to where his granddaughter was waiting. His breath came with more difficulty than usual and that old pain in his chest was back. He ignored these things and drew himself up to his full height as he reached the bottom of the stairs.

Fiona rushed to greet him. She curtsied and took his hands in hers.

"Oh Grandfather, I have good news," she trilled.

"And what is that, lass?"

She held up her left hand to him and there, on the third finger, was a gold ring with an emerald in it. "Why, I'm to be wed, of course."

Angus's heart beat irregularly and his mouth was dry as he asked, "And who might the lucky fellow be?"

"Don't worry, he's from one of the seven Families, it's William

McLaughlin. I know our families have had their differences in the past, but he really is the sweetest boy. If you just give him an opportunity, I know you'll warm to him too."

The dismay hit Angus's chest like a breaker smashing the prow of a ship. Angus felt the timbers of his heart collapse. The pain was liquid fire, burning down his arm, snatching his breath and weakening his legs.

The joy in Fiona's face gave way to concern and she put her hand to his cheek. "Oh Grandfather, speak, tell me your thoughts, give me your blessing, I beseech you."

Angus dropped to his knees, as if the Weorold Cyning himself had taken his shoulders and forced him to the ground. From his knees, he pitched forward with the sound of Mary's screams and Fiona's sobs in his ears.

He slipped in and out of consciousness for the next few days. They carried him back to his bed and summoned the physician, then the pastor. When their ministrations proved ineffective, the Shadowcasters took charge.

They carried him to the tunnels and down the shaft. The shaft that had been in place for as long as these lands had been inhabited. The shaft that held its own secrets and had called them from the Old World.

For as long as the Twelve Families had existed, they had always gathered in locations with deep subterranean tunnels. In Angus's youth, it had been the underground maze beneath St. Leonards. In his old age, it had been the subterrestrial secrets of Charlestown.

He had only hours left when they summoned the Scwyrm to take his last memories. This was at the McLaughlins' behest. He knew why they were doing it. They wanted to preserve their moment of triumph to savor it later.

They had outplayed him. Fiona was his principal heir and the scrolls and other records would go to her, but she was a McLaughlin now and the property of her husband. So the McLaughlins had control of all the sacred texts and had thwarted his efforts to resist them. It did not bode well for the Faith.

A shadow had been cast over the Shadows in the Cave.

CHAPTER 24

"**S**HOULD YOU BE here, honey?" The nurse was middle-aged with dyed red hair, an ample bosom, and a kind smile.

Linda was in a hospital smock, pulling her IV along on a mobile stand. Her words sounded a little slurred. "Yeah, it's okay, they . . . they, I'm expected."

The nurse raised her eyebrows, her look seemed to say: *Oh, really?* She took Linda's arm and was just about to lead her away from the meeting room and back to bed when a senior nurse appeared. "It's okay, Irene, she's with the um . . . " She made a circular motion with her hand.

Irene let go of Linda's arm, stepped away, and straightened her back. She looked at Linda with a renewed respect. "With the FBI?"

Linda nodded.

"They sure did a number on you, honey."

"I've had better days."

Irene chuckled. Linda shuffled past and opened the meeting room door.

She'd checked into Massachusetts General a day ago. According to the doctor who saw her, Linda had been found unconscious on campus along with Richard and McPherson. All three had been bleeding from the nose, ears, and eye sockets. Campus security found no sign of a terror attack, so the three of them were delivered to the hospital.

The doctor had tested Linda for hemorrhagic telangiectasia and tumors of the lacrimal apparatus, but found she was fine. She decided that Linda had a right and left-sided haemolacria and a bloody otorrhoea in the context of simple epistaxis.

In plain English, the doctor explained, this meant she'd had a bad nosebleed and because of the connection between the nose, eye and ear, an increase in pressure in the nasal cavity and auditory tube had caused her to bleed from those too. Linda wondered what the diagnosis would have been if they'd seen the thing the Shadows stuck on her face.

According to the bloodwork the doctor ordered, Linda's lungs and other major organs were all fine. They were keeping her another forty-eight hours in case of other complications.

The bill was already taken care of, Linda imagined the FBI had seen to that. This was a blessing because she didn't have any insurance at the moment. She'd been meaning to renew it off the back of the paycheck she was getting for this job and the increased sales of *Doom Divine*, but there hadn't been time. Lucky really, because she couldn't afford the hospital time otherwise.

The meeting room was not extravagantly furnished. There were a few plastic chairs, an old coffee table with out-of-date magazines, a jug of water, some plastic cups, and a TV screen that didn't look as though it worked. Richard and McPherson were seated when she entered. Richard also had an IV drip. It was the first time she'd seen them since they were in the cavern with the Shadows, or should she call them Shadowcasters?

McPherson got to his feet when she entered. "How you feeling?"

"Rough, the front of my face is still throbbing. It's like I have the worst case of sinusitis."

Richard held up his hand in agreement. His voice was hoarse. "Copy that."

Linda stumbled to a chair and sat down, taking her IV with her. "So, you guys got one of those giant larvae things too, huh?"

Richard put his head in his hand. "And I never want to go through that again. I don't know what was worse, having it invade my brain, or having it dump a whole memory in there. I didn't realize it was going to feel that horrible. I mean, they're memories, right? What could be so bad about that? But they were so alien. Being inside someone else's mind and body, I felt violated."

Linda sighed. "You and me both. Do you remember your memory?"

"Every second, it's more real than the things that actually happened to me."

"Yeah, me too."

McPherson crossed his arms and sat back down. "This

probably isn't going to be pleasant, but I think we need to talk about what we experienced. It could contain vital information."

Richard shifted in his seat. "Actually, I think it would really help to talk about my experience, kind of like a purge, y'know. I mean it's currently stuck in my brain, playing over and over on a loop, it would help to get it out there, to bleed off the poison if you know what I mean."

Linda stretched her back. "I know exactly what you mean, I hadn't thought about it till now, but I feel the same. I think it *would* help."

McPherson uncrossed his arms, put his hands on his knees and leaned forward. "Which one of you got the three-hundred-year-old, um, thing?"

Linda raised her hand. "That would be me."

"Chronologically, we should start with you then."

Linda cleared her throat, which was still sore. She poured herself a cup of water from the jug while she collected her thoughts. Then she told them both about Angus McKay, how he and the seven families, as he called them, came to the Massachusetts Colony from Scotland. She told them of the secret scrolls and the power and influence they brought over the Thirteen Colonies and even the course of American history. She told them of the strange heretical beliefs of the seven clans, of the power struggle between the McLaughlins and the McKays, and how Angus was betrayed by his granddaughter.

"The thing is, I got the feeling that the Shadows in the Cave might not have started out bad. It's just that there was this big schism and the side that wanted power won out." Linda paused and thought for a moment. "There was lots of stuff I didn't quite understand though. About the . . . what did they call it? The Weorol . . . the Weo, um, Weorold Cyning. It's so strange trying to say it. I heard the word so clearly in Angus's mind but I can't quite get my mouth to say it properly. It's from some old language I think."

McPherson pushed his glasses up the bridge of his nose. "It's Anglo-Saxon, or it's something much older but very like it. I heard similar words in my memory, but I knew what the language was, or the person whose memories I shared did."

"Okay, that makes sense, but I don't understand why they have to move to a place with underground tunnels."

Richard rubbed his nose. "I think I can answer that. It was in my memory, among other things. It goes back to the Allegory of the Cave again. We ascribe that to Plato, because that's the first record we have of it, but the Shadowcasters believe it was very, very old when it was taught to Plato. It originally comes from this Qu'rrm Saddic Heresy. As a race we emerged from the caves, that's why this allegory has survived for so long, why it resonates with us. Some of these caves were natural, some of them were apparently created by prehuman intelligences. The Shadows in the Cave believe this makes them centers of power."

Linda sat back in her chair and folded her arms. "Do you think the allegory really does come from this Qu'rm Saddic Heresy?"

"I think *they* believe it does."

"They certainly have some strange ideas, or Angus did. But sorry, I think you were going to tell us about your experience."

McPherson turned his attention to Richard. "Yes, I think it's time we heard what you learned from your . . . " McPherson cleared his throat, "Ordeal."

CHAPTER 25

RICHARD SAT FORWARD in his seat. His malaise fell away. Now the attention was on him and he was like an eager middle schooler presenting his homework to the class.

"I was a guy called Iain McCauley, it was 1940, so America hadn't entered the war yet, but there was talk of the conflict in Europe. I was in New York, in a comic studio, surrounded by Golden Age artists. Totally in my element, right? *I* would have been thrilled, but McCauley wasn't, he was in his early fifties and everyone in the studio was at least thirty years younger. He was a WASP and a bigot, most of the kids in the studio were immigrants, mainly Jewish or Polish, but there was also one Mexican kid and a black guy."

Richard paused. "Should that be—African American? I never know these days."

McPherson breathed heavily through his nose. "I think they're both fine to use, go on."

"So anyway, McCauley, who was well dressed and a bit of an athlete in his youth, is turning his nose up at all these skinny, young kids in their shirtsleeves whose only exercise was sharpening their pencils. He's standing at a drawing board with a pencil in his hand, drawing a complex esoteric diagram, involving two-dimensional directions and three-dimensional orbits. He's drawing the diagram because he wants this cover artist to convert it into a picture of the Crimson Coyote punching Mussolini in the face and knocking him out. He has to get this twenty-two-year-old wunderkind to draw the picture with all the vectors just right, without ever once explaining to him what the purpose of the picture really is."

Linda leaned forward. "I think I know that cover, I always thought it was simply a rip-off of the more famous picture of Captain America punching out Hitler."

"It wasn't a rip-off, it was all part of the same occult working. They were in league with an organization in the UK, founded by a woman called Dion Fortune, a novelist recognized by Aleister Crowley as one of the most powerful magicians in the world. It was called the Fraternity of Light and it was based in Glastonbury, the seat of Arthurian Britain. They aimed to 'seed ideas in the group mind' of the nation. They created these archetypal guardian angels to patrol the psychic shores of the UK and keep the people safe from the occult warfare practiced by Heinrich Himmler. The writer Arthur Machen did something similar in WWI, when he created the fictional Angel of the Mons, but it became so real soldiers in the trenches reported seeing it come to their aid.

"All of this was in McCauley's mind and when I came round, after the . . . after what happened to us, as soon as I could get a signal I looked this up on my phone and it's all true, it really happened."

Richard held up his hand before the others could ask a question.

"Okay, you might think I'm getting off course but I'm not. It turns out the Shadows in the Cave were doing something similar. But unlike England, the US didn't have any thousand-year-old national myths lying around, so they had to invent new myths about patriotic heroes with godlike powers. According to McCauley, that's where we get the superhero from. The Shadows in the Cave had to be careful to cover their tracks, they didn't want to give the game away before the US had even entered the war, so they funded the whole superhero publishing industry by channeling money through criminal sources like the Mafia and small-time pornographers like Harry Donenfeld who published Superman."

Linda's mouth fell open in shock. "You're telling me that the Shadows in the Cave created the superhero boom. What about Jerry Siegel and Joe Shuster, I thought they created Superman?"

"They were carefully maneuvered into place over a period of years by guess who?"

"But they came up with the idea years before war broke out. Are you telling me the Shadows in the Cave knew there was going to be another world war?"

McPherson, who had been cleaning his glasses, put them back on. "To be frank, just about everyone around that time knew there was going to be another world war, it was just a matter of time. Go on, Richard."

"A lot of historians have noted how much comics helped in the war effort, the GIs even read them on the front lines. But there were other motives behind the superhero, they were training the minds of the next generation of US children."

Linda frowned. "Training them for what?"

"Training them to accept the idea of American hegemony. They aimed to rule the world by secretly ruling the US. The superhero is a subliminal symbol of a world power, we even call America a 'superpower.' Think about it, before WWII the US was non-interventionist in foreign policy, it had no plans to found an empire, but after the war, it found itself as the most powerful nation on earth and it had actually proven itself to be a force for good, joining the war to defeat Hitler. Like Billy Batson or Steve Rogers . . . "

McPherson frowned. "Who?"

Linda scratched her arm. "They're the secret identities of Shazam and Captain America."

"Oh."

Richard resumed. "So anyway, like America, they didn't ask for great power, they had it thrust on them because they were pure of heart. They were specially chosen by magical forces to wield this power for good. So they put on the costume and act as unofficial police. McCauley thought he was putting these archetypes into kid's minds at an early age, so when they grew up they'd accept America's place as the unofficial policeman of the world."

Richard raised both his hands. He reminded Linda of a revivalist preacher, proselytizing to his flock.

"But there's more to it than even that. After the war, McCauley and the Shadows planned to use superheroes to seed the idea of an American god in the minds of the nation. You said the scrolls they brought over from Scotland contained the secrets of creation, right? Well, their grand plan was not just to create monsters, like those larvae things. It was always to create a god, a living American god! They even had a name for it, an ancient name from their scrolls—the Midswégan. The project to create the Midswégan was ongoing, even at that point. McCauley called it—get this— 'Operation Consciousness.'"

McPherson tilted his head and cocked an ear. His eyes

narrowed as he seemed to focus on the word Richard had said twice—'Midswégan.'

Richard dropped his hands into his lap, his shoulders sunk, and he looked at the floor, muttering, almost to himself. "That's it, that was the memory that thing gave me."

Linda placed her hand on Richard's shoulder. All the energy that had filled him moments ago seemed to have ebbed away. "Hey, are you okay?"

Richard shrugged. "I don't know, y'know. I mean, my whole life I've studied and written about comics and superheroes. And all my life I've been trying to find out what happened to my father, to prove that something really happened, that his death wasn't suicide, it was homicide. Now, here I am, with the answers almost in my hand, and I find the two driving forces in life are, I don't know, diametrically opposed. It's like I'm my own worst enemy or something.

"You know, Jerry Siegel's dad was shot when someone robbed his store. So Jerry creates this ideal super-protector who can repel bullets. They just bounce off him. I've always thought it was Jerry's way of coming to terms with his father's death. But superheroes didn't protect my father, they killed him. I guess it's just hit me and it's kinda hard to take."

Linda squeezed Richard's shoulder with affection. "All the more reason to get these bastards for what they've done."

Richard met her eyes with a disconsolate look. "Can we actually get them though? I mean, isn't what this big display of power was all about? Showing us they're too powerful and have been in charge for too long for us to do anything about that?"

McPherson steepled his fingers and rested them on his gut. "Ostensibly, I think they've been toying with us ever since they learned we were interested in them."

"When was that?"

"Could have been at the compound, when we were followed, could have been when you were looking into them online, could have been even earlier. But they may not be entirely untouchable."

"What do you mean?"

"I mean the memory I experienced might point to a weakness, a weakness we could still exploit."

CHAPTER 26

MCPHERSON PAUSED, it seemed, for dramatic effect. Linda and Richard leaned forward in their seats.

When Linda first entered the room, there'd been a general air of despondency hanging over them. In all the confusion, Linda hadn't stopped to consider her emotional well-being. But she realized she'd been suffering the general funk she usually experienced after dental surgery or some minor medical operation.

McPherson's last comment had given them something they'd been missing until now. It gave them the tiniest glimmer of hope.

Linda glanced at Richard and then back at McPherson. "What weakness would that be?"

McPherson held up his hand like a teacher quieting a class. "I think I should start at the beginning and tell you the whole thing while it's fresh in my memory, just like you guys did."

"Okay."

"My memories came from a guy called McKinney, he was a scholar of ancient languages and was especially fond of the Gaelic spoken by his ancestors, that's why he liked to sign his name as Mac Cionaodha, when writing to friends and family. He was at Bethesda Naval Hospital and he was instructing the doctor what to write on a patient's death certificate. The patient was a man who's come up several times in our investigation."

Richard was hanging on everything McPherson said. "Who was it?"

"Former Presidential candidate Estes Kefauver."

"No way."

McPherson nodded, "I'm afraid so."

"What was he doing at Kefauver's deathbed?"

"Well, that's where it gets interesting. It seems that the Shadowcasters had slipped Kefauver something on the Senate floor while he was attempting to get an antitrust amendment placed into a NASA appropriations bill. His constitution was stronger than they thought, because it only caused him a mild coronary. He was rushed to the naval hospital where they induced an aortic aneurysm with a massive dose of stimulants."

Richard was breathless. "Wait, is this Estes Kefauver who chaired the Senate Subcommittee into juvenile delinquency, the televised hearing that killed crime and horror comics in 1954?"

"And the Senator who rose to national prominence when he headed the US Senate committee investigating organized crime, taking down top mobsters like Frank Costello on national television for the first time ever. He was being groomed as presidential material even at that point."

"Who was grooming him?"

"The Shadows in the Cave, this is how we operate, we . . . " McPherson stopped and a mild panic crossed his face. He put a hand to his temple and opened his eyes wide as he took a deep breath. "I'm sorry, I just realized what I said. It's having someone else's memory in your head. It gets you confused about your own identity. About what you actually remember and what they put there."

Linda looked sympathetic. "That's okay, go on."

"This is how they operate, they choose candidates they can control, from both sides of the political spectrum, left and right, and they groom them for power, pulling strings to get them into office and get them noticed by the public and the party bosses. Kefauver is nearly forgotten these days, but back in 1939, he looked like the perfect candidate. He was an all-American college football star. He graduated from Yale Law School and entered Congress at thirty-six. After getting him into the Senate in 1948, the Shadows organized the US Senate hearings on organized crime and got Kefauver to head it up. The hearings were the first to be televised, just at the point where everyone in America was buying TVs for the first time. The hearings were shown coast to coast and made Kefauver into a household name. In the 1952 Democratic primaries, he won over eighty percent of the primaries, getting four times the number of votes that the other front runner, Adlai Stevenson did."

Linda had never heard any of this before. "So what happened, did he win the nomination?"

McPherson shook his head. "No, it seems the Shadows in the

Cave aren't as all-powerful as we might think. They have enemies at every level of government. In this case, they couldn't get the party bosses to back their candidate and in spite of his electoral gains the bosses snubbed Kefauver in favor of Stevenson."

"Are they allowed to do that?"

"There's no rule that says if you win the primaries you automatically win the nomination, not in the Democrats. Here's where it gets interesting. To get their man back in the public eye, the Shadows organized another Senate subcommittee, this time it was on juvenile delinquency, a hot topic back in the 1950s. But the real target was the crime and horror comics that had replaced the superheroes on the newsstands. The Shadows in the Cave whipped up a moral panic in the press, even paying to get a best-selling book written condemning comics."

Richard nearly leaped out of his plastic chair. "Not *Seduction of the Innocent*?"

"That's the one."

"The Shadows in the Cave were behind Dr. Frederic Wertham, the child psychologist who wrote a best-selling book condemning horror comics in the fifties?"

McPherson held out his hands. "This is what I'm telling you. They wanted to bring back the superheroes they'd created. Horror and crime comics were read by wisecracking teens and guys who came back damaged from the war. They were cynical and subversive. Superheroes taught younger kids to respect authority and obey the law, they created the psychological atmosphere among the young that the Shadowcasters wanted. Their scheme worked, the subcommittee put an end to horror and crime comics for over a generation and superheroes made a comeback. Plus their guy Kefauver was back in the public spotlight. In 1956, he swept the primaries once again in another landslide."

"Did he get the nomination this time?"

McPherson pursed his lips and shook his head. "They gave it to Stevenson once again. The Shadows still didn't have enough pull with the party bosses, but they did get him chosen as the vice-presidential candidate and they got a young senator by the name of Kennedy dropped from that ticket. Stevenson lost to Eisenhower in a landslide."

Linda was puzzled. "So, why would they kill him if he was their man?"

"Because he was too much his own man. Kefauver always acted according to his principles. Sure he played politics, that was part of his job. He courted the support of influential men like the newspaperman Edward J. Meeman and future president Lyndon Baines Johnson, but he was led by his conscience. He was one of only three southern senators who didn't sign the Southern Manifesto—a legal document arguing in favor of segregation, and his Senate investigations into organized crime brought down members of his own party, like New York Mayor William O'Dwyer and Senate Majority Leader Scott Lucas. That's how he made so many enemies among the Democrat bosses."

"You sound as though you admire him."

McPherson put his fingertips to his temples. He grimaced slightly, wrestling with some inner conflict. "It's hard to know what I think about him. All of this information was just dumped in my mind, in one big go, and then it sort of unraveled. I'm sure you both experienced the same thing. McKinney took years to amass all this information, he lived through it. So his perception of the events inevitably colors my understanding, but that changes my own feelings and thoughts about people."

McPherson paused, put his hand to his chin and looked down at the floor as he thought about his next words. "The key thing here is that Kefauver couldn't be controlled. When he first ran for the Senate he made an enemy of the corrupt Democrat boss Edward Crump, who ran Tennessee. Crump disparaged Kefauver, saying he was bringing in communism 'with the stealth of a raccoon.' Kefauver wore a raccoon skin hat on television and proudly said 'I may be a pet raccoon, but I'm not Boss Crump's pet raccoon!' The voters loved it and they elected him.

"He made a virtue of being his own man throughout his career. He knew the Shadows in the Cave could eventually make him president, but he came to see that compromise was too great. In 1960 he seemed a shoo-in for the nomination, but he stepped aside in favor of the young senator he'd beaten to vice-presidential candidate—John F. Kennedy, who was definitely not the Shadows' guy, and we all know how that played out.

"Some people think Kefauver had the most success after he gave up his presidential ambitions, but he definitely turned against the Shadows in the Cave. Not so they noticed, he was subtle about it, he collected information on them by stealth. He compiled the most comprehensive dossier on Operation Consciousness and the creation of the Midswégan outside of the Shadows in the Cave.”

Now it was Richard's turn to cock an ear. “So, that's why you took such an interest when I mentioned the Midswégan.”

“I realized there was a pattern developing in our memories, a map through the labyrinth of all this mystery. It explains what happened to your father, what became of Carver, and why those people, like Linda's editor, disappeared so mysteriously.”

Linda perked up at this. “Where does this map lead us?”

“To the Midswégan.”

“What is that?”

“I'm afraid McKinney didn't know, any more than McCauley or McKay. But he did know one thing, it was important the Shadows in the Cave keep the Midswégan and Operation Consciousness a secret. So important they killed JFK's biggest presidential rival, and maybe JFK himself, to keep it secret.”

CHAPTER 27

LINDA BREATHED OUT heavily and shook her head in disbelief. "I never expected our investigation to take this turn. Then again, I never expected a prehistoric larva to lay a memory in my brain in an underground cavern."

Richard hunched his shoulders and smiled awkwardly. "Even saying that out loud should get the three of us committed."

Linda tossed her head. "Tell me about it." She looked thoughtful for a moment, her mind trying to latch onto something. "Do you know what memory those things took from you?"

Richard shrugged. "No I don't, but I guess I wouldn't."

"I keep looking for gaps in my memory to see what it took, but it's all seamless, or as seamless as anyone's jumbled memories can get."

McPherson ruminated on this for a moment. "Maybe the memories we lost are like the missing people we're investigating. Maybe they're taken so completely from our minds that even our memories don't have a memory of them. If that makes any sense."

Linda's eyes widened with excitement. "It does, actually. Hey, you don't think some weird larva ate our missing persons right out of the memory of the world do you?" Linda put her hands up to her face. "What am I even saying, every time I try to get my head around this I just sound crazier and crazier."

Richard pulled a sympathetic face. "It's a lot for us to take in, every time I try to make sense of it I start going out of my mind. We've seen a lot of crazy stuff the past few months."

"Maybe we should get back to the case. What happened to Kefauver's dossier? Did the Shadows in the Cave destroy it?"

McPherson set his jaw. "They never found it. As far as they discovered, only three people knew about the dossier and what it contained. Kefauver, his wife, Nancy, a good Scottish girl from

Glasgow, and one of his aides, a man called Charles Patterson. The Shadows always believed that one of them hid it."

"What happened to them?"

"Nancy died four years later, in Washington. She was attending a dinner in the Mayflower Hotel's grand ballroom and she fell face first onto the banqueting table. They called an ambulance and rushed Nancy to the hospital, but it was too late—she was dead."

"What killed her?"

"No one ever asked and no one ever found out."

"You think the Shadows got to her?"

"Well, they never got their hands on the dossier, maybe they needed her out of the picture."

Richard scratched at his beard. "What about the aide, this Patterson guy?"

"He disappeared within weeks of Kefauver's death, went off the grid, got a new identity. A bit like the Caldwell woman we interviewed."

"You mean Pat?" Linda felt a warmth when McPherson mentioned her.

"Yeah, her. Only Patterson disappeared completely, never came out from under cover. And the dossier vanished with him."

"Did he have any relatives?"

"Only a daughter, she disappeared with him. His wife died of cancer a few years after his daughter was born and he raised her alone."

Richard narrowed his eyes and pursed his lips. He looked as if something were nagging at him. "Hold on a minute, all of this stuff, Nancy's death and Patterson's disappearance, it all happened after Kefauver died, right?"

"Right."

"So, it happened after the memory they gave you took place. How come you know about it all then?"

McPherson furrowed his brow, and his jaw moved as if he was grinding his teeth. "I don't honestly know. Maybe they gave me a memory of a memory, from much later in McKinney's life. Maybe that thing took two memories from me and gave me two in return. I have no idea how those things work. This is as new to me as it is to you. There is one thing that's been preying on my mind since I woke up in the hospital."

"What's that?"

"Like I said, I don't know how those things work, whether they knew what memories those things would give us or if they selected them at random. I don't know what memory they took from me either. But that Scwyrm thing rooting around in my brain might have stirred something up. Something I hadn't thought about in decades. It was triggered by the name—Charles Patterson. In my first year at the Bureau, there was a storage unit raid in Queens. It belonged to a terror suspect linked to several domestic incidents. The storage unit was said to contain vital intel on homeland attacks.

"The unit contained nothing of interest. What they'd left behind was of no import, it was meant to slow us down or throw us off their trail. Even still we had to copy and catalog every sheet of paper we found. The top brass were looking for specific intel, a series of documents, known to us by their file code numbers, if we found any we were to inform them straight away. As far as I was aware they weren't located in the raid. For me, it was another example of the long hours and tedious work that went with being an agent. The suspect was known to us as William Blighty, but he had many aliases, including Francis Dumbarton, Frederick Witherspoon, and Charles Patterson. It wasn't till a moment ago that I even recalled this, I mean it's over thirty years ago.

"Looking back, it has to be the same person. There's no way the Shadows knew I had such a minor part in that case unless they really do keep tabs on everyone. The most pertinent detail is the unit was booked in a woman's name. A woman known as Anna Farthingale, his daughter."

Richard tapped his steepled fingertips together. "Do you think she's still alive? I'm guessing Patterson probably isn't with us, but this Anna lady, or whatever her real name is, might just be."

"She could be and if she is, she might just know where the missing dossier is."

Linda cupped her chin in her palm. "Is there any way we could trace her so we could get in touch?"

"That would depend on how good she is at living off the grid. It's not as easy as it once was, but she may be very effective. The Bureau probably has a list of her aliases on file. I've no idea if any of them are current. If she's going under a name that we don't know about, she may be untraceable."

"So, you're saying we can't find her?"

"No, I'm saying it's going to be hard."

Richard's mood was lifting, as he dared let himself hope. "If we *could* find her, and she does have this dossier, she might have the answers we need. She may be able to tell us what Operation Consciousness was all about. She might know what happened to Carver and my dad. We might even explain these disappearances."

McPherson held out his hands in a calming gesture. "I don't want anyone to get their hopes up, this is a long shot. It might not work."

"But if it does, if we find this dossier, we might not only get answers, we could make them pay for what they've done."

McPherson made a pained expression. "Or we could spend the rest of our lives on the run like Patterson."

"But you're the FBI."

"And Patterson was a Washington insider, an aide to a very powerful man, and look how it turned out for him."

Linda didn't want everyone's mood to drop. "If you could find her, do you think the Bureau would pay our travel, so we could go talk to her?"

McPherson's expression grew even more pained. "I honestly couldn't tell you, I certainly hope so. I mean they've been pretty good so far, but that's because they don't want to know about me or anything I do. So long as I'm doing this, I'm out of their hair and they're happy to pay for that. But I always figured we only had so long until they started asking questions. I think we might have made some powerful enemies. If they have the sway they claim and put pressure on my bosses, they'll shut us down straight away. Either way, I think this is our last shot at solving this case."

Linda stood and held up the bag her drip was attached to. "You know what, this is the closest thing I've got to a shot of bourbon at the moment. So, here's to our last shot and finally solving this case."

Richard also stood and held up his drip bag. "I'll drink to that." He gave his bag a squeeze and grimaced. "Ow, ow, that actually hurts."

McPherson looked a little solemn. Linda wondered if he was looking ahead to a lifetime on the run from the Shadows in the Cave. They'd certainly put on a display of power.

Could the three of them honestly expect to take on a cabal with such reach and influence and expect to win? Could they even expect to come out unscathed? Linda supposed that depended on Patterson's daughter and the secrets she might reveal.

CHAPTER 28

L INDA KICKED HER apartment door shut, staggered through
to the kitchen, and dropped her groceries on the counter. She
never knew what to buy these days, because she never knew
how long she'd be staying home.

Linda had come back from Boston to find everything in her
refrigerator was rotten. She had to throw it all out and restock.
After days of grabbing take-out and rushing through diner
breakfasts, she was craving fresh fruit and vegetables. She wanted
to sit and digest a healthy meal and regain her balance.

Linda ended up buying one of every fruit and vegetable from
her organic food mart, plus a bag of salad greens. She could make
several salads and maybe even a fruit platter out of her haul.

She also planned on taking a long bath by candlelight, followed
by some aromatherapy. Linda had splurged on a room diffuser and
a selection of essential oils. She could afford to indulge herself with
her current income. She needed to engage in a significant self-care
program after the events of the last few weeks, not to mention the
last few months.

She'd gotten so used to the threat of physical danger that
Manhattan at night no longer made her apprehensive. In fact, it
felt like Disneyland. She'd been held at gunpoint, climbed down a
sheer rock face to a cavern miles underground, and strapped to a
wooden altar.

Linda deserved a lot of pampering and self-love. Her poor body
was aching in places she didn't want to think about. She'd been
neglecting herself in favor of working the case for too long. She
needed to soothe her muscles, calm her nerves, and take proper
care of her own needs before it all became too much for her. She'd
coped with more than anyone should expect to cope with, even in
a dangerous frontline profession. She was owed a break.

The work with the FBI was an exciting change of pace. Linda's life had been pretty sedentary for years. She sat at a drawing board, worked on her tablet, and occasionally traveled to a convention, when she could afford it or when they paid her airfare.

Now she was crisscrossing the country, interviewing everyone from Silver Age comic creators to monks and militiamen. All these hidden subcultures were opening up to her, each one part of a modern America she had no idea about.

The people she'd met had their own view of what it meant to be American, and it was different from Linda's. If she was honest, she wasn't certain she had a personal view of what it meant to be a US citizen. She'd taken on this case hoping to find herself in her quest to discover R. L. Carver. Along the way, she discovered an America she never knew existed.

Was it possible to truly know yourself unless you knew your own country? How much of her identity came from the nation in which she was raised, a nation that considered itself the greatest on earth? What did all these new Americas mean to *her* identity?

Linda didn't have an answer to any of these questions. Greater minds than hers had grappled with these issues and come up with just as few conclusions. But if she didn't know what it meant to be American, she did know what she wanted for lunch. So, she set about fixing it.

Later, as Linda selected essential oils to accompany her bath, she thought about her emotional needs and her mental health. The extra income was giving her a greater sense of financial security at a time when she really needed it, but the stress and physical danger were affecting her anxiety. She wasn't certain how much more of it she could take and the case was taking an increasingly hazardous direction.

Like Richard and McPherson, Linda was desperate to know what had happened to Carver out in that desert. So far the case had left her with nothing but questions, from why Paul had vanished without a trace, to what her country meant to her today.

The more questions she asked, the more hollow and insubstantial she felt, lacking any substance or definition. Each time the vacuum inside her grew, she feared it would be filled with her old existential dread. The sense that she was a stranger in her own life. That she was in the wrong place, the wrong time and the wrong body and nothing would ever be right again.

This was Linda's greatest fear, and she'd go to any lengths to avoid it. That's why she was taking on the Shadows in the Cave, even if it meant a lifetime on the run. She needed a definitive answer to anchor her life back to reality. To make sense of a world that was looking more complex, chaotic and unreal every day.

A long soak and a good meal would only do so much for her sense of well-being. She needed to talk this through with someone. Given her circumstances and the sensitive nature of what she wanted to discuss, a therapist was out of the question. Plus she didn't want analysis and professional courtesy, she wanted genuine sympathy and understanding.

She needed a big sister or a mother figure to hear her problems. Her own mother was always hopeless in these situations. Whatever Linda asked for, her mom would give the opposite.

It was as though her mom couldn't help herself. She wasn't unkind or unfeeling, but she'd always show kindness at exactly the wrong time. If Linda wanted to be heard, her mother would lecture her, if she wanted advice, her mom would just listen and nod. When she needed sympathy, her mother would be firm and if she wanted a kick up the backside, her mother would give her a hug and tell her everything would be all right.

At times like these, Linda would normally call Weezie, but she was reluctant. It wasn't how she'd left things with Weezie, she was fairly certain they were good. She cared too much about her and Walt to get them mixed up in this. She couldn't bear the thought of such dear friends being in harm's way.

There was a tight lump in her chest as she realized this. She found it hard to breathe and when she did fill her lungs they sent out cool tendrils of melancholy that chilled her body. Couldn't anyone help her? It was like being out at sea, on the tip of a promontory, with no welcoming lights on the shore.

Linda sensed there was something wrong with this image. There should be a welcome light and a safe haven to provide shelter. Hadn't there always been? She was forgetting someone who had always been there for her when she needed them most. But who was it and why was their name on the tip of her tongue but still out of reach?

A brief conversation Linda had with McPherson in the airport flashed into her mind. They'd just disembarked at JFK and were in line to collect their luggage when he turned to her and said, "You swapped cell numbers with Patricia when we interviewed her, right?"

"Yeah, there's nothing wrong with that is there? I mean, she's not a suspect or anything."

"It's fine, I was just thinking she spent several decades on the run. She knows how to go underground and stay off the grid. She might give us some insight to help track down Patterson's daughter. She'd pick up if you called wouldn't she?"

Linda frowned, wondering why he asked that. "I think so."

Seeing the frown, McPherson qualified his question. "It's just that she didn't seem to take to Richard or me like she took to you."

"Do you want me to give her a call?"

"That might be really useful."

"Okay."

As soon as she recalled the conversation Linda knew why it had sprung to mind. The tight lump in her chest was replaced with a sudden flood of warmth at the thought of Pat. There are people who make you feel like you've known them your entire life the minute you meet them. Pat was one of those.

Linda dug out Pat's number on her cell and gave her a call. The phone rang for a while, but no one picked up. Linda's shoulders sagged with disappointment. She couldn't take the thought of not talking to Pat. She phoned the number again.

It rang for a long time and just when Linda thought it would cut out, Pat picked up. She sounded breathless and anxious. "Hello, who is this? How did you get this number?"

"Pat, it's Linda, you gave me this number when we called on you, remember?"

"I gave you *this* number. Oh God, that means they could trace it."

"Listen, if this isn't a good time . . . "

"No, no, I'm sorry, I'm being rude. It's good to hear from you, but we can't talk long on this number, it puts us both at risk."

"At risk of what? Pat, has something happened?"

"I thought you'd know about it with your FBI contacts."

This wasn't going at all how Linda had imagined. "Know about what?"

"About the murders of Emma and Cicely."

"The what now?"

"You really don't know?"

"No."

"They happened recently. Less than twenty-four hours after you called. That's what tipped me off, I'd thought they'd have informed you at least."

"Pat, I haven't heard a thing, that must have been . . . I can't . . . I can't imagine."

"Oh the things that were done to them."

Linda's stomach turned over, she didn't even want to imagine what Pat might have seen. "What did you do?"

"I called the police, and lit out."

"Why did you leave, won't that make you a suspect?"

"Oh please, there's no way a woman my age could have done that."

"So why go?"

"For my own protection. Whoever it was who did this was sent there to silence me. Poor Cicely and Emma were just collateral. After all these years, I thought I was safe, but they must have been worried about what I said to you, what I might have let slip."

"By 'they' do you mean the Shadows in the Cave?"

"Yes, I've been resisting them my whole life."

Bile burnt the back of Linda's throat. "Oh Pat, I'm so sorry, if I'd known this would happen, that I was putting you at risk, I'd never have let them near you."

"You weren't to know, you were acting with the best intentions. Besides, I'm glad I met you, I felt we connected, on a deeper level."

"I know, right? I was phoning because I needed to hear your voice. I had no idea you were going through all this, or I'd never have bothered you."

"That's okay, it's good to hear from you. I was only rattled because I thought I got rid of this phone. I'm mad at myself for being so stupid. We've probably talked too long as it is. So listen, this is important, you're probably in danger yourself. You need to give me the names and addresses of all the people you've spoken to so far, I think they're also in danger and I'll try and help them. Don't send anything to this number. I'm going to destroy this phone and the sim card as soon as we hang up. I'll text you a burner number, send the info to that."

"I can send you names, I'm a bit hazy on addresses and phone numbers."

"Whatever you can remember, this is important."

"Okay."

"I'll contact you as soon as I think it's safe. In the meantime, will you do me one last favor?"

"Anything."

"Look after yourself and be safe out there. I've only met you once, but I feel like I've known you for years and I care about you."

"I care about you too," Linda said, and the line went dead.

Linda was torn. Her heart leaped when Pat said she cared about her. But she was in serious danger. Two lovely women who Linda thought charming had been murdered. And it might be all her fault.

Was Linda in as much danger as Pat thought she was? Was it too late for her to run and hide from the Shadows in the Cave? Or was exposing them the only protection left to her?

Linda had the sense that the ride had already started and it was far too late to get off. She had no choice but to see this through. To find Patterson's daughter and unearth that dossier.

CHAPTER 29

"**S**O, ARE WE in Chicago or not?" Linda stared through the windshield at Fairfield Avenue, wondering if she could imagine a more suburban street.

Richard looked up from his phone. "Actually, Elmhurst is a city in its own right. *Family Circle* ranked it as one of the ten best US towns for families."

"Regularly read *Family Circle*, do you?"

"My mom did, especially after my dad died. I think she wanted to make up for the family life we never had."

Linda mouthed a silent "oh."

An uncomfortable silence descended on their rental car. She took in the four-bedroom, rehabbed, ranch-style house they were staking out, a few doors down from where they were parked. She listened to her heart and tried counting the beats, slowing her breathing as she did so. It was a technique one therapist had taught her to deal with panic and anxiety.

When they'd climbed on the plane at JFK, Linda had not been able to cross the runway to the steps. Colors had become brighter and the noise of jet engines unbearable. She'd gripped a temporary metal barrier to stop the ground from spinning, as though she were a fixed point and the whole airport revolved around her.

Strangely, it had been Richard who came to her aid. She hadn't credited him with much empathy, but he spotted she was in trouble before she said anything and placed a gentle hand between her shoulder blades.

"You okay?"

Linda shook her head.

"Panic attack?"

Linda nodded.

"Thought so, I get them too. Boston was pretty rough, huh?"

Linda nodded again and it didn't feel like her head was so heavy or her neck so fragile this time. The noise of the jet engines stopped echoing so loudly in her head. Richard's presence was grounding her.

"Let's just try this one step at a time. That's what I do. It's easier if we don't think about the plane, just the next step we have to take."

Richard had gotten her across the runway and onto the plane, where the brisk efficiency of the flight stewards had quelled her fears and helped Linda into her seat. There were no further incidents on the flight to Chicago, but the threat of another had hung over Linda since that moment.

Sitting in the rental car, Linda had phantom premonitions looking at the wooden door behind the screen. She thought of herself leaving the car to go knock on the door, a sniper's sights following her down the street. She thought of the door swinging wide when she knocked and wizened hands reaching out to grasp the front of her top. Something skittered below the porch, something with teeth and claws hungry for her ankles.

This was the problem with combining an active imagination and freeform anxiety. Like Richard said, Boston was pretty rough, but it wasn't just Boston. It was the fear and mistrust of the people they'd been interviewing. The case had started out with them chatting to old hands from the comic industry, but it had soon gotten weird. They'd been followed and menaced by men in black and held at gunpoint multiple times.

And then . . . no, Linda had no words to describe what had happened in Boston, no context to explain it. She would be processing it for a very long time. Along with Pat's warning that she was in danger. Had someone really tried to murder Pat? Were the other people they'd interviewed really in danger?

When Linda had raised this with McPherson he'd agreed to look into it, but he hadn't seen any murder reports on the people they'd spoken to. Nevertheless, it didn't help Linda's stress. The investigation was taking its toll. Things had gotten scarier since she'd come back, yet she couldn't let go.

Linda remembered a summer's day when she was twelve years old. Her family had been visiting an aunt in Connecticut. Her aunt had no children either, but she hadn't adopted like Linda's mom and dad. As a consequence, she doted on Linda.

She always made Linda her favorite, French toast with maple syrup and bananas, and she spoiled her with other treats. She was the first to show Linda how to use make-up and fix her hair. Linda's mom disapproved, probably because she couldn't give Linda that attention herself, and that was why Linda basked in it.

That morning she was up early with her aunt, waiting for the mailman. Her aunt had ordered Linda something special and they were eager for him to deliver it. Linda saw the mailman approach her aunt's house with a package that was too big for the mailbox.

As he made his way across her aunt's yard to ring the bell, next door's dog, a tiny Jack Russell named Patch, escaped the house and charged the mailman. The dog clamped his jaws around the mailman's ankle and he howled and dropped the package (which, it turned out, was a wooden easel that her mom insisted they leave in Connecticut for some reason).

The mailman shook his leg and used some choice language that eventually encouraged her aunt to take Linda away from the window. But before she did, she saw Patch draw blood. The mailman in his desperation began to punch the Jack Russell, obviously hurting it from the whines the animal gave off, but it refused to let go of his ankle. The more he hurt it, the deeper it sunk its teeth into him.

Linda felt like that Jack Russell now. No matter how many times this case punched her, metaphorically, in the face, she couldn't let go. She only sank her teeth in deeper. She had no idea why. It wasn't great for her mental or emotional health, but she couldn't leave it alone.

It had taken McPherson a week to find Anna Patterson. Apparently, he'd followed a paper trail from the rental of the storage unit and the many identities she'd used before settling in Illinois.

It wasn't easy, McPherson had told her, but Patterson's aliases followed a pattern. They were based on family names and her father's aliases and once McPherson had those she was easier to track than she might have realized. Anna had fallen off the FBI's radar long ago. She was no longer a wanted radical, or even a person of note. Maybe this was why she got sloppy. She probably thought she'd been forgotten and no one was watching.

"Someone's always watching these days," McPherson had said. Given her current paranoia, Linda hadn't found this reassuring.

Anna Patterson was now Anna Kruger. She had settled in Illinois and worked as an administrator in the City Manager's office in Elmhurst. So they'd flown into O'Hare International, hired a Honda Civic so they didn't draw any attention and they'd driven to Elmhurst. With its many parks, museums and art galleries, Linda could see why a magazine like *Family Circle* would rank it as one of the ten best towns for families.

Did they even publish *Family Circle* anymore? Linda was pretty sure she hadn't seen it on sale in a while. She imagined Richard's mother rushing to the newsstand on the day the magazine was canceled and waving her fist in the air, shouting, "No, now I'll never raise the perfect family in Elmhurst!"

She smiled to herself at the thought, and then checked to make sure neither Richard nor McPherson had caught her smirk. Richard was rotating his right shoulder and grimacing.

"You okay?"

Richard grunted. "My shoulder's been killing me ever since we left California. It's all these motels we stop in. I don't know what they do to their beds, but every time I sleep in one I end up pulling a muscle in my back or my arms."

Linda turned away and tried to stop herself from rolling her eyes. Richard could be a real hypochondriac, but he'd been sweet to her at the airport.

"I've got some Tylenol in my purse if that would help."

Richard shook his head. "I've got my own pain meds, but they make me woozy sometimes, so I'll hold off till after the interview."

No one spoke for twenty tedious minutes. Linda was wondering if she'd be able to go get her sketch pad from the trunk. "I thought you said she had a half day."

McPherson glanced over at her. "She does, according to her schedule."

"How were you even able to look at her schedule? Isn't that, like, a private, internal document?"

"It's an internal document in a local government department. You don't think the Bureau worked out how to monitor civil servants decades ago?"

"Don't suppose there'd be much point asking you how you do that?"

"Don't suppose there would."

"So where is she?"

"Could be shopping, at the hair salon, fixing her nails, seeing some guy, who knows?"

"And in the meantime, we just sit here and wait till she turns up?"

"Welcome to the glamorous world of surveillance."

Linda sighed with frustration and turned to snipe at Richard in back of her. "How come you get to stare at your phone when we're supposed to be staking this place out?"

Richard looked up from his phone. His hurt expression made Linda regret her petty outburst. It changed in seconds to one of surprise and recognition. He pointed at the ranch house. "Wait, isn't that her?"

A short woman, in her early sixties, was approaching the driveway, carrying a bag of groceries in her arms. Her hair was cut short and dyed chestnut brown, she was wearing thick glasses and just the sort of cheap suit Linda imagined all provincial bureaucrats wore.

McPherson unbuckled his seat belt and opened his door.

"Are we just going to door-step her?" Linda said.

"It gives us the psychological advantage. She won't have time to evade or avoid us."

He climbed out of the car and Linda followed suit. The air was chilly and she regretted not grabbing her jacket. Richard stumbled along behind them, slinging his backpack, with his tablet and notes, over his shoulder and pushing his glasses up his nose. The car bleeped as McPherson locked it.

McPherson headed Anna off before she could enter her driveway. "Excuse me, Ms. Patterson. Agent McPherson, FBI, can we have a word?"

Anna stopped and peered at him over the top of her glasses, she was smiling but she appeared a little confused, playing the part of an amiable grandmother. "I'm sorry, young man, I think you have me confused with someone else. My name's not Patterson."

"It's not the name you go by now, but it is the name you were born with."

"I'm afraid I don't follow you, what's this all about?"

"Sixty years ago your father disappeared with a dossier that could implicate a powerful cabal. A cache put together at the behest of his employer, Senator Estes Kefauver. He went underground and you've spent your life hiding from the authorities under a series of assumed identities."

"I assure you I've done no such thing. My name is Kruger, not Patterson, I'm a public servant and I've lived my entire life in Elmhurst."

"Except you haven't, ma'am. You moved here seventeen years ago from Freeport, Kansas, where you'd lived for nearly a decade as Anna Parkinson. Before that, you were Annette Jones, an accountant from Hermann, Missouri. And prior to that you called yourself Irma Hemingway and worked for a solicitor in Leadville, Colorado. I can go on if you like, I've mapped every single identity you've ever held and every place you've ever lived, and I have the paper trail to prove it. I can show you if you want?"

Anna's back straightened and her brow knitted into a frown. "I don't care to see it, you're entirely mistaken and if you'll excuse me I have to put my groceries away."

She made to leave and McPherson blocked her way. Linda tried a different approach. "We're after them too, the Shadows in the Cave, the people your father compiled the dossier about. We're not interested in your past. The fact you've had to hide like this, reinvent yourself just to stay ahead of the authorities when you've done nothing wrong, well, frankly it's an injustice. We want to make the people who did this pay."

Anna wavered for the first time, her expression softened, her shoulders dropped, but she said nothing.

McPherson pressed their advantage. "The bottom line is, Ms. Patterson, if *we* can find you they *will*. You got sloppy, it's been a long time since anyone took an interest in you, I'm sure your father taught you how to monitor official channels and you probably thought you'd fallen off the radar, but you hadn't. The cabal's power waned for a decade or so, but I can assure you it's now in the ascendant. They have very long memories and you're at risk. We know this because we're investigating them and they're not making it easy for us. Your only chance now is to tell us what you know and let us protect you."

Richard stepped forward and held out his arms for the bag she was carrying, like a dutiful son. "Can I help with your groceries?"

Anna snatched the bag away and her back stiffened again. "I can carry my own shopping, thank you." She considered them for a moment, making some mental calculation, then said, "I think you better come inside."

CHAPTER 30

ANNA UNLOCKED THE front door and showed them into her house. After the crisp, outside air, the hallway felt hot and close. It smelled of lavender air freshener.

Anna showed them into her living room, a large, well-lit space with leather couches, house plants, and Mesoamerican prints on the wall.

Anna took a deep breath and closed her eyes for a moment. She remained still, as though she was composing herself. When she opened her eyes her mood had softened. Her manner was more hospitable and her voice was low and gentle. "Won't you please take a seat? Give me a minute to put these groceries away and I'll make us a nice jug of lemonade."

McPherson lowered himself into a plush recliner. "That won't be necessary, we don't want to put you to any trouble."

Anna waved away his protest with her free hand. "Don't be silly, I invited you in so you're my guests, and I treat my guests properly, that's how I was raised. So, who's for lemonade?"

It was very warm in the living room and Linda's throat was dry. "Actually, that would be lovely."

Richard looked up from rummaging in his backpack. "That would be great."

McPherson adjusted his tie. "Could I just have a glass of water?"

"And miss out on the best lemonade in Illinois? I don't think so. It's an old family recipe. You're gonna love it."

Anna disappeared into the kitchen. The sound of cupboards opening and closing and glasses rattling could be heard as she hummed to herself.

Linda glanced around the living room. The whole house had a vacant quality, as though someone inhabited it, but didn't live there. It reminded her of a film set dressed to resemble the home of an aging woman.

It seemed as if Anna had carefully studied what her interiors ought to look like without ever buying into them. Not wanting to invest too much of herself in the place because she knew that at any moment she might have to pack up and haul ass to another part of the country.

Linda wondered what that must be like, never putting down roots or making any meaningful relationships because that could put your whole life in jeopardy. To discard your whole identity at a moment's notice, as if you were clearing out old summer outfits that no longer fit.

Linda couldn't imagine living like that, but Anna had been raised that way by her father. Not out of choice, they were forced to by a cabal that wanted to know what her father's employer, the senator Estes Kefauver, had found out about them. No wonder she'd been so wary of them.

Anna returned a few minutes later with a large pitcher and four glasses on a tray. She poured everyone a glass and handed McPherson his last. "Well, go on, try it, tell me I'm right. It's the best lemonade in Illinois."

He took a big swallow while she stood over him and tried to smile. "It's very good."

"Can you guess the special ingredient?"

McPherson took another drink. "There is something, I can't quite put my finger on it."

"It's mint, and a few botanicals, plus the secret family ingredient."

Richard drained his glass and asked for another. Linda sipped hers. It was cold and sweet but it had a strange bitter undertone she couldn't quite place. It reminded her of tonic water, she supposed that was the botanicals.

Anna sat in an armchair opposite them all, crossed her legs, and rested her chin in her palm. "Now what is it you think I'm supposed to have done?"

McPherson put his half-drunk glass on the low coffee table. "Not done, ma'am, it's what we think you possess, a dossier detailing the activities of a shadow cabal known as the Shadows in the Cave."

Richard finished his second glass and wiped some drops from

his beard with the back of his hand. "We think the dossier might contain information about a case we're working. We're looking into a black site in the Chihuahua desert, that's linked to a string of national disappearances. It's part of a clandestine government project with the highest levels of security, a project called Operation Consciousness."

Anna blinked five times in rapid succession, but her face betrayed no other emotion until she broke into a bored smile and affected a jaded voice. "What a fascinating set of documents you think I have, and what a fascinating life you think my father and I had. I can assure you he was as boring and ordinary as I am."

McPherson lifted his chin and looked skeptical. "I don't think you're the least bit boring or ordinary, Ms. Patterson."

"Call me Anna, please. And you must realize any papers my father might have owned are legally protected by estate law and I'm not obliged to show them to you without a court order."

"I don't think we'll need a court order."

"But I think you will."

Linda felt an unpleasant tingling in her legs and wondered if it was from sitting so long in the Honda Civic, she never found sedans comfortable. "Anna, we don't want to force you to do anything you don't want. We were hoping you'd freely share it with us. This case has touched all of us, personally, just as it's touched you. I lost someone, he wasn't my closest friend, but my life hasn't been the same since. I need to solve this case so that my life can start making sense again and I was really hoping you could help us."

Linda saw Anna's resolve waiver. Her gaze softened and the muscles around her mouth relaxed. McPherson saw this too and pressed his advantage. "Ms. Patters . . . Anna, I can understand why you're protecting the dossier, I think it's your insurance. I think you're saving it for that moment when you can't run and can no longer hide. Well, that moment has come. If we're here, the Shadows in the Cave won't be far behind. We can help you, I can organize protection, but you have to let us know what's in the files your father and Estes Kefauver compiled."

Anna's expression was almost wistful, melancholic. "Well, that's all well and good, but you've drunk the Kool-Aid now."

"What do you mean?"

Linda heard Richard's throat rattle, followed by the sound of his shirt fabric rubbing against leather. She glanced over and saw he'd fallen onto his side.

The sardonic tone crept back into Anna's voice. "I told you I was boring, I've put your colleague to sleep."

McPherson held up his near-empty glass and considered it, his head rocking from side to side. He looked alarmingly drunk all of a sudden. Linda had never seen him lose control, not in any situation, and to see him this way alarmed her.

McPherson fixed his unsteady gaze on Anna. He was having trouble getting his sluggish lips and uncooperative tongue to speak. "That shecret ingre . . . dient, itsh . . . itsh . . . "

"Flunitrazepam," Anna confirmed.

The tingling in Linda's legs was unbearable. She tried to uncross them but found she couldn't. Her brain was telling her legs to uncross but they wouldn't respond. The couch started to sway and Linda had the sensation of being on a storm-tossed ship far out at sea. She wanted to vomit, but didn't have the energy.

McPherson pitched forward and hit the floor, spilling the last of his lemonade. Linda tried to say something but her jaw simply fell open.

Everything was too much effort. It took too much energy for her eyelids to blink, breathing was strenuous for her chest and lungs. Unconsciousness pressed down on her like a lead-lined blanket.

The nausea stopped Linda from fully losing consciousness. It would hit her in waves, washing her to the darker depths of slumber. She came to briefly to see Anna pull Richard off the couch by his ankles and marveled at the strength of the tiny woman in her early sixties.

The next thing Linda was conscious of was a sharp pain in her skull. It felt as if someone was hitting her repeatedly on the back of her head with a plank. She opened her eyes and saw she was being dragged backward down a set of basement steps by her ankles.

She had no way of protecting her head or wriggling free. Her body had lost the ability to come to its own aid. Linda couldn't even cry out.

The concrete basement was lit by a single bulb. Linda lay on her side, fighting to stay awake. She glimpsed three stout oak chairs. Richard and McPherson's limp forms were draped over two of the chairs. Their wrists and ankles were bound by duct tape.

Sleep had its dark hands on her, dragging her further into lightless pits. All Linda had left to fight it with was panic. But even her terror wasn't enough to keep her awake.

It followed her down into a drug-induced coma. Knowing she was entirely at a stranger's mercy and there was nothing she could do to stop it.

DRAW YOU INTERLUDE 2

THE HATCHET MAN
PART ONE

JACK EDGAR PULLED up to the beach house and killed the engine. No one would have guessed he was over the limit, but alcohol rarely affected his driving.

He climbed out of the Porsche 911 and popped the trunk. He loved the sound it made. He loved everything about the Turbo S. It was a pussy magnet, for sure. Which was why his bitch ex-wife was trying to claim it. She already had the house and half his income, if she thought she was going to get the beach house and his cars she could go screw herself. Though she had plenty of pool boys to do that for her.

As he reached into the trunk to grab the battered portfolio, Jack felt something on the back of his neck. His hand went reflexively to the collar of his Armani shirt. His fingers brushed fur and leathery skin.

Jack pulled his hand away and swung around. The portfolio was still in his hand. He heard wings flapping and he went cold. He looked into the twilight sky and there it was.

A bat.

Jack swung the portfolio at it. The bat took off into the night. He tasted bile and felt his stomach clench. He thought of the parasites in its fur and the germs on its claws. He thought of beady eyes and wrinkled noses, distended ears and venomous teeth.

Jack swung the portfolio up into the air, again and again. He didn't stop until he heard the leather around the handle tear and he remembered how valuable the contents were. He stumbled back until his calves were resting against the Porsche's back bumper.

He could hear the blood singing in his ears and the veins throbbing in his temples. His heart was trying to punch its way out of his chest and his lungs burned.

The ground was spinning. Or was it the Porsche? The sea was too loud against the shore. The security lights were burning a hole in the back of his retina. He needed to scream but his jaw was clenched shut.

Stop. Jack told himself. *Stop. Hold your breath. Close your eyes. Feel the ground at your feet. Remember your Porsche, your beautiful Porsche.* Jack reached behind him and touched its still-warm hood. His breathing slowed. His heart rate lowered. Jack opened his eyes.

A bat. What the hell was a bat doing at the beach? Hadn't he bought a beach property to stay away from them?

Jack took a ragged breath and a wave of nausea overcame him. He dropped the portfolio and bent forward, his hands on his knees. He thought he might vomit, then remembered what he paid for his Gucci brogues and got ahold of himself.

Jack straightened up. His head had stopped spinning, but his legs still shook. He closed the trunk, picked up the portfolio, and went inside.

Chiroptophobia. Jack had paid a shrink five figures for that one-word diagnosis.

"It means 'fear of bats,'" the shrink had told him.

No shit, Jack had thought. *And here's me thinking I was in love with the critters.* All the same. He wasn't sure which he'd rather touch—a bat or his ex-wife.

Jack shook his head at the memory. And people thought lawyers were crooked. He could learn a thing or two about charging from his shrink.

The beach house was a sprawling property over two floors. The ground floor was open plan, except for the bathroom in back, with a kitchen/breakfast room, dining room, living room, and gym. There was a small swimming pool and large jacuzzi on the terrace overlooking the beach. Upstairs were three bedrooms, all of them en suite, and his home office with a breathtaking view of the bay.

Jack dropped the portfolio on the couch. He would get to it sometime tonight, it contained important material he'd been asked to check for legal reasons. But first, he headed for the drinks cabinet. He poured himself three fingers of a single malt that cost him twice what his shrink had charged. Then he opened the wall-safe, pulled out a bag of Bolivian and cut himself two thick lines. He'd earned it.

Tonight was a night for celebration and he wasn't going to let his ex-wife, or a flying rat, spoil his buzz.

Jack had just settled a multi-million-dollar suit for his employers without setting one foot in a courtroom. No, he'd more than settled it, he'd murdered it.

To his employers, it meant a saving of millions and control of a valuable intellectual property. To Jack, it meant promotion, pay raise and a huge increase in his end-of-year bonus. He was set to make a killing.

Jack's good fortune began when his employer, a multinational telecommunications conglomerate, purchased a media group. A significant part of this group included a film studio and several publishers, one of whom specialized in comic books.

Fox Comics was one of the "Big Three" comic book publishers, going all the way back to the forties and the days of the pulps. Since their acquisition in the eighties, they were mainly seen as a loss leader, a way of incubating intellectual property that would be more profitable in other markets, like film and video games.

Jack didn't know a thing about funny-books or any of that nerdy stuff. He was more of a sports guy, even as a kid. But he knew an opportunity when he saw one. That's why he'd asked to be transferred. Sooner or later, he knew he'd get his chance to shine, and it came sooner than anyone thought.

***

The movie studio who owned Fox Comics had a surprise hit with a film about the superhero *Black Lion*. Originally a big game hunter who turned to hunting criminals, *Black Lion* had become an African American character in the late eighties. The most recent creative team had used the character to explore themes relevant to the Black Lives Matter movement. This had given a huge boost to the readership and the filmmakers had decided to follow a similar line, albeit not quite as radical as the comics.

The studio had committed to two more sequels and a spin-off featuring one of the most popular characters from the film, the *Black Lion's* love interest—*Yemaya*. Based on an African goddess, or Orisha, or whatever, she could control the ocean and had other water powers. The actress playing the character had a platinum-selling R'n'B album, so the franchise was basically a license to print money.

Until everyone hit an unforeseen problem. Fox Comics didn't actually own the character.

Yemaya had been created in the nineties by Joanna Crawford and Scott Poe, a writer/artist team, for Fox's creator-owned imprint *Velocity*. Creator rights were big in the nineties and, for some stupid reason, the whole industry flirted with letting creators own their characters, rather than working for hire. All the Big Three had a creator-owned imprint. Marvel had *Epic*, DC had *Vertigo*, and Fox had *Velocity*.

Fox wound up *Velocity* in the mid-oughts, but as early as '99 they were making changes to the contracts they issued. They moved from giving full rights to their creators, to giving partial rights, then no rights but a preferential royalties system. When they wound up *Velocity*, Fox added the most popular characters to their regular continuity, with the understanding that the creators would get first refusal when it came to working on any titles that included them.

Yemaya hadn't sold much in her first incarnation and the title had been canceled after a year. Joanna Crawford left comics to become a children's author and college lecturer and didn't pay attention to what was happening at Fox, or comics in general. So she didn't notice when *Yemaya* was revamped and redesigned and brought back in the pages of *Black Lion*. As there were no editors at Fox who'd worked for *Velocity,* neither Crawford nor Poe were asked if they wanted to work on the character and no one checked who held the copyright to the character.

Someone messed up big time.

It wasn't until the release date for the *Black Lion* movie was announced, and the studios revealed that *Yemaya* was also going to be in the film, that Crawford first threatened legal action. Fox's lawyers dismissed Crawford's claims, and her request for a share of the profits, out of hand, assuming she had signed the standard work-for-hire contract. An assumption that might have been very costly.

Crawford and her legal team took Fox to court. Fox's lawyers moved to have the case dismissed on the grounds that Crawford had assigned copyright of the character to Fox when they employed her to create the character. It was then that Crawford produced the paperwork she'd signed with Fox. To everyone's surprise, the contracts showed Crawford and Poe owned one hundred percent of the rights to the character. The judge found in favor of Crawford, denied the dismissal, and set a date for the trial.

That's when everyone at Fox and its parent company panicked. The comics were a minor issue, but the film franchise and the merchandising were worth millions of dollars and now it came to light that Fox did not have any rights to that income. If they'd cut Crawford in on a percentage of those profits, as she'd originally suggested, they might have kept the majority, but now it looked as if they might lose them all.

It was at this point that Jack stepped in. While the rest of the legal team pored over the contract to see if there was any loophole they could exploit or any legal precedent they could cite, Jack looked at the bigger picture and he saw the one detail everyone else had overlooked, the other creator, Scott Poe.

Jack hired a firm of private investigators to look into every aspect of Poe's life. It didn't take them long to find the leverage Jack needed. Poe hadn't left comics. He'd never become a fan favorite and he certainly hadn't pulled in the big bucks, but he'd had a solid career and he even did the odd job for Fox Comics. Jack got in touch with Fox EIC, Roger Fielder, and asked him to offer Poe an exclusive contract with full health benefits.

Fielder argued that Poe wasn't exactly a hot artist. His style was old-fashioned and out of sync with the direction Fox, and comics in general, were taking. Nevertheless, Jack insisted and brought a lot of pressure to bear on Fielder from higher up the food chain. Fielder was forced to concede. Poe was offered the contract and put to work on several minor titles.

Next, Jack had gotten in touch with one of the pediatricians at Doernbecher Children's Hospital in Portland, Oregon. She was having certain legal problems and Jack offered her his services pro bono. It was a small matter that wasn't hard for Jack to clear up and all he needed in return was a small favor. The pediatrician was more than happy to oblige.

With that sorted, Jack caught a flight to Portland, Oregon. He picked up a hire car at Portland International and drove southeast along the I-84. He turned off just after the intersection of Seventh Avenue and Sandy Boulevard and pulled up to a dive bar whose exterior was decorated with fairy lights and barbed wire.

The interior had even more fairy lights but no barbed wire.

Jack put down his briefcase, took a stool at the bar, and ordered a Maker's Mark with ice. It was just after four on a Wednesday afternoon and there were only five or six people in the joint. Sitting at the other end of the bar was a tall, stooped guy in a blue denim shirt and jeans. He was in his late forties and both his beard and his hair, which was tied in a ponytail, were going grey.

Jack sipped his drink, got up from his stool and moved to sit next to the guy, taking the briefcase with him.

"Excuse me. But aren't you the artist, Scott Poe?"

Jack knew exactly who the guy was and, thanks to his investigators, he knew the man's weekly itinerary—which hardly changed. So Jack had known just where to find him.

Scott, who'd been sitting with his head down, quietly nursing his beer, turned to regard Jack with open surprise and a tiny hint of suspicion.

"Who wants to know?"

Jack smiled and offered his hand. "Jack Edgar, I work for Fox Comics, same as you."

Scott's mood mellowed and he smiled for the first time, taking Jack's hand and shaking it. "Oh, well in that case it's good to know you, Jack. You'll excuse me if I don't recognize you. I haven't been to Fox's new offices and I don't do the convention circuit much anymore. So I'm not up to date on who works where anymore. You in editorial, or are you a creator?"

Jack shook his head. "Neither, I represent their legal affairs."

Scott's smile disappeared. His shoulders slumped and he turned back to his beer, his tone sullen. "Oh, a suit."

"Aren't you going to ask me what I'm doing in Portland?"

Scott shook his head. "Can't imagine you're here to do me any favors."

"How long is it since you split with Darlene?"

Scott looked up and glared at Jack. "What business of yours is it how long I've been divorced?"

"She throw you out? Was that what happened? Were you tomcatting around behind her back?"

Scott's hand tightened around his beer glass. "Seriously man, you better back off. You got no idea what went on in my relationship, what kinda pressures we had to face. I'm just here trying to have a quiet beer by myself and I'd appreciate it if you let me be."

"Oh, I get that. Wasn't trying to be impolite or anything. I was just wondering if you caused any problems in your relationship, maybe with another woman. You certainly caused *me* a problem with another woman, you and Joanna Crawford."

Scott smiled sardonically. "That what this is all about—the court case? I don't have to talk to you about that. Joanna says I should get myself a lawyer, a good one."

"And yet you haven't, why is that?"

"None of your damn business."

"Maybe I'll hazard a guess and say it's because you don't want to bite the hand that feeds you. Not yet, anyway. My guess is, you've got it good at Fox, so you're sitting back and waiting to see how this court case plays out. If it goes well for Joanna, then maybe you'll make your own play for a slice of that pie."

"Think what you like, no skin off my nose."

"I beg to differ, Scott. You have a lot of skin in this game. You might say you're right at the heart of it."

"Look, why don't you just beat it and let me finish my beer in peace?"

"Oh, I will, but first there's something I need you to hear."

Jack reached into his pocket and took out his phone. He pulled up the audio file he wanted, pressed play, and set it down on the bar between him and Scott.

It sounded at first like a clock heard through a wall, only wetter and more organic. Its rhythm was like a kindergarten drum student, struggling to stay on the beat.

Lub-Dub . . . Dub, Lub, Lub-Dub . . . Dub, Dub, Lub-Dub . . . Dub, Lub, Lub-Dub . . .

"Do you know what that is, Scott?"

"Your latest Drum 'n' Bass track? Wouldn't give up the day job."

"No, it's Timothy, or Timothy's heartbeat to be more specific."

Scott sat up and swiveled around on his stool. He looked ready to punch Jack. "Where the hell did you get . . . ?"

Jack held up a hand to quiet Scott. "I got it from Dr. Hansen, perfectly legitimately. She also told me a little bit about his condition—Complete Atrioventricular Canal Defect. Did I say that right? As she explained it to me, your son has a hole in his heart, between the left and right chambers, and the oxygenated blood from the right is mixing with the less oxygenated blood on the left causing congestive heart failure."

"You bastard . . ."

Jack raised his index finger. "No, no, hear me out, I've done a lot of reading up on this. It *can* be addressed with open heart surgery, especially if caught early, but it's a tricky procedure. I believe Timothy was under for more than six hours. Normally, that would fix the problem, but in certain rare cases, more surgery is needed. Certain rare cases like your son's. It's lucky you've got such comprehensive medical cover with Fox, isn't it?"

"Are you threatening me?"

"No, simply stating the facts. Does you good to count your blessings every once in a while, wouldn't you say?"

Scott turned away from Jack. He unclenched his fists, his arms went limp, and the anger drained from his body. He leaned on the bar with his head bowed. "What do you want?"

Jack increased the volume on his phone, ever so slightly.

Lub-Dub . . . Dub, Lub, Lub-Dub . . . Dub, Dub, Lub-Dub . . . Dub, Lub, Lub-Dub . . .

"Do you remember a woman called Cassandra Gunderson?"

"No."

"She remembers you. She was an assistant editor when Fox's offices were in New York, not over in LA. A glorified filing clerk really, back before paperless offices were all the rage. You made quite the impression on her. You see why I asked about your extra-marital activities, given your way with women."

"Where are you going with this?"

"Cassandra looked after the filing department, such as it was back in the nineties, keeping track of all the paperwork, invoices, contracts, that sort of thing. Says you used to pop in and see her whenever you called in at Fox to drop off pages. Saved having to pay for a courier—remember those? Used to play havoc with downtown traffic. Any of this ringing any bells?"

"Only about the couriers. Had a flatmate, when I lived in Queens, who rode his bike all over Manhattan."

"Well that's a convenient lack of memory. Because Cassandra claims while you were down there flirting with her she left you alone, to run errands, on many occasions. Left you alone long enough to go through the contracts and swap a real document for a fake one you and Joanna drew up."

"Now just a minute . . . "

Jack picked up his briefcase, opened it, and produced four documents. "I have a sworn affidavit from Cassandra detailing everything I've just told you."

"That's bullshit, I don't even remember this Cassandra and that statement doesn't prove anything."

"Maybe not, but it becomes a lot stronger when it's considered with this affidavit from Avi Friedman, who used to practice law but has since been disbarred for misconduct, who claims he drew up a fake contract for you. The same fake contract Joanna Crawford has just produced and that you sneaked into the files at Fox Comic's Manhattan office, when you took the real one you actually signed and destroyed it."

"Again, bullshit. No one's going to believe this guy's story. You said yourself he's been disbarred, so he's a proven liar."

Jack held up his hands. "Fair point, and I'm sure that's what Ms. Crawford's lawyers will argue, perhaps a little more eloquently than you have. And, to be fair, we'd have a hard time proving it. But that's where this last document comes in."

Jack handed Scott the document. Scott frowned. "What's this?"

"It's *your* sworn affidavit wherein you outline everything I've just explained. How you paid Avi to draw up a fake contract, sweet-talked your way past Cassandra, and swapped the real contract for the fake one, hoping to blackmail Fox with it someday. It also states that Ms. Crawford knew all about what you did and it was her idea. You're going to sign it before I leave this bar. And later, you're going to testify to it in court."

"Why the hell would I do that?"

"Because if you don't, then I'll give you the final document I have with me. Your letter of dismissal canceling your contract and the medical coverage that's paying for Timothy's next operation."

"But it's a lie. All of it's a lie. If I signed this I'd be perjuring myself. And what you want me to say, I'd be admitting to something criminal. I could go to prison for something I didn't do."

"Don't worry about that, Scott. We won't press charges. We're willing to be quite magnanimous about your little misdemeanor. We'll even keep you on the payroll until we've been to court. Of course, your career will be over afterward, but it'll be worth it to save Timothy's life. And it'll be worth the cost of keeping you on, to us, because we'll get to save millions."

"So, what's stopping me from getting a good lawyer and going after those millions with Joanna? I wouldn't need your crummy coverage then. I could pay for Timmy's operation out of my own pocket."

Jack steepled his fingers and rested them on his chin, fixing Scott with a homicidal stare. "The window of opportunity, that's what's stopping you. Little Timmy needs this operation in the next couple of months. He won't survive without it. This case won't come to court for over a year. We'll do everything to delay it. Even if you do win we'll appeal it in every court we can. If you win all those appeals and we're forced to concede, you'll have to hire an army of accountants to work out just exactly what we owe you. It could be a decade before you see any significant payout, and by then Timmy will be nothing more than a tragic memory. Sure, you'll be rich, but you'll wake up every morning knowing you let your son die when you could've saved his life with a simple stroke of the pen."

Jack turned his phone up to full volume. It was so loud, even the barman looked up from his paper.

Lub-Dub . . . Dub, Lub, Lub-Dub . . . Dub, Dub, Lub-Dub . . . Dub, Lub, Lub-Dub . . .

"Listen to that, arrhythmia they call it, doesn't it just break your heart?"

"Will you turn that damn thing off!"

"Sure I could turn it off, but pretty soon that poor little heart might stop beating altogether, and then this recording will be all you have to remember it by. Do you really want to risk that? Here, you can even use my pen."

Jack handed Scott the pen, like he was cutting out his heart, and in a way he was. Scott took the pen and put his hand up to his face to hide his tears from Jack.

Lub-Dub . . . Dub, Lub, Lub-Dub . . . Dub, Dub, Lub-Dub . . . Dub, Lub, Lub-Dub . . .

When he first began in the business, Jack had the good fortune to be mentored by one of the toughest and most ruthless lawyers he'd ever known—Henry Wrightson, known to his friends as Hank. If ever Jack knew someone with a killer instinct, it was Hank.

Hank had told him that rational argument was one of the best weapons in a lawyer's arsenal, but it wasn't the most effective. To really land a killing blow you had to go for the jugular, and that lay in their emotions.

Didn't matter if it was the plaintiff, the defendant, the judge or the jury, everybody's weak spot lay somewhere in their emotions. Everyone has something to which they're too attached to let go. Something they care about too much. Could be God, family or country, doesn't matter, it's there, and once you find it, you own them.

"Always go for the emotions, Jack," Hank would say. "In the end, it's always the heart that betrays you."

Jack had proved that once again. And Scott lay bleeding at his feet.

***

Jack did another line and rubbed the residue on the front of his gums. His nose and top lip were numb, his synapses were firing. This was really good stuff. He chased the line with a mouthful of single malt, savoring the burn as it went down.

Jack smiled as he thought of Scott Poe handing him the signed affidavit. He couldn't look Jack in the eye. He'd hung his head and his whole body radiated dejection and defeat.

There was no doubt about it, Jack was a stone killer. It had taken him a mere twenty minutes to trap the artist and end his life forever. He'd taken Crawford's suit, dismembered it and buried it in an unmarked grave.

He was feeling very pleased with himself, but he couldn't overdo the partying. He still had a bit of work to do this evening. He retrieved the portfolio from the couch and made his way up the stairs to his office.

He'd let the Fox execs know that he wanted more oversight of editorial. If he knew what the company was putting out, he could head off potential problems before anything was published. The editorial staff saw this as outside interference, of course, and resisted any attempt to curtail their freedom of speech. After all, they claimed, this was their area of expertise. A fallacy that was blatantly exposed by the shit show he'd just had to clean up.

So, Jack was taken aback when one of the editors in the reprints department had reached out to him. As part of its new deluxe line, Fox was planning to print a notorious, unpublished horror comic from the seventies that was long believed lost and had become legendary as a result.

The editor, Stephanie Allan, had been contacted by an anonymous party claiming to have the original pages. When

Stephanie asked for copies, to verify their legitimacy, she was surprised to receive the actual artwork.

She wanted to know where Fox stood legally with regard to negotiating a price for the artwork, when no proof of ownership had been given and Fox possessed the artwork. She also wanted Jack to look over the stories, which were strong even by today's standards. She wanted to make sure they wouldn't get into trouble publishing them.

All this was discussed via email and Jack had arranged to come by the offices to pick the pages up. For some strange reason, Stephanie demanded to meet him in the parking lot. She wasn't bad looking, even if she dyed her hair, and Jack would have been happy to invite her back to the beach house. But she was totally uncommunicative.

She didn't say a word to him. She just drifted over and handed him the portfolio with the pages in it. Her expression was totally blank and her eyes glassy, like she was in a trance. Jack suspected she was on something, like most of the editorial department. Another reason to keep a careful eye on them.

It was her loss for cutting him dead. Jack could do a lot for someone's career at Fox, if they were willing to show a bit of gratitude. Especially after the stone-cold slaying he'd just executed.

He put the portfolio down on his desk and unzipped it, moving the angle-poise lamp to get more light on the pages. The answer to Stephanie's first query was quite simple. Possession, as every first-year law student knows, is nine-tenths of the law. If this schmuck had handed over the pages to Fox already, and couldn't prove legitimate ownership, they didn't owe him a damn thing. They were Fox's pages now, to do what they liked with. So long as Jack approved them first.

As to legality, well the splash panel, on the opening page, was already pushing the boundaries of taste and legality.

DRAW YOU INTERLUDE

THE HATCHET MAN
PART 2

JACK COULDN'T SAY for sure what it was about the pages that bordered on illegality. So much law was a matter of interpretation and precedent. He spent a good five minutes trying to pinpoint what the problem was and he couldn't find anything specific.

It was more the way everything was presented, its execution. The shadows that filled the page were blacker than any ink should be able to make them, especially ink that was forty or fifty years old.

There was something wild and dark in the characters' eyes and Jack couldn't work out how the artist put it there with only a few lines on an old sheet of Bristol board. Their skin seemed too sweaty, their breath too hot. The whole opening scene was just too close and tactile for a comic book. This wasn't just the coke talking either.

This comic had affected Jack in a way that shouldn't be legal. Even if there were no laws preventing it.

The first story he read was about a guy who got trapped inside wallpaper. It sounded stupid, laughable even, but it made Jack increasingly uneasy. The second story was about a boy who was eaten by a book. Again the idea sounded preposterous when you put it into words, but he was left feeling nauseous and deeply disturbed by the time he finished it.

Jack wasn't a reader by nature. He followed the news, checked the sports pages, and read law journals to keep on top of his field, but that was all. He'd had to read a lot of books to graduate law school and that was enough for any lifetime. Reading these comic pages made him wonder why anyone would read this for fun.

The work appalled and disgusted him. It was the first time he'd ever wanted to punch a page of anything. There was no way he was going to allow this to be printed.

In fact, he wasn't even going to finish reading it. He was going to take all these pages down to the beach, gather up some driftwood and have himself a nice little bonfire. He didn't care whether these pages were worth a lot of money or not. *Jack* didn't like them and he was going to put an end to them once and for all.

His mind was made up. He was resolved. He had every intention of lifting the pages off his desk and heading straight for the beach. But he didn't.

He turned the page and began reading the next story. Something, way at the back of his mind, was screaming that this was wrong. That he'd already decided to burn this godforsaken piece of filth.

That part of his mind wasn't in control. Instead, it seemed as if the story had taken him over. That it wasn't letting him look away. It was demanding his attention.

The first page of the new story had three panels. The first was the largest. Jack thought they called them 'splash panels.'

The panel was almost entirely in shadow. It showed an ancient alleyway, like the type you'd see in the East End of London. The only thing the reader could see in the darkness of the alleyway was a pair of bloodshot eyes and crooked teeth, twisted into a sardonic grin. A single hand was illuminated by a streetlight. It was holding a large meat cleaver that was soaked with blood. This was the story's narrator. Maybe it was the shape of the word balloon, or the way the words were written, but Jack could almost hear the narrator's thick cockney accent:

HATCHET MAN: WOTCHA MATES, IT'S YER OLD MUCKER THE 'ATCHET MAN 'ERE. BACK WITH ANOTHER SALUTARY LESSON IN THE SUBTLE ART OF SERIAL KILLIN'. IF I 'AVE ANY PEARLS OF WISDOM TO PASS ON TO YOU TERRIFIERS IN

TRAININ',IT'S 'OW TO KEEP DOIN' IT WITHOUT GETTIN' CAUGHT. THE BEST WAY FOR ME TO DO THIS IS TO SHOW YOU THE SLAYERS WHAT FELL FOUL OF THEIR OWN MISDEEDS. TONIGHT'S SUBJECT IS JACK EDGAR, BETTER KNOWN AS THE TELL-TALE KILLER! PUT YERSELF IN 'IS POSITION AND SEE IF YOU WOULD'VE DONE ANY BETTER ...

The next panel showed the interior of a bedroom in a modest apartment. The focus was on a man in a long raincoat, wearing a trilby with the brim pulled down to hide his eyes. He was standing in the corner of the room holding an antique lantern with shutters, which he was opening and closing.

CAPTION:SOME MIGHT THINK YOU MAD, JACK EDGAR, BUT COULD A MAD MAN EXECUTE A PLAN LIKE THIS?

The third panel was bigger, showing the whole of the bedroom. Jack Edgar was flicking the light from the lantern into the eyes of a man in bed. The man in the bed was tall, with curly hair and an overbite. He was transfixed by the light and obviously in a trance.

CAPTION:THE MAN IN THE BED IS JOHN ALLAN, A DEMOLITIONS EXPERT.

CAPTION:YOU'VE BEEN STANDING IN HIS BEDROOM FOR HOURS, SLOWLY MESMERIZING HIM WITH THE ANCIENT LANTERN.

As if this lousy comic couldn't get any weirder, now the lead character had Jack's name. This was one coincidence too many. What was the matter with him? Why was he still reading this crap?

He should be down on the beach right now with some kerosene and a Zippo. Yet here he was about to turn over and read the next page.

The first panel on this page showed a:

Close up of JOHN sitting up in bed, wearing pajamas. His mouth hangs open, his eyes are wide, and his arms hang limply at his side.

CAPTION: IT'S ALL PART OF THE RITUAL ISN'T IT. THE MYSTICAL CEREMONY THAT INDUCES LIVING DEATH IN YOUR VICTIM.

JACK has put down the lantern and approached the bed, carrying a sack and a large carving knife.

CAPTION: YOU HAVE TO FOLLOW EVERY STEP METICULOUSLY. EVEN ONE MISTAKE COULD SPELL DISASTER.

JACK looms over John, his knife raised to strike.

CAPTION: YOUR VICTIM IS COMPLETELY DEFENSELESS. TOTALLY UNABLE TO STOP THE BUTCHERY YOU HAVE PLANNED.

John lies on the bed. JACK has hacked off both of JOHN'S legs, their bloody stumps are sticking out of the sack. JACK is using the carving knife to remove JOHN'S right arm. The sheets and mattress of JOHN'S bed are soaked with blood.

CAPTION: ONCE YOU'VE CUT OFF THE ARMS AND LEGS YOU CAN MOVE ON TO THE HEAD.

JACK places JOHN'S severed head in the sack along with the dismembered arms and legs.

CAPTION: BE CAREFUL NOT TO LET A SINGLE DROP OF BLOOD FALL ON THE FLOOR. THAT'S ESSENTIAL.

JACK is using the carving knife to slice away the skin covering the left side of the chest, revealing the ribcage beneath.

CAPTION: NOW YOU CAN MOVE ON TO THE MOST VITAL PART OF THE RITUAL.

JACK cracks open the ribcage and reaches in to cut out the heart.
    Close up of JACK holding the amputated heart, still pumping, in his hand.

SFX: LUB-DUB! LUB-DUB! LUB-DUB!

CAPTION: IT'S STILL BEATING. THE RITUAL HAS BEEN A SUCCESS.

JACK places the heart in an ornately carved, silk-lined wooden box, which also looks very old.

CAPTION: NO MATTER HOW MANY TIMES YOU DO THIS, IT'S ALWAYS A THRILL. BUT THE MOST FUN IS WHAT COMES NEXT.

Cut to EXT. outside the apartment building on the street, across the road from a park. JACK is lugging the sack to his car.

CAPTION: YOU STILL HAVE TO DISPOSE OF THE BODY PARTS. IT'S A GRIM JOB, BUT YOU HAVE A STRONG STOMACH. THERE'S NOT MUCH THAT FRIGHTENS YOU.

A BAT swoops down from a tree in the park and flies right at JACK, who leaps back in terror.

CAPTION: ONLY ONE THING IN FACT.

JACK: OH JESUS!

JACK swings the sack at the BAT who flutters out of its way.

JACK: KEEP AWAY FROM ME!

The next panel, is a close shot of the BAT. The streetlight picks out its tiny eyes, its furry body, and its sharp, bared teeth.

Jack stepped back from his desk. He managed to tear his eyes away for the first time in about an hour. It was the bat that did it.

The dismemberment of the still living body was bad enough. It was only a comic but the detail was like an anatomical manual. Jack had seen every layer of fat and muscle tissue as the body was taken apart. He'd seen the blood pumping from severed arteries and the marrow at the center of the dissected bones.

The bat was worse though. It was like a specimen preserved on the page. Held in suspension just below the surface, waiting to break out as soon as Jack looked at it.

Well, it could stay there and die in the flames to which he was going to consign this whole comic.

His mouth was dry and the back of his neck was damp. *Not the best combination*, he thought. He stepped back to the desk to grab the pile of boards. His hands hovered over them. He was almost too scared to touch them. What was wrong with him?

Don't look down, don't let it grab your attention, he told himself.

Too late, he tried to avoid seeing the page as he reached for the boards but his eye moved reflexively toward them and he glanced at the next panel. Then he couldn't pull his sight away. It was like the page had its own weird gravity, dragging his gaze down like light into a black hole.

On the next panel he saw:

A BEAT COP approaches JACK, with his hand on his weapon.

BEAT COP: ALRIGHT BUB, HOLD IT RIGHT THERE. I'M GONNA HAVE TO SEE WHAT'S IN THAT SACK.

JACK holds out one hand to reassure the COP and reaches into his jacket pocket with the other.

JACK: OKAY, OFFICER, BUT BEFORE I DO ANYTHING I NEED TO SHOW YOU MY I.D.

JACK pulls a police badge out of his pocket and shows it to the cop. He also has photo I.D. identifying him as a plain clothes lieutenant.

JACK: THIS IS SENSITIVE EVIDENCE, WHICH IS WHY I'M AFRAID I CAN'T SHOW IT TO YOU. I HAVE TO TAKE IT DOWN TO THE STATION AND BOOK IT IN.

The COP takes his hand off his weapon and acts very apologetic. JACK shrugs it off, understanding.

BEAT COP: I'M VERY SORRY, SIR. I HAD NO IDEA. WHEN I SAW YOU SWING THAT SACK AROUND, I JUST THOUGHT ...

JACK: NOT A PROBLEM, OFFICER, YOU'RE JUST DOING YOUR JOB. I'M AFRAID I WAS JUST STARTLED BY A BAT.

The BEAT COP looks surprised and a little bemused, JACK appears sheepish, as he makes an admission.

BEAT COP: A BAT, SIR?

JACK: I HAVE A PHOBIA OF THEM. IT'S A BIT EMBARRASSING. LISTEN, I SHOULDN'T KEEP YOU AND I'VE REALLY GOT TO GET THIS EVIDENCE BOOKED IN.

The COP tips his hat and leaves.

BEAT COP: VERY GOOD, SIR, YOU HAVE A SAFE NIGHT.

JACK: YOU TOO, OFFICER.

JACK is in his car driving out of town, a grim and determined look on his face.

CAPTION: THAT COP WOULD NEVER HAVE GUESSED YOU WERE ON THE FORCE, WOULD HE JACK? ESPECIALLY IF HE'D SEEN WHAT WAS IN THAT SACK.

CAPTION: NO ONE WOULD HAVE GUESSED YOU WERE A COP IF THEY SAW WHAT YOU'VE BEEN UP TO, AND THEY CERTAINLY WON'T GUESS WHAT YOU'RE GOING TO DO WITH THAT HEART.

CAPTION: BUT FIRST YOU HAVE TO BURY THE REST OF THE BODY, IN A VERY SECLUDED PLACE. BUT YOU KNOW JUST THE SPOT, DON'T YOU, JACK? IT'S THE PLACE YOU ALWAYS USE.

This was getting very strange. The main character having his name was a simple coincidence. It wasn't like he was the only person with that name.

But there was all this business with his namesake being scared of bats. What was all that about? This comic was written and drawn in the eighties, when he was an infant. How would anyone have known about Jack, or his phobia of bats?

Why was he still reading it? Why couldn't he put it down? It was like the comic had him under some kind of spell.

Jack took a deep breath and rubbed his eyes. No, that was ridiculous. He was tired and he'd had a little too much nose candy. There was no spell. He was simply doing his job, assessing a prospective property for Fox. It was well written and well drawn, that was all. The artist had a certain twisted talent that was compelling to read.

In the morning Jack would return the comic with a note saying that under no circumstances would Fox ever publish this work. Burning it was an overreaction brought on by stress.

Jack turned the next board over and saw that the scene had changed to:

An interrogation room at Police Headquarters. A YOUNG MAN sits alone behind a table with a tape recorder on it. He is in his early twenties with fair hair, wearing an open-necked shirt and jeans. He's sweating and chewing at his fingernails with a nervous expression. A single light shines on the table, the rest of the room is in shadows. Behind the table is a large mirror.

CAPTION: THE NEXT EVENING …

The door opens and JACK walks in carrying a briefcase. The YOUNG MAN looks over at him.

JACK sits down and switches on the tape recorder, checking his watch.

JACK: INTERVIEW WITH TIMOTHY POE COMMENCING 6:15 PM. LIEUTENANT JACK EDGAR CONDUCTING.

JACK lights a cigarette and leans back, eyeing TIMOTHY.

JACK: MR. POE, AS AN ENVIRONMENTAL ACTIVIST, WOULD I BE RIGHT IN THINKING YOU'RE PASSIONATE ABOUT ECOLOGICAL ISSUES?

TIMOTHY: WELL, OBVIOUSLY.

JACK leans forward, and blows smoke in TIMOTHY'S face.

JACK: PASSIONATE ENOUGH TO KILL FOR THEM?

TIMOTHY: COUGH! COUGH! WHAT DO YOU MEAN?

JACK leans in close, to intimidate TIMOTHY.

JACK: DOES THE NAME JOHN ALLAN MEAN ANYTHING TO YOU?

TIMOTHY: NO, SHOULD IT?

JACK: YOU JUST GOT A COURT ORDER TO STOP A FREEWAY BEING BUILT THROUGH LAND YOUR FAMILY OWNS JUST OUTSIDE THE CITY LIMITS.

TIMOTHY: THERE'S A PRESERVATION ORDER ON THAT LAND. THE CITY HAS NO RIGHT BUILDING A FREEWAY THROUGH IT.

JACK smiles sardonically.

JACK: THAT MIGHT NOT HAVE BEEN HOW JOHN ALLAN SAW IT. HE WAS A DEMOLITIONS EXPERT, EMPLOYED BY THE CITY TO CLEAR THE TREES ON THAT LAND.

JACK opens the briefcase, takes out some black and white photos, and places them on the table in front of TIMOTHY.

JACK: JOHN ALLAN WENT MISSING LAST NIGHT. THIS MORNING A CLOSE FRIEND FOUND HIS BEDSHEETS AND MATTRESS SOAKED WITH BLOOD.

JACK: WHERE WERE YOU LAST NIGHT, MR POE?

TIMOTHY frowns, but he also looks nervous.

TIMOTHY: I WAS OUT CELEBRATING THE COURT ORDER WITH FRIENDS.

JACK: AND AFTER THAT?

TIMOTHY: I WENT HOME AND SLEPT, NEXT TO MY GIRLFRIEND. I WAS WITH SOMEONE THE WHOLE TIME.

JACK stubs out his cigarette.

JACK: YOUR GIRLFRIEND IS A MS. ANNABEL LI, RIGHT? WE SPOKE WITH HER EARLIER AND SHE TOLD US SHE GOT UP AT 5 AM TO GO FOR A JOG.

JACK: THE DOORMAN AT YOUR COMPLEX SAYS NO ONE SAW YOU TILL AFTER 11 AM.

TIMOTHY: I SLEPT LATE, I WAS HUNGOVER.

JACK reaches into his briefcase.

JACK: SO YOU SAY, BUT IT DOES MEAN THERE ARE SIX HOURS OF YOUR TIME THAT ARE UNACCOUNTED FOR. SIX HOURS IS PLENTY WHEN YOU WANT TO MURDER SOMEONE AND HIDE THE BODY.

JACK takes the bloody knife he used to dismember John Allan out of the briefcase. The knife is bagged as evidence. JACK puts it in front of TIMOTHY, who is startled and confused.

JACK: WE GOT A WARRANT TO SEARCH YOUR APARTMENT AND WE FOUND THIS UNDER YOUR SINK. I'M ABOUT TO TAKE IT TO FORENSICS, AND WHEN I DO, I BET THEY'LL MATCH THE BLOOD TO JOHN ALLAN.

TIMOTHY: WHAT? I'VE NEVER SEEN THAT KNIFE BEFORE.

Close up of the inside of the briefcase, containing the ornately carved box in which JACK put the heart.
JACK opens the box and the HEART is still beating inside it.

SFX: LUB-DUB! LUB-DUB! LUB-DUB!

TIMOTHY looks around him, trying to locate something in the room. He looks perturbed.

TIMOTHY: WHAT'S THAT NOISE?

JACK: I DON'T HEAR ANYTHING.

TIMOTHY: IT'S LIKE THE SOUND OF A CLOCK HEARD THROUGH A WALL. THERE'S NO CLOCK NEXT DOOR IS THERE?

SFX: LUB-DUB! LUB-DUB! LUB-DUB!

JACK gives TIMOTHY a fierce, hard stare. TIMOTHY is distracted and increasingly frantic.

JACK: NO.

JACK: YOU WEREN'T SATISFIED WITH JUST GETTING A COURT ORDER WERE YOU? YOU HAD TO MAKE JOHN ALLAN PAY FOR WHAT HE WAS GOING TO DO TO YOUR FAMILY'S LAND.

TIMOTHY: I DON'T EVEN KNOW WHO JOHN ALLAN IS. ARE YOU SURE YOU CAN'T HEAR THAT? IT'S LIKE A HEARTBEAT. IT'S MAKING ME FEEL REALLY GUILTY.

SFX: LUB-DUB! LUB-DUB! LUB-DUB!

JACK points an accusing finger at TIMOTHY who breaks down and begins to cry, his head in his hands.

JACK: IT'S YOUR CONSCIENCE, TIM. CONFESS, YOU'LL FEEL BETTER WHEN YOU DO. YOU KILLED JOHN ALLAN IN THE EARLY HOURS OF THE MORNING.

JACK: YOU CUT HIM UP AND YOU HID HIS BODY.

TIMOTHY: ALL RIGHT, ALL RIGHT, I DID IT. IT WAS ME. I KILLED HIM.

SFX: LUB-DUB! LUB-DUB! LUB-DUB!

TIMOTHY is shocked and appalled by what he's saying, but he can't help himself.

TIMOTHY: WHAT? WHY DID I SAY THAT? IT WASN'T ME. IT'S THAT NOISE THAT'S CONFUSING ME.

JACK: WHAT NOISE? THERE IS NO NOISE, TIM. YOU KILLED HIM.

TIMOTHY: YES I DID. I KILLED HIM AND I CHOPPED UP HIS BODY!

SFX: LUB-DUB! LUB-DUB! LUB-DUB!

CAPTION: WHAT WAS IT YOUR OLD PARTNER AND MENTOR, HANK USED TO SAY? IN THE END, IT'S ALWAYS THE HEART THAT BETRAYS YOU.

Cut to the room adjoining. We can see the interrogation room, through a window in the far wall. In the foreground are THREE MIDDLE-AGED MEN, all well-dressed. One, who looks like an older version of TIMOTHY, has his head in his hands.

CAPTION: YOU KNOW WHO'S ON THE OTHER SIDE OF THAT DOUBLE MIRROR, DON'T YOU, JACK? AND YOU KNOW THE MAYOR AND HIS LAWYER ARE JUST ABOUT TO PUT THE SCREWS ON SCOTT POE.

The MAYOR, a tall, fat man with heavy jowls, has his hand on SCOTT'S shoulder. SCOTT is imploring the MAYOR. The LAWYER, a skinny guy in shirtsleeves and a vest, raises a finger to contradict SCOTT.

MAYOR: WE'VE GOT HIM BANG TO RIGHTS, SCOTT. YOUR SON'S GONNA GET THE CHAIR IF YOU DON'T PLAY BALL.

SCOTT: BUT HE'S INNOCENT. HE HAS AN ALIBI.

LAWYER: AND WE GOT A TAPED CONFESSION AND A MURDER WEAPON THAT'LL TIE HIM TO THE CRIME SCENE. THERE ISN'T A JURY IN THE COUNTRY THAT WON'T CONVICT.

MAYOR: ESPECIALLY WHEN WE PUT JACK ON THE STAND. YOU WON'T GET A MORE CREDIBLE WITNESS. HE'S CLOSED MORE HOMICIDE CASES THAN ANY COP IN THE STATE.

SCOTT looks crushed, despondent. The MAYOR and his LAWYER appear very smug and pleased with themselves.

SCOTT: WHAT DO YOU WANT FROM ME?

MAYOR: YOU KNOW WHAT WE WANT. YOU AND YOUR SISTER ARE SITTING ON A VERY VALUABLE PROPERTY AND THE CITY NEEDS A FREEWAY.

SCOTT: JOANNA WILL NEVER SELL.

LAWYER: SHE WILL WITH A COMPULSORY PURCHASE ORDER.

SCOTT: BUT THERE'S A PROTECTION ORDER ON THE LAND.

The LAWYER is holding out a typed statement and a pen to SCOTT, who looks very reluctant.

LAWYER: THAT'S WHY YOU NEED TO SIGN THIS.

SCOTT: WHAT IS IT?

LAWYER: IT'S YOUR CONFESSION, WHEREIN YOU ADMIT THAT YOU HAD A FAKE PROTECTION ORDER DRAWN UP AND YOU BRIBED A CLERK AT COUNTY HALL TO FILE IT FOR YOU.

SCOTT is nervous and appalled. The MAYOR has his arm around him to reassure him.

SCOTT: YOU WANT ME TO CONFESS TO FRAUD AND BRIBING A PUBLIC OFFICIAL. THOSE ARE SERIOUS CRIMES.

MAYOR: DON'T WORRY SCOTT, WE'LL MAKE SURE YOU GET A SUSPENDED SENTENCE, IN RETURN FOR GIVING US THE LAND FOR NOTHING.

LAWYER: AND YOUR BOY WILL GET SIX MONTHS IN A COUNTRY CLUB PRISON BEFORE HE'S OUT ON PAROLE.

The MAYOR becomes stern and menacing.

MAYOR: BUT IF YOU DON'T THEN I CAN'T DO ANYTHING FOR YOUR SON, EXCEPT MAYBE SEND A WREATH TO HIS FUNERAL.

SCOTT is signing the confession, his shoulders are slumped and he looks like a beaten man. The **MAYOR** and his **LAWYER** are patting **SCOTT** on the back.

MAYOR: YOU'RE DOING THE RIGHT THING, SCOTT.

SCOTT: I DON'T KNOW HOW I'LL EVER EXPLAIN THIS TO JOANNA.

LAWYER: SHE'LL COME AROUND. ESPECIALLY WHEN YOU GET TIMMY BACK HOME.

The AC was on full in Jack's office, but sweat ran down his back, his shirt clung to his skin. He could smell the smoke that hung in the air of the interrogation room and the waxy scent of the floor polish. His beach house never smelled of anything except cleaning products and air freshener. He paid the maid enough to ensure that. So where had these smells come from? Was the art that evocative?

Or was it the uncomfortable parallels he was seeing in the story? Was it just synchronicity that tonight, of all nights, he should read a story where a character with *his* name forces a confession from a character called Scott Poe?

Surely there was an explanation for all this. If he just kept reading, maybe he'd find it. Jack looked at the next page. It was a kind of a flashback. A montage of scenes from nearly a century and a half of history. The panels had no borders, each image flowing into the next. The first one showed:

JACK shaking the **MAYOR'S** hand, holding up the commendation he's been presented with, as they pose for **PHOTOGRAPHERS.**

CAPTION: SO, NOW WE KNOW THE DARK SECRET BEHIND YOUR STELLAR CAREER, JACK.

CAPTION: YOU KILL ONE CRIMINAL, THEN FRAME ANOTHER BY FORCING HIM TO CONFESS TO YOUR CRIME.

Flashback. In a dark alley, HANK, an older, plain-clothes cop in his sixties is handing a younger JACK the ornately carved wooden box with a still beating heart in it. Behind him is the CORPSE of a drug dealer who HANK has obviously just killed and butchered in order to procure the heart.

CAPTION: YOU WERE INITIATED INTO THE SECRET THAT CREATES THE HEART BY HANK, BEFORE HE RETIRED.

CAPTION: THAT'S HOW YOU BECAME THE MOST RECENT, IN A LONG LINE OF COPS, WHO BEAR THE MANTLE OF THE 'TELL TALE KILLER.'

Flashback. A bedroom in a nineteenth-century house, walls are lined with ancient books. A YOUNG MAN with madness in his eyes and drool hanging from his chin is holding up a still-beating heart that he has taken from the chest of a dismembered CORPSE. TWO POLICEMEN are trying to wrestle the heart from him, while a THIRD POLICEMAN looks on in shock and disgust.

CAPTION: THIS LEGACY BEGAN IN **1843**, WHEN THE POLICE WERE CALLED TO INVESTIGATE THE MURDER OF AN OLD MAN WHO TURNED OUT TO BE A NECROMANCER.

CAPTION: THE OLD MAN'S HEART WAS STILL BEATING, EVEN THOUGH HE WAS DEAD, AND IT FORCED THE YOUNG MAN WHO KILLED HIM TO CONFESS.

SFX: LUB-DUB! LUB-DUB! LUB-DUB!

A few nights later, the THIRD POLICEMAN has returned to the bedroom in the tiny house. He has taken a large tome of arcane law from off the bookshelves and is reading it by candlelight.

CAPTION: ONE OF THE POLICEMEN STUDIED THE OLD MAN'S SECRETS UNTIL HE LEARNED HOW TO MAKE AN UNDEAD HEART THAT WOULD FORCE A CONFESSION FROM AN INNOCENT MAN.

The THIRD POLICEMAN stands over the corpse of a BURGLAR he has just stabbed to death, holding the still-beating heart he has just cut from his body.

In a holding cell in the Police Station, the POLICEMAN is holding an ornately carved wooden box with a still beating heart in it, while a BANK ROBBER signs a confession in tears.

SFX: LUB-DUB! LUB-DUB! LUB-DUB!

CAPTION: THE POLICEMAN USED THE RITUAL TO SLAY CRIMINALS, SO OTHER MEMBERS OF THE UNDERWORLD WOULD CONFESS TO THESE MURDERS.

We see a line of POLICEMEN, down through the ages, starting with the THIRD POLICEMAN and ending with JACK.

CAPTION: THE SECRETS OF THE 'TELL-TALE KILLER' HAVE BEEN PASSED DOWN, FROM COP TO COP, THROUGH THE GENERATIONS, KEEPING HIS LEGACY ALIVE TO THE PRESENT DAY.

Out of flashback. The Forensic Lab. JACK is handing the bloody knife to a LAB TECHNICIAN.

CAPTION: BUT THIS IS THE FIRST TIME YOU'VE EVER USED THE RITUAL ON TWO PEOPLE WHO WEREN'T CRIMINALS, ISN'T IT JACK?

TECHNICIAN: OKAY, JACK, LET'S SEE IF THE BLOOD ON THIS KNIFE MATCHES THE VICTIM'S.

CAPTION: WHICH IS WHY YOU NEED FORENSIC EVIDENCE, FROM THE KNIFE YOU PLANTED, TO BACK UP THE CONFESSION.

The TECHNICIAN rubs some clear liquid on the bloody knife blade with a swab.

TECHNICIAN: I'LL JUST TREAT THE DRIED BLOOD WITH A DE-COAGULANT SO I CAN TAKE A SAMPLE.

The TECHNICIAN accidentally knocks the knife off the bench she is working at, onto the floor, she looks distraught.

TECHNICIAN: OOPS! OH NO!

The TECHNICIAN picks the knife off the floor, looking more relieved, unlike JACK.

TECHNICIAN: IT'S OKAY, THE KNIFE'S FINE, IT'S NOT CONTAMINATED, WE CAN STILL DO THE TEST.

Close up of JACK'S face, he looks aghast.

CAPTION: BUT THAT'S NOT WHAT YOU'RE WORRIED ABOUT, IS IT, JACK?

Close up of a single drop of blood on the floor of the lab.

CAPTION: YOU'RE NOT SUPPOSED TO LET A SINGLE DROP OF BLOOD FALL ON THE FLOOR, ARE YOU, JACK?

CAPTION: OTHERWISE IT COULD AFFECT THE WHOLE RITUAL. THIS IS NOT GOOD, IS IT?

In a corridor, the MAYOR and the LAWYER stop JACK as he leaves the forensic lab. The MAYOR looks extremely happy, JACK looks preoccupied.

MAYOR: JACK, THERE YOU ARE. THAT WAS GOOD WORK YOU DID TODAY, YOU SAVED THE CITY MILLIONS.

JACK: THANK YOU, MR. MAYOR, BUT I WAS REALLY JUST DOING MY JOB.

The MAYOR claps JACK on the back.

MAYOR: YOU'RE TOO MODEST, JACK, I'LL SEE YOU'RE MADE CAPTAIN FOR THIS. I LOOK AFTER THE PEOPLE THAT LOOK AFTER ME.

JACK leans in conspiratorially to speak to the MAYOR.

** JACK:** DO YOU MIND IF I ASK A QUESTION?

MAYOR: NOT AT ALL, GO AHEAD.

JACK: WHERE IS THIS FREEWAY BEING BUILT? YOU MIGHT THINK I'M STUPID, BUT I DON'T KEEP UP WITH THE PLANNING DEPARTMENT.

MAYOR: I DON'T THINK YOU'RE STUPID, JACK. WHY, IT'S BEING BUILT JUST TO THE NORTHWEST OF THE CITY. A A LITTLE STRETCH OF LAND CALLED 'USHER'S FALLS,' DO YOU KNOW IT?

Close shot of JACK'S face, he seems extremely shaken and very nervous.

JACK: I, UH ... THAT IS, I THINK I MIGHT HAVE HEARD OF IT.

Cut to a country lane outside the city, late at night. JACK is driving his car. He is tense and on edge.

CAPTION: OH, YOU KNOW WHERE USHER'S FALLS IS, DON'T YOU JACK?

CAPTION: YOU'VE VISITED IT MANY TIMES. IT'S WHERE YOU HIDE THE BODIES YOU MURDER, WHEN YOU'VE TAKEN THEIR HEARTS.

JACK pulls up at a desolate stretch of land, gnarled oaks with twisted branches dot the landscape. He gets out of his car.

CAPTION: YOU'RE GOING TO HAVE TO MOVE ALL THE BODIES YOU BURIED. QUESTIONS WILL BE ASKED IF THEY'RE FOUND.

CAPTION: AS THE ARRESTING OFFICER YOU'RE BOUND TO DRAW SUSPICION.

JACK is taking a shovel out of the trunk of his car when an OWL flies over his head.

SFX: AAWOOOO!

Jack looks up from the page, startled by the sound of an owl right outside his window. The noise has broken the comic's spell. What is an owl doing down by the beach? That's even stranger than seeing a bat.

The cry was loud, too loud, as though the bird was in his office, just over his head. He glances about his office on the off chance there actually is an owl inside.

Something is wrong with his eyes. Like he's been struck color-blind. Is that even possible? He doesn't know, but he can't see any color in the room. It seems as if everything has been outlined in black. As though it has all been drawn by the artist he's reading.

That's ridiculous, isn't it? He glances around the room a few more times. Is this a medical condition? Does he need help? The room doesn't really look like the artist drew it, does it?

Jack's eyes dart back to the page to check. He realizes his mistake the minute he does this. He can't look away now. He's captivated by the drawing in the next panel which shows:

JACK approaches the graves he's dug in the bleak, tree-studded terrain, shovel in hand.

CAPTION: SOMETHING'S WRONG, ISN'T IT JACK? YOU CAN TELL THE MINUTE YOU SPOT YOUR HIDING PLACE.

CAPTION: THE GROUND IS MORE FRESHLY TURNED THAN IT SHOULD BE.

 A small mound of dirt builds up on the ground at JACK'S feet, as though something is pushing the soil up from within.

CAPTION: YOU'VE HAD AN UNEASY FEELING EVER SINCE THAT KNIFE HIT THE GROUND.

CAPTION: A DROP OF THE VICTIM'S BLOOD FELL ON THE FLOOR, THAT'S NEVER HAPPENED BEFORE, IN ALL THE CENTURIES THE TELL TALE KILLER'S BEEN AROUND.

Close shot of JACK'S face, as his eyes dart nervously around the makeshift burial ground.

CAPTION: YOU HAVE NO IDEA HOW IT WILL AFFECT THE RITUAL YOU JUST CONDUCTED.

CAPTION: OR EVERY OTHER RITUAL YOU'VE CONDUCTED.

Close up of a hand breaking through the earth and grabbing JACKS'S ankle.

Something grabs *your* ankle. It feels like rotting fingers in a tightening grip. You step back from your desk and stare down at the floor of your office, to see what's caught hold of you. Only you don't see the floorboards of your office, do you, Jack?

You see the freshly dug soil of a stretch of land. You reach out a hand to your desk, to steady yourself. But your desk isn't there. Your office isn't there.

The expensive furniture, the sea view, the high-speed broadband, all of it's gone. In its place, you see gnarled oaks and a cold, comfortless burial ground. Devoid of any color. The comic strip, the one you've been reading, it's no longer on the page. It's all around you.

You look down at your hands. They have no color either. They're just white, outlined and shaded in black as though drawn in ink. What's happening?

You're concentrating on the wrong thing, Jack. Don't worry about *your* hands. Worry about the other hands. The ones connected to the severed arms buried here.

CAPTION: ALL AROUND YOU, THE GRAVES YOU DUG, OLD AND NEW, ARE ERUPTING.

Rotting limbs and torsos are clawing their way out of the ground and crawling toward you. Every dismembered body you ever buried is coming back. How many bodies did you put into this ground, Jack? Do you even remember?

CAPTION: IT'S THE RITUAL JACK, YOU BROKE THE RITUAL. YOU SHOULDN'T HAVE LET THE BLOOD FALL ON THE FLOOR.

But you didn't. That wasn't you. It was a character in a story you were reading.

CAPTION: IT'S YOUR STORY NOW, JACK. IT ALWAYS WAS, AND IT'S BEEN WAITING SO LONG FOR YOU TO SEE IT THROUGH TO THE END.

A hand fastens on your other ankle. You kick out, trying to shake it loose, but it grips you tighter. You turn to run and the severed arms are joined by more.

They grab at your calves and your thighs. They tear the material of your trousers. You take two more steps and a disembodied leg kicks the back of your knee. You go down hard, forced to kneel, and a sharp pain shoots up your thigh as you hear your knee dislocate.

Ignoring the pain, you try to stagger to your feet, but another leg aims a swift kick to your groin. You double over, clutching yourself in agony.

You fall forward, onto your knees, bent over. You feel rotting fingers scamper up your back like decomposing spiders. More hands tug at your shirt, your tie, your belt. They force their way past your clothes and tear at your skin. Thick globs of rotting tissue smear the bruises they leave.

Hands claw at your face. Pushing their way into your nose, your mouth, and your ears. They stink of damp earth and tainted meat. Some of the flesh liquefies and falls apart in your mouth, coating your tongue, catching in the back of your throat.

You can't breathe properly. Your pulse is pounding. You feel dizzy and there are blotches in front of your eyes. You lash out, thrash, and kick but the mound of disembodied limbs holds you fast.

There's a huge pressure on your neck. Something is pressing against your carotid artery. Your head throbs, the blood whistles in your ears. Lights flash behind your eyes and then . . .

CAPTION: EVERYTHING GOES BLACK.

CAPTION: THANK GOD.

The first thing you see, when you come round is JOHN ALLAN. Only, he's not the JOHN ALLAN you mesmerized and dismembered last night.

He has JOHN ALLAN'S head and torso, but there are twenty legs fixed to his hips, like a millipede. Ten pairs of arms have grafted themselves to his shoulders, giving him the look of a Hindu god.

The skin of his face is grey and waxy, his eyes are glazed, and a beetle crawls out of his mouth as he speaks.

JOHN: AH, YOU'RE BACK, GOOD. YOU'RE JUST IN TIME FOR THE BIG DENOUEMENT.

You're lying on your back, pressed into the cold ground. You try to sit but your arms and legs are held down by disembodied limbs.

You try to say something but your mouth's too dry and your throat hurts. Then you hear it. The rhythmic beating like the sound of a clock heard through a wall.

SFX: LUB-DUB! LUB-DUB! LUB-DUB!

You look down at your body and see there's something wrong with your chest. The skin and muscle tissue has been sliced and peeled back, but it's worse than that. Your breastbone has been cracked open and your ribs have been retracted. An improvised retractor is holding them open. There seem to be several wires running from the hole in your chest.

You crane your neck for a better look. You see the pink and red muscle of your heart exposed and beating in your chest cavity.

SFX: LUB-DUB! LUB-DUB! LUB-DUB!

The wires you saw are hooked up to sensors embedded in your heart. You turn your head to see where the wires are going. They run from your chest, across the barren ground, to connect with a small, black, electrical device. The device sits atop a large pile of red tubes, bound by black straps, to which it's also connected.

This has been done without any anesthetic. Until now, you'd been viewing JOHN ALLAN'S handiwork with cold detachment, as though you were outside your body and not connected to it. The horror of what's been done to you sinks in, and so does the pain.

You feel the night air on your internal organs, as it blows through the hole in your chest. Every beat of your heart drives the sensors deeper into the muscle tissue.

There is no threshold to this agony. It mounts in wave after wave, with every breath you take, every beat your heart makes.

SFX: LUB-DUB! LUB-DUB! LUB-DUB!

Something slaps at your cheek. Your eyes come back into focus and you see it's one of JOHN ALLAN'S many hands.

JOHN: DON'T PASS OUT ON ME NOW, JACK. TRUST ME, YOU NEED TO STAY AWAKE, TO STAND ANY CHANCE OF SURVIVING THIS.

JOHN: THIS IS WHAT HAPPENS WHEN YOU MAGICALLY DISMEMBER AN EXPLOSIVES EXPERT AND STEAL HIS HEART.

JOHN: HURTS, BY THE WAY, DOESN'T IT? I WAS AWAKE DURING EVERYTHING YOU DID TO ME. WE ALL WERE. WE NEVER DIED, THAT'S WHY WE'VE BEEN WAITING SO LONG FOR THIS.

You finally find your voice, though it's barely a croak as it comes out.

JACK: WHAT HAVE YOU DONE?

JOHN: I'VE WIRED YOUR HEART UP TO THESE EXPLOSIVES, ENOUGH TO TURN THIS WHOLE TERRAIN INTO A CRATER.

JOHN: IT'S SIMILAR, IN PRINCIPLE, TO A TIME BOMB. AS SOON AS YOUR HEART HITS 8,000 BEATS THE EXPLOSIVES WILL DETONATE.

JOHN: THE AVERAGE HEART BEATS 60 TIMES A MINUTE. THAT'S 3,600 TIMES AN HOUR. YOU'VE GOT TWO HOURS TILL SUNRISE AND APPROXIMATELY FOUR TO FIVE HOURS UNTIL THE SURVEYORS GET HERE AND FIND YOU.

JOHN: IF YOU CONTROL YOUR NERVES AND SLOW YOUR HEARTBEAT, YOU MIGHT LIVE LONG ENOUGH TO BE RESCUED.

JOHN: BUT IF YOUR PULSE ACCELERATES, AND YOUR HEARTBEAT GOES UP, THEN YOU WON'T SEE ANOTHER SUNRISE.

You listen to your heart, exposed to the night air, still pumping blood through your body.

SFX: LUB-DUB! LUB-DUB! LUB-DUB!

A calm resolve comes over you.

JACK: I CAN DO THAT. I CAN KEEP MY HEART RATE DOWN. HAVEN'T YOU HEARD? I'M A STONE KILLER.

JOHN: MAYBE, BUT YOU HAVE ONE FATAL FLAW.

JACK: WHAT DO YOU MEAN?

JOHN: DID YOU EVER WONDER WHY THERE'S A PROTECTION ORDER ON THIS GODFORSAKEN STRETCH OF LAND? WHY THEY WEREN'T ALLOWED TO BRING THE BULLDOZERS IN?

JOHN: IT'S BECAUSE THIS IS A BREEDING GROUND FOR AN ENDANGERED SPECIES.

JACK: WHAT ENDANGERED SPECIES?

JOHN: YOU'VE NEVER BEEN HERE AT THIS LATE HOUR, HAVE YOU JACK? OTHERWISE YOU'D KNOW. BECAUSE THIS IS THE HOUR THEY SWARM.

JACK: SWARM? WHEN WHAT SWARMS?

But JOHN ALLAN doesn't answer. He doesn't need to. You can already hear them approaching.

In seconds they'll be here. With their slick, leathery wings and their matted, furry bodies. Their hideously extended ears and their sharp, pointed fangs. Swarming in the air around you. Brushing your skin. Catching your hair. Flying into your chest cavity.

And now you have no control over your heart rate!

SFX: LUBDUB! LUBDUB! LUBDUB! LUBDUB!LUBDUB!LUBDUB! LUBDUBLUBDUBLUBDUB!!!

CAPTION: WHAT WAS IT YOUR OLD MENTOR USED TO SAY, JACK? IN THE END, IT'S ALWAYS THE HEART THAT BETRAYS YOU!

Stephanie found the beach house without a sat-nav. No one had told her about it, she just knew to get in her car and drive there.

The door was open, she knew it would be, but she couldn't have told you how. She walked through the ground floor and made her way up to the office.

On the desk, she found the stack of original pages she'd given

Jack. Next to them was the battered portfolio. One of the handles was coming off, and the leather around it had torn. It hadn't been like that when she handed it to him.

The last page of the comic was on top of the pile. Stephanie bent her head to peer at it. It had two panels. The first showed Jack, pinned to the ground by disembodied limbs. His chest was open and wires ran from his still-beating heart to a pile of dynamite. In the sky above him, a swarm of bats was about to descend.

The final panel was mainly in shadow. All that could be seen were two maddened eyes and a terrifying grin that had too many teeth. A bloody hatchet sat below them. This was the story's narrator.

HATCHET MAN: SO, MY MERRY MURDERERS, WHAT CAN WE LEARN FROM THIS GRUESOME GEEZER, AND 'IS MANY GAFFS? WELL, 'IS FIRST MISTAKE WAS USING SUPERNATURAL MEANS TO KILL 'IS VICTIMS AND FRAME OTHERS. SEE, THE PROBLEM WITH THE SUPERNATURAL IS THERE'S SO MANY CLAUSES AND CONDITIONS THAT EVENTUALLY YOU'RE GOING TO COME A CROPPER. WHEN IT COMES TO KILLIN', STICK TO THE CLASSICS, A GOOD LENGTH OF ROPE AND SEVERAL INCHES OF SHARPENED STEEL.

HATCHET MAN: 'IS SECOND COCK UP WAS 'OW HE DISPOSED OF 'IS BODIES. IF YER NOT GONNA STICK 'EM ON DISPLAY AFTERWARDS, TO TERRORIZE THE COMMUNITY, THEN YOU'VE GOTTA DISPOSE OF 'EM ENTIRELY. FEED 'EM TO PIGS OR GET YERSELF A NICE WARM ACID BATH.

HATCHET MAN: FINALLY, 'E SHOULD'VE NEVER GIVEN IN TO 'IS FEAR. YOU BECOME A SERIAL

KILLER TO DOMINATE AND VANQUISH YER FEAR. EVERY VICTIM BRINGS YOU ONE STEP CLOSER TO SAINTHOOD, TO **BECOMIN'** THE **FEAR** THAT GRIPS MEN'S 'EARTS IN THE DEAD OF NIGHT, NOT SURRENDERIN' TO IT! SO THERE YOU 'AVE IT, ME OL' MUCKERS. 'OLD ON TO YER 'OMICIDAL TENDENCIES TILL WE MEET AGAIN.

Stephanie shuddered. The drawings were brilliant but hideous. Was the narrator actually encouraging people to become serial killers? No wonder it never got published.

She slipped the pages back into the portfolio, took it downstairs and left the house. She climbed back in her car and began to drive. She had no idea what direction she was heading in. That was for the pages to decide.

They'd called her to the beach house. They'd been calling the shots for the last two days. Stephanie was a passenger in her own life.

***

Just over twenty-four hours later, Stephanie came to in an airport parking lot. She had no memory of where she'd taken the pages and no memory of what happened over the last three days. She was over a thousand miles from home.

On the drive back she pulled into a service station and had a panic attack in the bathroom. When she got home she went into therapy for two years. She had herself tested for rape, Rohypnol, and hypnotic suggestion, but nothing explained the memory loss or the journey.

Stephanie took a leave of absence from her job at Fox Comics on compassionate grounds. They were very understanding, especially her boss Roger. A week into her sabbatical she collected up every comic and graphic novel in her apartment and took them all to the Goodwill store.

She'd collected comics since she was in third grade, starting with Archie then moving on to superheroes and other genres. But now she found she hated them, and she couldn't quite say why.

When she'd been in college, she'd dated this guy for a couple of months. At first he'd been really sweet, dependable and attentive, but then he'd begun to question her on everything from the clothes she wore and the people she hung around with, to the courses she took. It was as if he were trying to get control of her life, subtly, by degrees. It wasn't anything she could put her finger on, just a feeling she had.

When she broke up with him he asked her what he'd done wrong. All she could think to say was that her heart wasn't in it anymore.

That's how she felt about comics. They'd taken over her life and she just didn't trust them anymore. Stephanie quit her job at Fox Comics and retrained as a Financial Advisor.

Around two years later, Stephanie was contacted by a young blogger for an interview about her time in comics. Surprised that anyone would even remember her, Stephanie wrote back that she'd be happy to answer a few questions.

When the blogger asked, as Stephanie knew she would, why she left comics, Stephanie paused for a moment, considering her answer.

An image came into her mind. It was a black-and-white line drawing of a man, a lawyer she thought, but she wasn't sure how she knew that. He was staked out on the ground at night and a swarm of bats was approaching him. His chest cavity was open and there were wires coming out of his heart.

She didn't know why, but she was certain the image was linked to the three missing days, for which she still couldn't account. The horrific image seemed to perfectly encapsulate the way she felt about comics, though she had no idea how to put that into words.

All she said in reply was: "My heart wasn't in it anymore."

CHAPTER 31

SOMETHING WAS HITTING Linda's skull again. It wasn't planks or steps and she couldn't work out if it was inside or outside her head.

Whatever it was, it wouldn't let her sleep. Linda's eyelids didn't want to open, they felt old and brittle. Her eyelashes clung to each other. Her eyes were dry, crusted with dirt at the corners. It hurt to tear them apart and when she finally did, the light stung them, even though it was dim.

No one, it turned out, was hitting her head, it was throbbing all on its own. Her stomach complained and Linda wondered if she could hold onto its contents. Was she hungover? She felt hungover. She didn't normally get that drunk. How long had she been out?

Linda's head hung forward. She lifted it, feeling the muscles in her neck protest. She was slumped in a chair. She tried to stretch her back and shoulders but she couldn't move her arms. Her wrists were bound with duct tape. She tried to stand and found her ankles were duct taped to the chair.

Her chest tightened and she started to breathe in too much air. Linda tried pulling at her bonds but she was held fast. She told herself not to panic but that only made things worse. *Relax*, she thought. *Take in your surroundings, try to remember how you got here.*

She was in a basement with a low ceiling. It was Anna's basement, she remembered now. Anna had slipped them something and dragged them all down here.

Linda hated basements, ever since she was a child. Nothing good happened in basements, Linda always avoided them. She steered clear of the basement in her parent's apartment block and the one in her own. She refused to frequent anything below ground level, clubs, restaurants, even bookstores.

The fact that she was tied to a chair in a basement did nothing to alleviate Linda's hatred of them. She wanted out. This was her worst fear, always had been. Ever since . . . ever since . . .

No, she wasn't going to go there.

Richard and McPherson were taped to the chairs on either side of her. Both were starting to stir.

Linda's eyesight came back into focus. Anna stood across from them on the other side of the room. She was wearing a white lab coat and holding a .38 semi-automatic pistol.

"Welcome back to the living. You'll excuse the roofie, but there's three of you and one of me and it was the best way to get you where I needed."

Linda bit back her nausea. "Why are you doing this? We only wanted to ask you some questions."

"I'll ask the questions, starting with why you really came here?"

"We told you, we want to talk about the dossier your father compiled. It might have some bearing on a case we're working. Why won't you believe us?"

"Because of what my father learned compiling that dossier. He warned me they'd come looking for it. They'd send official agents with seemingly innocuous requests. Well, here you are and, thanks to my father, I'm prepared."

Richard groaned as he tried to sit up. "Don't you think you're being just the tiniest bit paranoid?"

"Says the man who runs one of the country's biggest conspiracy sites?"

Richard blinked in surprise. Anna's face creased into a tight, self-satisfied smile. "That's right, I looked you up online, had plenty of time while I waited for you to come round, and I needed to sit down after dragging you all down here. You could do with eating less donuts, big fella."

Richard frowned and blushed. Anna chuckled, a low, mirthless sound. "In fact, you're exactly the type of people I'd expect them to send. A conspiracy theorist and a funny-book artist, special advisors to a washed-up agent."

Anna gestured to each of them with her pistol as she spoke. Linda's heart beat faster when Anna casually pointed the weapon at her. What had she done to have so many guns pointed at her?

Like most folk, Linda was used to seeing people wield guns on TV. She'd drawn plenty of firearms and hardly noticed if someone was carrying one. She thought she was used to the sight of them, but she flinched every time the pistol moved in her direction. The sight of a real weapon was terrifying.

Anna reached into the pocket of her lab coat and produced a vial of colorless liquid. "The dossier wasn't the only thing my father left me. He picked up a few things during his time in intelligence, including this, liberated from a Russian lab. Have you ever heard of SP-117? It's said to be the only effective truth serum."

Out of the corner of her eye, Linda saw McPherson sit bolt upright. He was genuinely agitated at the mention of the truth serum. "Look, okay, that's a serious controlled substance, and these are ordinary citizens. If you're going to use that on anyone, please, I'm asking you, politely, use it on me, not them. Use it on me. It could be psychologically damaging on an untrained person."

Anna raised an eyebrow. "And how easily you give yourself away, for all your training. You seemed to know what this was the moment I mentioned it. I saw it on your face. You don't seem the type to spook easily but this has got you worried. You say they're untrained, which means you're probably trained to deal with this type of interrogation, so I'm not going to use it on you. I want the unfettered truth."

Anna pointed the pistol at Linda's temple. Linda winced, turned her head as far as she could, and screwed her eyes shut, breathing heavily through her nose.

Anna stopped pointing the gun at Linda. "I'm going to put this down for a moment. If you do anything that gives me cause for concern I will not hesitate to pick it back up and use it on you. Do you understand?"

Linda nodded, not trusting herself to speak. Anna put the gun down, then she rolled up Linda's right sleeve. She undid her belt and wrapped it around Linda's upper arm, just above her elbow. She pulled the belt tight, produced a syringe, filled it from the vial and selected a vein.

Linda made a fist. "You don't have to do this. Really, I'm not a professional spy, or anything, I'll tell you whatever you want."

"I know you will, and this will ensure you do."

There was a sharp prick as the needle entered Linda's vein, then a slight pressure as Anna pushed the plunger and the serum flooded her system. The room seemed to expand around Linda, colors became sharper and brighter. Her headache lifted and the pain in her wrists and shoulders also went. It was like sinking into a hot bath.

Linda sat back in her chair, the tension slipped from her muscles and her anxiety just evaporated. Anna picked up the pistol, but it didn't bother Linda, nothing bothered her anymore. She didn't even care about the tape around her wrists and ankles.

The floor rocked and the chair swayed as though Linda were on a boat. She didn't mind, she enjoyed the sensation. The drug was a rising tide that lifted her mood and let her inhibitions drift out to sea.

Anna frowned, and pointed the pistol at her. Linda didn't mind, it must be hard to be so mistrusting, never letting your barriers down, keeping everyone out. "It says on your driving license your name is Linda Corrigan. Has that always been your name?"

Linda smiled, she liked Anna, in spite of the gun. She felt for her and she had a sudden urge to unburden herself. To communicate without any filters and unload every thought that flitted through her mind. "Oh that's a good question, you're good at this, you know how to interrogate. I see what you're doing there, because if I had a false identity, then I'd have to tell you even if I'd officially changed my name before I came and saw you."

"You haven't answered my question."

"No, no, I'm getting to that, you see it's complicated, and I want to tell you the full truth, I want to tell you everything."

"Go on."

"Corrigan is my adopted name, I was adopted when I was seven years old. I want to tell you my original surname, but I can't, I don't know it, I was too young, and nobody told me and it didn't bother me, because of what happened and I didn't want to go back and find out. In fact, Linda is only really five-sevenths of my first name. That was Belinda, but I didn't like it, and I didn't want to be that person anymore, I wanted to leave my old name behind. So, when I was ten years old, I had to move schools, and I decided I was going to have a fresh start with a fresh name and I told my parents, my adoptive parents, that from then on I was going to be Linda, just plain old Linda. My Dad always joked that even if I wasn't Belinda anymore, I could still 'be Linda.' Get it? 'Be Linda' as in Belinda. That used to crack me up. I really miss my dad, he died when . . . "

"Enough." Anna rolled her eyes. "How do you know about my father's dossier?"

Linda squinted and pursed her lips. "Ah, now that's even more complicated. See, we were sent to Boston by this whistle-blower, a sort of QAnon, deep throaty, kinda guy that Richard had the biggest man crush on. He had a codename, something like durned-grrr-something . . . "

Richard was fully conscious and listening, and he couldn't help interjecting. "Dierngewrit."

Anna trained her gun on him. "Be quiet, I am not talking to you."

Linda giggled. "That's right, Dee urny gurny something, isn't that silly? Boys and their codenames and their little intrigues, they never grow up, do they?"

"How does this pertain to me?"

"Ooh, 'pertain,' that's a good word, I like that. You are good at this, aren't you? I've said that before, but you are. Now, don't glower, you're showing your laughter lines, can you call them laughter lines when they're from frowning? Anyway, don't be cross, I'm getting to the point. This whistle-blower was part of the Shadows in the Cave and he sent us on this scavenger hunt all around Harvard, which was supposed to prepare us to penetrate the mysteries he was about to impart, or whatever. But we ended up in this ancient cave off a bottomless shaft, and they put these prehistoric creatures on our faces."

"They did what?"

"Put them on our faces, I know, I know, but it gets weirder. These creatures are like, part thoughtform and part organic and they feed off memory. So, they crawl up your nose, even though they're larvae that are like three feet long and just as wide and they attach themselves to your brain and they eat one of your memories. And they dump another memory they've already eaten into your brain so they can make room for your memory. I got a memory from some pilgrim father who'd come all the way from Scotland to form the Shadows in the Cave and McPherson got a memory about Estes Kefauver and the dossier he compiled about his former backers and how your father might have taken it. Then he remembered he'd raided your father's lockup when he was a newbie agent and it was in your name so we tracked you down and here we are."

Anna let the gun drop to her side and massaged her temple with her free hand. "Okay, either you *are* trained to withstand this stuff and this is all some big double bluff or you're telling the truth, because that is the most unlikely cover story I've ever heard."

"I'm telling the truth, I mean that's pretty much the point of a truth serum, isn't it? You're probably the only person who can tell us what happened to R. L. Carver."

"R. L. Carver?"

"Yeah, he's a cartoonist who drew horror comics back in the fifties."

"I know who R. L. Carver is."

"You do? That's great, most people have never heard of him, unless they're serious nerds. Are you a serious nerd? Never mind. Anyway, he's linked to a series of weird disappearances. I mean really weird disappearances, these people haven't just disappeared, it's like they never existed at all, and we're probably the only people who know about this, but we don't know why it's happening and that's why we've been researching him. Carver took part in a government program to test psychic ability back in the eighties, we think it might have been secretly run by the Shadows in the Cave and that's why we want to look at your dossier."

Linda finally drew breath. Anna's lips tightened and her eyes narrowed. Linda noticed a slight tic in the corner of her eye that suggested some internal conflict. Anna's brow furrowed and Linda could see her mean side had won out.

Anna lifted the gun once again and pointed it directly at Linda's face. Linda knew it was a threat, but the gun seemed such a strange object. What had been so intimidating now appeared to have such an abstract and arbitrary form. Linda leaned forward and sniffed the barrel on a whim. It smelled of nickel, oil and cordite.

"Is this thing loaded? Do you know how to fire it?"

There was a hard edge to Anna's voice. "Trust me, you don't want to find out."

Linda sat back. "I suppose not."

"Why are you involved in this case, Linda? How does a comic artist end up working with the FBI?"

"Because a friend of mine disappeared. Not just disappeared, like I said, it was like he'd never existed in the first place and the only person who remembered him was me, and I know that sounds crazy, but it wasn't crazy and I wanted to prove that. Same thing happened to Agent McPherson with a case he was working. Both disappearances were linked to Carver and so we set out to investigate him. But that's not the whole truth, there's another part to it, and I know you want the whole truth, so the other part is that I'm involved because of the Li'l Ghost Girl."

Anna shook her head. Her expression was less implacable, she looked bemused. "Who's the Li'l Ghost Girl?"

"She's this character who's been haunting my work. I mean literally haunting it for months now. I wasn't aware of her at first, but she's been in the background of everything I draw. Sometimes I go into these trances while I draw and she appears and tries to tell me things. It's like she's guiding me and there's something really important she's trying to tell me, but I haven't worked out what it is. But that's not the whole truth, there's another part to it and that other part is that the Li'l Ghost Girl is . . . the Li'l Ghost Girl is . . . "

"Yes?"

"The Li'l Ghost Girl is . . . she's me. She's me, aged six."

This last truth struck Linda like an anvil dropped from a cliff top. She'd been hiding it from herself since she'd first seen the Li'l Ghost Girl. It had been right there in front of her, but she hadn't wanted to know. Now that she was full of truth serum she couldn't dodge it any longer.

"She's me aged six, when I escaped from Henry McLaughlin."

"Henry McLaughlin?"

"Yes, he was my father, my biological father."

Maybe it was the drug, but Linda was hit by a sudden recollection, it came at her like an ocean breaker, knocking her off her feet and washing her out to sea. Her mind was pulled to a distant moment of her life, far from the cramped and threatening basement.

She was six years old, standing on a dusty sidewalk in a distant suburb. The scents of fall were in the air, burning leaves and the subtle promise of an early frost. A tall man with thick glasses who smelled of peppermints bent down to ask Linda if she was lost. Mr. Stukeley, that was his name, she hadn't thought about him in decades.

She saw the denim skirt she was wearing. The same skirt the Li'l Ghost Girl wore. It was tight and ill-fitting, the fabric reeked of sweat and neglect. But Linda had loved that skirt more than anything. It was one of the few she owned.

Something prodded insistently at Linda's chest. She tried to raise her hand to stop the jabs but her arms were taped down. The memory melted around her and the sights and sounds of the present rushed back.

" . . . said can you hear me?" Anna was jabbing her with the barrel of the gun. "You floated away for a moment there, where'd you go?"

"Back to my childhood, back to me aged six. I think this drug is really strong."

"I gave you quite a dose, I want to be certain you tell me the truth. What do you mean you're Henry McLaughlin's daughter? Who are you really?"

The question hit Linda right where she lived. It was the one question she most feared, because it triggered her worst doubts. She didn't know who she really was. Sitting behind everything she'd ever said and done her whole life was the terror that she wasn't who everybody told her she was. She was someone different who had woken up and found themselves trying to live someone else's life.

It was the bitter root of all Linda's anxiety. The thought that one day she'd be exposed as an imposter inside a stolen life, that someone would finally strip away the disguise and ask her who she really was.

And here Linda was, pumped full of truth serum and taped to a chair with a hostile stranger asking her that very question. The rising euphoria of the drug was the only thing keeping her heart from racing and her chest from heaving.

"I don't know who I really am. I've spent my whole life trying to find out. I know it might sound selfish but I think I joined this investigation to find out, as much as anything else."

"Why are you avoiding my questions?"

"I'm not avoiding them, you're asking direct questions and the answers are bigger than you realize. My biological mother was one of the girls McLaughlin kidnapped and . . . and raped. For some reason, he didn't kill her. She became pregnant with me and he let her live. I spent the first six years of my life inside a tiny cell, just me and the woman I called Mommy. I slept there, ate there and went to the toilet in a small potty I shared with my mom.

"Then one day, something happened and he stopped feeding us. I got the cell door open, I don't know how, I just did. I've always had a knack with locks. I tried to show my mom, but she was scared of what McLaughlin would do if we left, so she wouldn't let me open it. We starved for days and she made me come and lie down beside her. I went to sleep and when I woke up she was dead.

"I left the cell and soldiers came in the house. They came down to the dungeon. I was scared and I hid. They went into another room and there was lots of shooting. Then it stopped, and there were strange lights coming from behind the room's door. There were colors I'd never seen before and still can't name, they cast shadows that didn't seem possible. I knew I had to open the door. I knew I had to go into the room and I knew when I did it would change everything, for everyone I'd ever known. Forever."

The gun was back at Anna's side, her shoulders hung lower, less tense. Her eyes were wide and Linda could see a dawning recognition in them. "What was in the room?"

Linda could see the scene in her mind, but it was blurring, as if she wasn't allowed to remember. "Soldiers," her voice cracked. Something inside her was pushing back against the serum, stopping her from going there. "Soldiers, they were all dead and he was there."

"Who?"

"Him."

"McLaughlin?"

"Yes, McLaughlin and *him*. He was there too. And that's when I learned . . . that's when everything was opened up and explained to me . . . "

Linda wanted to go on. She was lifted, like a piece of flotsam, on the momentum of the drug, compelling her to speak. But then the drug crashed against the barrier, deep inside her. Deeper than her DNA. Deeper than her soul, and that barrier wasn't letting her continue.

Linda was caught between the unstoppable force of the SP-117 and the immovable silence within, and it was crushing her.

There was conviction in Anna's eyes and a hunger for the revelation Linda couldn't reach. "What was explained to you?"

And that was the last straw. The final compulsion that finished her.

Everything went black.

Linda was aware of the soft tissue in her throat tearing, caused by her shrill and piercing screams. They seemed to reach her from a great distance.

She vaguely heard the concern in McPherson's voice. "That's enough, stop it! Stop it, you're killing her."

Then she wasn't aware of anything at all.

CHAPTER 32

THE CORRIDOR WAS bare and stark with strip lighting. It had gray vinyl floors and beige walls punctuated every hundred yards by bright orange roller doors.

Anna stopped in front of a door. "This is it."

Linda had no idea how she picked it out. It was identical to the other orange roll doors in the warren of corridors they'd been walking.

Anna's right hand was in her coat pocket to hide the .38. She reached into her jeans pocket with her left, pulled out a bunch of keys, and unlocked the storage unit.

As the door rattled upward the floor began to sway beneath Linda. Her left leg wasn't working, it had gone numb and wouldn't support her weight. She reached out to steady herself on the roll door but it was still moving.

Anna grabbed Linda with both hands to stop her falling. Linda felt the hard metal of the pistol in Anna's coat bump her stomach.

Anna saw Linda's eyes drop to the gun in her pocket. "Don't get any ideas."

"What kind of ideas? What would I want with your gun? I *asked* to see the papers you've got stored here, remember? We all did. I don't know why you even have it."

"It makes me feel safer. I'm about to show you something I've never shown anyone." She patted the weapon in her pocket. "This means I'm more secure in that decision."

"I'm surprised you even got it past reception."

"Are you kidding? Have you seen the things people keep in their storage units? Besides, some people in this country still believe in the Second Amendment."

"Didn't have you figured as a gun nut."

"Didn't have you figured as a liberal."

"Wasn't your dad a liberal?"

"Touché."

Anna was still holding her up. "C'mon, let's get you a seat, you're still feeling the effects of the serum."

Anna's attitude and treatment of Linda had altered since Linda came round on the couch in her living room. It seemed that while Linda had been unconscious, Anna had freed Richard and McPherson and made them carry Linda to the living room at gunpoint.

Anna had sent Richard for a bucket from the kitchen while she injected Linda with something to counteract the SP-117. Linda had come to a few minutes later and thrown up in the bucket. Without relinquishing the .38, Anna told them she was going to share some limited documents from her dossier, but only those that were relevant to their case.

She didn't explain why she was doing this, but as soon as Linda could walk, Anna handed Richard her keys and made him drive her slate metallic Toyota Corolla. McPherson rode in the passenger seat and Linda sat in the back with Anna who kept her pistol trained on Richard. They drove into Chicago and all the way around the Loop till they got to the storage unit in Streeterville.

Anna lifted a wooden chair from the clutter and set it down. Linda collapsed gratefully into it. The unit was ten feet by twenty and lined with shelves containing box after box of documents. The floor and the shelves were littered with furniture and bric-a-brac.

None of the furniture matched and the bric-a-brac seemed chosen at random. If you inspected it closely, it didn't look like a bunch of junk someone couldn't bear to throw out. It looked like a carefully arranged movie set. The junk was there to distract you from all the boxes, to disguise what was really a meticulously compiled archive.

None of the contents had any emotional value to Anna, they were meant to distract a casual viewer and make them think there was nothing to see. Like all the trappings of Anna's life, it was a mask, a disguise.

A wave of melancholy overcame Linda as she took in the unit. It struck Linda that her existential fear of being exposed as an imposter, living inside someone's life, was the stark reality Anna faced every day of her life.

"You have a lot of papers here. This dossier is far bigger than we thought."

Anna smiled, not a warm smile, more of a knowing one. "This isn't half of it, this is just one of several units, in different locations with just as much in them. After Kefauver died, my father added extensively to the research and I've continued that since he died."

"I don't know how we're going to go through it all."

"You're not. Like I said, I'll share some choice information that pertains to your case only."

Linda looked around at all the boxes of documents. She'd collected comics her whole life, she was a bit of a hoarder herself, but this was just insane, and this was one of several units. The pressure of looking after so much forbidden info must be immense. It wasn't a pressure Linda would ever want. "So, how did you and your father put all this together?"

"You want to know about our research methods? They're a little different from researching a mid-term paper or an article for the local rag. To understand how we unearth all this evidence, you have to understand how an organization like the Shadows in the Cave works. And to understand how an organization like that works you have to unearth the sort of evidence that we do."

"Well, that clears that up—not!"

"Okay, I admit it's a bit of a closed circle, but that's the nature of the beast here. My father had to dig deep. He used his contacts at the CIA and Washington, but he also employed PIs, other researchers, and the odd psychic."

"Psychics, for real?"

"Only as a route to evidence, and the key thing here is that we've always collected evidence. I've adapted his methods for the internet age."

"You're still researching, after all these years?"

"Someone has to, someone needs to bear witness, because one day they're going to be called to account. I'll admit knowing all this, and adding to the damning pile of evidence makes me cynical about how power is really wielded. But, despite that, I'm still a patriot and I still believe in our system of democracy. I know it's flawed, look at this evidence if you want to see its flaws, but it's still a good system. And it's a system worth fighting for. One day there's going to be a reckoning, and all of this," she indicated all the boxes with her arm. "All of this is going to be crucial when that day comes."

Linda was silent for a moment, her arms folded, trying to weigh

Anna up. That was the most passionate Anna had been in their company. Her manner had changed since Linda came round. She was slightly less aggressive and abrupt, it was probably the closest she came to conciliatory, but Linda still couldn't get a handle on her. "Do you mind me asking why you're doing this? I mean, a few hours ago you taped me to a chair to interrogate me. Now you're sharing your life's work."

Anna regarded Linda with quiet amusement, her head tilted to one side, her face pulled into an expression that seemed to say *you really don't get it, do you*? "I'm doing this for you, Linda. I don't give a damn about the FBI, or any cockamamie missing persons investigation. I'm doing this because you're inextricably linked to the history of the Shadows in the Cave and you have no idea what you have or how much danger you're in. I'm doing this because I believe you have a right to know."

Anna turned away and began lifting objects off one of the shelves. "Are you okay to stand now?"

Linda got to her feet. "I think so."

"Good, cos we're going to need to take this box with us."

She handed Linda a cardboard box full of manilla folders. It must have weighed more than ten pounds. Then she took two more off the shelf. "And these two."

Linda was surprised at Anna's strength, given her age and height. She felt like she was going to have a hernia just holding the box. "There's no way I can carry this to the car."

"Don't be silly, put it on the floor, I'll go get us a trolley."

They loaded the boxes in the trunk of Anna's car and Anna climbed into the backseat with Linda. She took her .38 out straight away and stuck it in the back of Richard's head. "Okay, get going, big guy."

Richard held up his hands to show his compliance and then started the engine. "You want I should take a left and get us back on the Loop?"

"No, take a right, we're going to Lincoln Park."

"What's in Lincoln Park?"

"Only the best pizza in Chicago, probably the best pizza in the country. I'm starving and we've got a long night ahead of us."

CHAPTER 33

THE PIES HAD a caramelized halo of cheese around the rim of the crust. The sauce tasted of sweet, ripe tomatoes. A single slice was a meal in itself.

Linda had two. Where had deep dish been all her life?

Richard had finished his pie. He pointed to the remains of Linda's. "Are you going to eat those last slices?"

"Hands off, I'm saving those for later."

McPherson gave a slight shake of his head. "The smell of old pizza, that's just what the car's upholstery needs."

"It's a rental, they price that stuff in."

Anna caught Linda's eye, her face relaxed, and the corners of her mouth turned up. Linda realized she might actually be smiling. "You like the pizza, huh, New York? Do we have a Chicago-style convert?"

Linda chuckled. "You might have."

Anna had put away the .38, on the condition that McPherson leave his gun in the car. McPherson had grudgingly complied.

Anna was less antagonistic when they got back. She even opened a bottle of wine to go with the pizza. The meal became a truce. A watering hole where they put their differences aside. They broke bread and drank wine to seal the peace.

After Anna had Richard and McPherson clear up, she perched on the edge of a leather La-Z-Boy and opened the oldest-looking box. She had them all brought in before they were allowed to eat and guarded them zealously throughout the meal. She opened the box with a certain amount of reverence and ceremony. Linda couldn't help feeling honored she was sharing it with them.

"This is some of the last research my father did, before a heart attack took him in '93. He lived long enough to see Clinton elected. An idealist to the end, he never saw the Lewinsky affair."

Linda sat forward and frowned a little. "Clinton did a lot of good things for the economy."

"Yes, he did."

"But you don't share your father's idealism?"

"Our idealism is similar, with one fundamental difference."

"What's that?"

"My father was an idealist in spite of the secrets he uncovered. I'm an idealist because of them. After Kefauver died he continued to carry this torch. He passed it on to me and I've carried it ever since."

Richard took out his phone. "Is it okay if I record this?"

Anna glowered. "No, it's not okay. Put that away or you can leave right now. This is all off the record. I'll let you see these files to verify what I'm saying, but you can't keep them or make any copies."

Richard put his phone away and raised his hands to show they were empty. "Fine, but do you know what was really going on out in the Chihuahua desert in the eighties?"

"It had been going on for a long time by the 1980s."

"The psychic testing, you mean?"

"That wasn't what they were doing out there in the desert."

"But we interviewed one of the men who conducted those tests and that's what he seemed to think he was there for."

Anna drew in a deep breath. "That's just how the Shadows in the Cave work, the true meaning of most of their plans are entirely unknown, even to the principal actors. That's how they remain in control."

Richard scratched his chin. "I can buy that. So, if a bunch of parapsychologists and psychics were led to believe they were testing the existence of psi-powers, what was it they were really doing?"

"To answer that, we have to go back to 1902."

Anna pulled out a manila folder filled with aging documents and photographs. She showed them a map and six black-and-white photographs. The map showed a plot of land in the Chihuahua desert. The photos showed four women and two men in turn-of-the-century dress. One of the men was Indian and wore a turban, another woman was dressed in traditional African garb. They looked at the camera with the pride that comes from accomplishment and yet this made them seem tragically doomed.

"This is the site of the compound in 1902, forty years before it was built. It was simply a failed ranch, bought cheaply while still part of Mexico."

Anna indicated the photographs. "These are the six leading psychics of their day, spiritualists, mediums, a yogi and a mambo."

Linda stared at the photo. "R. L. Carver's grandmother was a mambo, that's a voodoo priestess, isn't it?"

"That's right. They were invited to this remote location, by an anonymous benefactor, to prove the scientific existence of the afterlife. They were paid handsomely to keep very quiet about it."

"Did they find any proof?"

Anna shrugged. "No one knows. That was the last anyone heard of them. All record of their existence disappears. These well-known people were fêted in their day. They had families, friends and followers, but no one reported them missing. No newspapers or journals mentioned them again, almost as if there was a purposeful blackout, wiping all six from the public record."

Anna put the folder away and took out another. The documents in this one looked about eighty years old. She unfolded blueprints for a military compound stamped 'Classified.' Then she placed six more black-and-white photos on the coffee table. Linda saw five men and one woman, three of the subjects were in uniform and the other three sported forties fashions.

"Just after we entered the war, the Office of Strategic Services, the CIA's forerunner, built a private compound on the site of this ranch. They requisitioned two Marine platoons to guard it. The official purpose of the compound was to investigate occult warfare. Hitler's armies and the British secret service were locked in a clandestine magical battle. Winston Churchill had pitted Aleister Crowley, Dion Fortune and her Fraternity of the Inner Light, against Heinrich Himmler's dark forces."

Richard picked up one of the photos. "We've heard of the Fraternity of the Inner Light. Would I be right in thinking all six of these people disappeared just as mysteriously?"

"Officially they're listed as 'missing in action,' even though three of them were civilians. None of them have an official grave and their remains were never returned to their families. The date of their deaths is marked as the second of September."

Linda gazed at the blueprints, admiring the detail in the design. The artist in her was filing them away for future reference.

Something was becoming clear to her. "There's a pattern forming here."

"There is indeed." Anna opened the final folder, which wasn't as thick as the other two. Among the papers was a headshot of a middle-aged African American, with the most piercing brown eyes Linda had ever seen.

She recognized him instantly. "Oh my God, that's R. L. Carver."

Linda had never seen such a clear image of Carver. She'd only come across a couple of fuzzy snaps from the sixties. She couldn't tear her eyes away from the photo. It was like looking at a picture of her father, or her husband. It seemed like she'd known him her entire life, or maybe longer. The more she stared, the more it seemed she was going to recollect things she couldn't possibly know, like the sound of his laugh, or how he smelled when he needed a shower.

Linda was aware of a hand on her shoulder, gently shaking her. It was Anna. "Linda, are you still with us?"

"Sorry." Linda put a hand to her brow. "I think I zoned out there for a moment."

"I said: care to guess when the next lot of experiments took place?"

"Um, the second of September?"

"Exactly forty years after the previous set of experiments and eighty years after the ones before that."

Richard became animated. "So, Operation Consciousness wasn't confined to the eighties, it was part of a project that went right back to the nineteen hundreds."

"It goes back further. These three events are the culmination of a plan that was centuries in the making."

"And what were they planning?"

Anna adopted the manner of a tutor encouraging a promising student. "You've been researching this incident for a while now, am I right?"

"Yes."

"So, if you've been paying attention, you might already know. Why did the Shadows in the Cave secretly sponsor the Senate Subcommittee on Juvenile Delinquency?"

Richard seemed eager to answer her. "To revive Kefauver's campaign for President, to get him national coverage."

"And . . . ?"

"To put crime and horror comics out of business."

"Because . . . ?"

"People weren't reading superhero comics anymore and the cabal had secretly spent a lot of money getting them published in the forties."

"And why did they do that?"

"This was in the memory the Scwyrm gave me, you know, the prehistoric thing Linda mentioned. As I understand it, they wanted to focus impressionable minds on the idea of an American god, that's why they put all those star-spangled deities in the comic books they sponsored. That was the effect superheroes were supposed to have on the collective consciousness."

Anna sat back for a moment, her head cocked, a look of pleasant admiration on her face. "What if I told you they were laying the groundwork for the real thing and that was the plan all along?"

"Are you saying the Shadows in the Cave were trying to create their own American god?"

"They were fulfilling an ancient prophecy, their goal was to initiate the coming of the Midswégan."

Linda clenched her interlocked fingers, not certain if she should ask this: "We've heard that name before. What exactly is the Midswégan?"

Anna's face took on a severe tone. "Very possibly the end of everything we know."

CHAPTER 34

LINDA HELD UP her hands. "Okay, this just got real scary, real quick. And given what I've seen these past months, that's saying something."

Richard nodded, unconvinced. "Even with the things we've seen these past months, are you asking us to believe a shadow-government cabal was trying to build a god out in that desert?"

Anna was irritated and dismissive of this question. "I'm not asking you to believe anything. This isn't about what you do or don't believe. This is about the Shadows in the Cave and what *they* believe. If you ever hope to understand them and the things they do, you have to understand what they believe."

Linda wanted to placate Anna. "Can *you* tell us what they believe?"

"I'll try, but to fully understand what the Shadows in the Cave believe, you have to be part of them. I can only give you the historical facts and some educated guesses."

Anna unfolded a photocopy of a map of the Scottish Highlands from the eighteenth century. She pointed to a small town that was clearly marked Dunballan.

"This is the last known recording of this small Scottish town. After this, it disappears from all visual and written records."

Richard squinted at the map. "Was it abandoned?"

"No, it's inhabited to this day, but you won't find it on any maps, there are no road signs, and it's missing from satellite photos of the area."

"Can I ask why?"

"It was the last location of the Twelve Families who could manifest the Thirteenth."

Linda sat forward in her chair. "Wait, that was in my memory from the Scwyrm. I think I mentioned it."

A ghost of regret passed across Anna's face. "I recall that, yes."

"Anyway, the memory was from an old man called Angus McKay, he was part of the Twelve Families. He called himself a Shadowcaster, whatever that meant. But he was in Boston, while it was still an English colony, and there were only seven families there. What *are* the Twelve Families?"

Anna placed a photograph of an ancient clay tablet on the coffee table. The tablet had cuneiform writing on it, along with a relief showing twelve men and women holding hands. Standing above the twelve men and women was another figure. It seemed to be shining and it didn't appear human. The impression was very faint and had faded altogether in places. Someone had filled in the outline with a red pen. Below the relief was a strange symbol that looked very familiar to Linda. It was in the shape of a lopsided diamond, filled with intersecting lines.

Anna tapped the coffee table. "This photograph was taken in the British Museum. It's part of their collection of Mesopotamian tablets, the oldest surviving human writings. This tablet is from the city of Uruk in the Indus Valley, on the borders of what are now Iraq and Iran. It was created more than four thousand years before the birth of Christ. It's the oldest depiction of the Twelve Families summoning the Thirteenth."

"What does the writing say?"

"It describes how the Shadowcasters of the Twelve Families would summon what they called the Thirteenth. A non-corporeal being who only appeared when the Twelve Shadowcasters came together."

Richard pointed at the shining figure in the photograph. "So this is the Thirteenth and it's like some kind of egregore?"

Linda wrinkled her nose in bewilderment. "What's an egre-thingy?"

"There's a theory that whenever a group of people come together to do something, that group creates its own collective spirit, it can be anything from running a regular poker game to campaigning for a cause. The name for this group spirit is an Egregore and it draws its energy from the group and at the same time guides the members."

"Oh."

Anna indicated the cuneiform writing on the photograph. "That partially describes the Thirteenth. The writing is propaganda, by enemies of the Twelve Families decrying their activities. It says the group's collective spirit was inhabited by a pre-human consciousness that prophesied the future. This was what they called the Thirteenth and it gave them many gifts. Each of the families produced one delegate per generation who could help summon the Thirteenth, the other members of the family helped to safeguard the Thirteenth's prophecies and gifts."

"What do you mean by gifts exactly?"

"According to the writings on the tablet, the Thirteenth led them to a secret trove of knowledge that existed before humans walked the earth and it taught them how to understand and profit from this knowledge. The Twelve Families claimed this knowledge once guided all of humanity, but humans broke from its teaching and fell from grace. They perverted the knowledge and this led to every religion from the birth of civilization."

Richard fixed Anna with a quizzical stare and pushed his glasses off the bridge of his nose. "We've heard people use the phrase—'faith before man' or 'the faith that came before man.' Are they referring to this knowledge you mentioned?"

"That's one of many names for it. It's also referred to as the Qu'rm Saddic Heresy. The tablet says the Twelve Families had guarded the knowledge and profited from it for millennia, even before the first cities of Mesopotamia were founded."

"What happened to them?"

"They seem to have gone underground as the Sumerians, Assyrians, and Babylonians built and lost their empires. Sporadic reports of the Twelve Families or followers of the Qu'rm Saddic Heresy surface throughout history. They're mentioned in texts from the ancient Greek colony of Massalia, now known as Marseille in France. A Roman colony of Neo-Platonists in ancient Britain was said to have harbored them for a time in what is now the English county of Wiltshire. They were said to have fled their Pyrenean stronghold in the mountains of Northern Spain in 1329, during the last crusade against the Cathars."

Anna retrieved the seventeenth-century map of the Scottish Highlands and tapped it with her finger. "The last known location of the Twelve Families is in Dunballan, just north of St. Leonards."

Linda pointed to the lopsided diamond symbol. "I recognize this symbol. It was drawn on the side of the tank they kept those

Scwyrm things in. It looked familiar even then. I think McLaughlin drew it on the wall of my cell, when I was a tiny child."

Anna furrowed her brow. "It's called an Eorcanstán. If I remember, it's a visual summary of the Twelve Families' most sacred secrets. That's all I can tell you."

"What are their most sacred secrets?"

"I have no idea."

Linda shifted her gaze to the map. "So, I'm trying to put this information together with everything else I've learned. Am I right in thinking the Seven Families that came to Boston were once part of the Twelve Families who can summon the Thirteenth, this spirit guide, or whatever?"

"Yes, from what my father and I could find out, it seems there was a schism in the group, over ideological issues."

"Angus, the guy whose memory I have, seemed to think they had split before. He was aware of antiquated scrolls with information that gave them power and influence among the settlers, was that what you called 'the knowledge?'"

"Some of it, I expect. The Seven Families who left Dunballan took many records with them. Some of the remaining records are said to be in the catacombs under a church in St. Leonards. There may be other caches of forbidden knowledge hidden around the globe."

"So, those Seven Families have secretly been behind some of the key moments in American history and they eventually became the Shadows in the Cave."

"Yes, but because they only have seven Shadowcasters they could never summon the Thirteenth, even if they hoped to fulfill its prophecies."

Richard lifted his glasses and rubbed his eyes with a knuckle. "So, it was the Thirteenth who prophesied this American god they were aiming to build. What did you call it again?"

"The Midswégan, yes the Thirteenth prophesied it and gave their forefathers the knowledge to bring it about."

"And they're doing this to bring about the end of the world?"

Anna looked very grave. "Oh no, I think they have much worse plans."

CHAPTER 35

NNA PAUSED, picked up the wine bottle and examined the dregs. "I think we're going to need more wine."

Linda grabbed her wrist as she got up to go to the kitchen, and pulled her back down. "Hey, you can't just leave it hanging like that. What do you mean by 'much worse?'"

Anna patted Linda's cheek, Linda wasn't certain if it was affection or condescension. "Trust me, hon, for this we're going to need more wine."

She returned with another bottle of red and filled everyone's glasses. McPherson held his hand over the glass. "I'm driving."

For all his size, Richard was looking glassy-eyed and didn't seem able to hold his liquor. "Are you sure I can't record this? You've no idea how valuable this info is."

Anna raised an imperious eyebrow. "Oh, trust me, I know just how valuable it is. I've lived a double life since childhood because of how valuable this information is. And that's why I can't just give it away and let you record me. If you ask again, I'm going to have to ask you all to leave."

Richard looked chastened. "Sorry, of course, but we can protect you now." He looked at McPherson. "Can't we?"

McPherson finished the wine in his glass. "If you're prepared to give a full affidavit outlining everything you know, and hand over all your files to the FBI, I can arrange you a new identity and round-the-clock protection."

Anna wagged a dismissive finger at McPherson. "Oh no, you don't get anything from me except for what I tell you tonight. As for a new identity, I've become very proficient at creating those, even in the digital age."

McPherson looked puzzled. "So why are you telling us all this? I thought you wanted to make a deal. Like I said, if we can find you, they won't be far behind. We're the only option you have left."

Anna let out a short bark of a laugh. "Ha, I have plenty of options, and the minute you drank that mickey I was putting my plans to disappear into effect. I admit I got a little sloppy there. After so many years, I assumed people had stopped looking for me, I won't be making that mistake again. No, as soon as you're gone, so am I and the files along with me, and trust me, this time no one will find me."

McPherson frowned, there was genuine anger in his eyes as Anna spoke, but he held his silence.

Linda noted the tension and attempted to circumvent it. "Can we get back to building a god, please? There's a lot of this I'm not getting, such as why they made three separate attempts."

Anna swilled the wine in her glass. "It wasn't three separate attempts, each event was part of the same working. They had to perform the same ritual three times, with six gifted psychics, forty years apart."

"Why forty years?"

"According to my father, it had something to do with the position of the continental shelves."

"The what now?"

"The position of the continents in relation to each other. The big land masses are moving all the time, at the rate of a centimeter or two a year. Because they're so big and we live such a short time, we don't notice it. That's why the ancients measured time and distance by the stars, because they noticeably move. But, if you walked the earth when the continents were all one, if you were used to making plans that lasted for millennia, you'd measure things by the position of the continental shelves, not the stars. When they're in the right place, then certain energies are in play that you need for your ceremonies. The stars are way out in space, some of them are dead by the time we see them. The earth is right at our feet. That's why the earth holds so much power for the Shadowcasters."

"I guess that makes sense. So, every forty years the continents are in the right position for this ceremony?"

"That's right."

"And the six psychics, what was all that about? I mean, why six?"

"It has magical significance to them. Three sixes are eighteen, numerologically, eighteen is the number of independence, and building something that will last forever. In Angelology, the eighteenth angel is sent when your thoughts and prayers are about to become reality. My father seemed to think this very relevant to their goal."

Richard took a drink and wiped wine from the corners of his mouth. "So, how did the Shadows in the Cave learn all of this? Did these god-making rituals come from this ancient knowledge they're supposed to have?"

"I think that was one of their sources, but they incorporated more modern techniques with every ceremony."

"What sort of modern techniques?"

Anna reached into another box and produced a color photo of a tall, bearded man with sandy blond hair, wearing a mauve turtleneck and a blue blazer. "I'm guessing you've come across Anton Le Corbusier and his theory of multi-modal consciousness?"

Richard nodded in a knowing fashion. "It's similar to Sheldrake's Morphogenic Field Theory."

"That's what I've read too. But Le Corbusier's hypotheses were more wide-ranging than Sheldrake's. He suggested that thoughts and memories were not only contained in invisible energy fields that surround all living things, but these fields have their own unique inhabitants, what we might describe as "thought forms." He was attempting to explain everything from Angels and Demons to Egregores with this hypothesis. Egregores have a symbiotic relationship with their group. They're nourished by the thoughts, beliefs, and actions of a group. To create a god, you need to go one step further, you need to make a sacrifice."

"A sacrifice?"

Anna nodded. "Haven't humans always made sacrifices to the gods when they needed their help? And a human sacrifice was always the ultimate way of petitioning the gods."

"So, you're saying these psychics were killed in some kind of ceremony?"

"No, what was done to them was much worse than being killed. Their minds, their psychic abilities, and their souls were ripped from their living bodies and grafted onto one another to create a larger gestalt consciousness, a being of unimaginable power."

"Is that even possible?"

Anna rifled through the files in one of the boxes and pulled out a large typewritten manuscript. The first page read: 'UNI-

CONSCIOUS TO MUTLI-CONSCIOUS EXISTENCE by ANTON LE CORBUSIER.'

"According to Le Corbusier it is. This is an unpublished book where he outlines some of his more radical ideas. His basic hypothesis is that just as unicellular beings, like protozoa and algae, eventually evolved and developed into increasingly complex multicellular beings, like fish, reptiles, and mammals, uni-conscious beings, like animals and humans, will one day evolve into 'multi-conscious existences' of increasing complexity. The Shadows in the Cave were trying to speed that process along."

"We heard as much, but how would they even do that?"

"Well, I'm certainly no expert. But, from what I understand, as a layman, the basic idea was to contain the stolen minds and souls of the psychics in a morphogenic holding field, until all eighteen consciousnesses could be harmonically calibrated to create one giant, unified consciousness which would become the prophesied Midswégan."

Linda nibbled a slice of pepperoni off her pizza "Do we know what happened to the psychics afterward, to their bodies, I mean?"

Anna sighed. "I don't know what happened to the first twelve. I imagine they were more or less braindead, everything had been sucked out of them. I don't know what they did with their bodies. Locked them in a sanitorium or put a bullet in their heads, I guess."

Richard flicked through a few pages of the manuscript. "You said you didn't know what happened to the first twelve. Does that mean you *do* know what happened to Carver and his five fellow psychics?"

Anna refilled her glass and took a big gulp. "My father was able to piece together a fairly comprehensive account and it isn't good."

"You mean they ended up mindless vegetables too?"

"Oh no, what happened to those other psychics would probably have been a blessing compared to Carver's eventual fate."

CHAPTER 36

LINDA DIDN'T WANT to ask her next question, but couldn't help herself. "What could have been worse than what they'd done to those other psychics?"

Anna bit the inside of her cheek. "Let's just say things didn't go according to plan."

"What do you mean?"

"My father believed, in order to conduct the experiment over an eighty-year period, they had to keep the emergent Midswégan pretty rigorously imprisoned. They couldn't have it breaking out and ruining all their plans."

"Why would it do that?"

"For a start, can you imagine how much psychic pressure would have been generated by imprisoning all those minds in one holding field, for over eighty years, until the barriers between them were shattered and they began to bleed into one another? What would it have been like to feel all your thoughts, memories and emotions subsumed by a new being? A being created by having your psyche crushed together and imprisoned with five or eleven others. To have everything that was unique about you consumed. To have your mental, emotional, and spiritual essence stitched together to create some creature of pure thought. It's like Doctor Frankenstein stitching bodies together while they were still alive, only this would be infinitely more painful and invasive."

"That sounds like the worst kind of torture."

"Yes, it does. And you have to understand that these minds were capable of reading other minds. They would have known what their captors had in store for them, they would have been able to read their thoughts."

Richard scratched at his ear, querulously. "Why didn't the

psychics read their minds in the first place, and stop all this before it began?”

“I imagine the Shadows in the Cave had developed ways of masking their thoughts.”

Linda was still thinking about the souls of the psychics, torn from their bodies and held inside a morphogenic field, slowly melting into one another as they transformed into what Anna called the Midswégan. She held back a shudder. “So what did the Shadows have in store for them, or the Midswégan?”

“My father seemed to think that changed over the course of eighty years. He believed the original aim was to fulfill the prophecy and immanentize the Forhwyrfan.”

Richard was puzzled. “Shouldn’t that be immanentize the eschaton?”

“No, the Forhwyrfan was a crucial part of the Twelve Families’ beliefs. It’s kind of hard to explain, partly because it’s an extremely complex concept and partly because it’s a carefully guarded secret, so it’s not like there’s any experts we can call on to flesh out our knowledge. I think it’s the closest thing the Qu’rm Saddic Heresy has to an apocalypse.”

Linda’s eyes grew wider. “You mean they’re trying to end the world?”

“Not quite end the world, so much as change it, transform it so completely that nothing of the old world will remain and all life in the cosmos will move on to its next stage of development. At least, that’s how I understand it.”

“So, that’s what you meant earlier when you said the Midswégan was ‘possibly the end of everything we know?’”

“Yes.”

Richard bit his top lip pensively. “If that’s what they started out to do in 1904, how did their plans change?”

“They evolved gradually, from what I can tell. This is outside the remit of what I agreed to tell you, but like any powerful cabal working behind the scenes, their influence waxes and wanes. We think of them as these master puppeteers, pulling all the strings, but they’re actually fighting, gaining and losing control all the time. This means there’s power plays inside the organization as well as outside of it. Key members within the inner circle come to power and lose favor all the time, the same as in any powerful institution. By the 1980s, the Shadows in the Cave had ditched the progressives and were backing the forces of conservatism, so it's no surprise that those forces were in the ascendancy. The people at the fore of the Shadows were some of the most ruthless operators the cabal had ever seen. How they planned to use what they saw as their pet god had changed."

Linda found herself zoning out. She looked over at McPherson. He was trying hard to hide his disapproval of what Anna was saying. Did he dislike the political implications of what Anna was saying, or was the conspiracy stuff a little too much for him?

"How did this affect their new plans?" Richard said. He was lapping this up, even if he couldn't record it.

"According to my father, the new leadership of the Shadows in the Cave wanted more. What they now wanted was immortality."

"And how did they plan to become immortal?"

"It seems that years of studying the forbidden lore at their disposal had uncovered new knowledge and darker arts. They now believed they had the ability to create an over-mind, one that would control and bend the Midswégan to their will by burning their own psyches onto the multi-consciousness of the Midswégan, like an engram."

Linda frowned. "What's an engram?"

"It's a permanent change in the brain," Richard said. "Like a vivid memory you can't forget, or a personality change."

Anna pointed at Richard to confirm what he said. "They wanted to change the Midswégan's personality to their own. Imagine if you could upload your consciousness to a cloud on the internet. That's what they were planning. Only this wasn't a cloud of information, it was an impossibly powerful psychic being. They would rule it, they thought, as a group mind. They would become gods and live forever."

Linda drained her glass and held it out for a refill. "I'm guessing there was a fatal flaw in their plan to become gods."

Anna topped up all their glasses, except for McPherson's. "The flaw was their overconfidence. They thought because they held the Midswégan captive that they had control over it. But it had access to their thoughts and knew what they were planning. So, my guess is it put its own plan in motion."

"Did this plan have anything to do with Carver's disappearance?"

"It has everything to do with Carver's disappearance. My father believed that in order for the psychics to be drained of their minds and souls, the holding field that kept the Midswégan captive had to be opened to create a conduit. But a conduit goes both ways. He thought that in the eighties, when they opened it for what the Shadows thought was the final time, the seminal Midswégan saw its chance to escape. We think it slipped from the holding field and took possession of one of the psychics at the crucial moment of the ritual, when the Shadows in the Cave least expected it."

Richard got quite excited. "We heard from one of the researchers that when they conducted this experiment, or ceremony, it went disastrously wrong, do you think this is what he meant?"

"I do."

"He also told us that four of the psychics died and the other one was left a vegetable."

"That's also what my father learned."

"So it's probably true. Did your father learn what happened to Carver and the Midswégan after that?"

"We think that when the Shadowcasters opened the conduit into the morphogenic field, the Midswégan saw its chance. Rather than let the last six minds and souls come to it, the Midswégan escaped from the field into one of the psychics."

"And you think that psychic was Carver?"

"Yes, I do. I think the Midswégan escaped from the compound inside Carver's body. It used its immense power to get off the desert base undetected and escape into the night, inside Carver. Now, no one really knows how it did this, where it went, or what happened next. My father was fairly sure of one thing though, no human body could survive with that much raw psychic energy inside them. If it was hell for the twelve other minds and souls crushed together in a holding field, can you imagine what it would be like for one human being to carry all that inside their body?"

Linda had a mental flash of what that would have been like for Carver. Staggering from the compound into the baking heat of the desert, filled with a howling maelstrom of psyches all crushed together inside of him.

There was a sharp pain in her jaw and Linda realized she was grinding her teeth. She hadn't noticed till now, but her hands were bunched into fists and there were beads of sweat on the back of her neck. The image seemed too real, like a memory she'd purposefully suppressed. She needed to distract herself. "Did your father have a theory about where Carver went, or what happened to him and the Midswégan?"

"We know what happened to Carver, but not the Midswégan. Our best guess is that it would have to have left Carver's body fairly soon after the escape, for both their sakes. You also have to bear in mind that it wasn't at its optimum power. It was supposed to be constructed from the minds of the world's eighteen leading psychics. Because it escaped, during the final ceremony, four of the psychics died. So, at best, it was missing about a fifth of itself. This means it wasn't at its full power. We probably can't consider it a god, just a powerful entity. We think it would need somewhere to hibernate and hide until it could become its full self."

"How would it do that?"

"It would have to find more energy."

"You mean more people to feed off?"

"Unfortunately, yes, that's exactly what I mean. It would take another forty years for the continental shelves to move into the right position for it to feed again, so it would need somewhere safe to hide, somewhere it couldn't be located, not even by the Shadows in the Cave."

"And I'm guessing the only person who knew where it hid was Carver."

Anna drained the bottle. She'd put away more than anyone, yet she seemed the most sober. "And Carver never told a soul."

Richard swilled the contents of his wine glass, trying to appear less drunk than he was. "You said you knew what happened to Carver, did he survive?"

"For a brief while, he did."

"Can you be more specific?"

"How Carver got off that compound in the first place is a mystery. Transport through the desert was tightly controlled."

"That's what we were told. Our contact informed us the jeeps and troop carriers were under military control, and they were the only way out of there. You certainly couldn't have walked across that desert."

"And yet Carver escaped."

Richard often squinted when he was thoughtful. "If this Midswégan is a near god-like entity, does it have magical powers? I mean, would it have been able to teleport Carver out of the compound?"

Anna frowned. "I don't know, maybe, if it was at the height of its power, but the Midswégan wasn't. I don't have any proof for this, but it's more likely that it helped Carver commandeer a vehicle and the military personnel covered it up to cover their asses. Either way, he did something no one else had ever done before. He eluded the Shadows in the Cave and he survived their ceremony.

"What's more, he got away with their most valuable asset. A proto-god they'd created by stitching together the minds of other psychics like him. An asset they'd spent almost a century trying to create. You'd better believe they'd want that back. He had to go into hiding, to evade them. But the weight of carrying a being that powerful inside him, feeling it take over his mind and body, it must have been excruciating, it would have driven anyone mad after a while."

"So you don't think he stayed missing for long?"

Anna rifled through another of the boxes and pulled out a slim manilla folder. She moved an empty pizza box from the coffee table and opened the file. It contained a small stack of press clippings. They were all about the same story—an incident in the city of Hobbs, New Mexico.

Linda saw one cutting from the *Hobbs-News Sun* dated 1985. It showed a picture of a run-down apartment block with the headline: '*STRANGE LIGHTS SEEN IN DOWNTOWN HOBBS.*' Another cutting, which looked like it came from one of Hymie Schmeling's UFO magazines, showed an artist's impression of the same apartment block, with a flying saucer hovering over it. The heading for this story read: '*PROOF THAT EXTRA-TERRESTRIALS WALK AMONG US?*'

Richard picked up some of the clippings. "This is the Hobbs Incident, right? When people think of UFOs in New Mexico, they always think of Roswell, but they forget that Hobbs had its own sightings and anomalous incidents."

Linda leaned in to get a better look at the folder's contents. She saw a photo of a S.W.A.T. team outside the same apartment block and it brought back unwanted memories. "Was this some kind of shoot-out with aliens?"

Richard shrugged. "No one knows exactly what happened. The official story is that the authorities sent a S.W.A.T. team to apprehend a dangerous drug dealer, working out of Hobbs. But the residents of the apartment block swore there was no evidence of drug dealing. Most of the team died of gunshot wounds during the incident, but reports suggest it was their own bullets.”

“You mean they shot themselves? Why?”

“That remains unexplained. Eyewitnesses, both inside and outside the building, report seeing strange lights, in colors they’d never seen before. What makes many researchers think there was extra-terrestrial involvement is that some eyewitnesses mention a figure who could change shape, a short African American.”

Richard slapped his forehead. “Wait, you don’t think that’s Carver, do you?”

Anna looked very pleased with herself. “I think the Shadows in the Cave tracked Carver down and sent a retrieval team to collect him. They cooked up the whole drug dealer story afterward, along with the UFO angle. What made me think of this story were the lights you mentioned seeing in McLaughlin’s basement, Linda. That was when I realized how important you are to this whole mystery.”

Linda blinked and her mouth fell open. “Me? Why am I important to all this?”

Anna fixed her clear, gray eyes on Linda. There was something approaching compassion in them. “You’re intimately involved in all this, and that’s the only reason I’m sharing this information with you.”

“Do you mean I’m intimately involved because I’m working this case?”

“No, you’re intimately involved because of your childhood.”

“My childhood?”

“Yes, you see, when they captured Carver, they needed him to talk, so they could retrieve the Midswégan. They needed to find out how to separate them. So they handed him over to their interrogation expert.”

“Who was that?”

“Henry McLaughlin.”

“The serial killer, the man who abducted and raped my mother?”

“Your birth father, yes. The minute you told me about your early life, I realized you’re in more danger than you know. I had to try and warn you.”

“But I don’t understand, why would the Shadows in the Cave hand Carver over to a psychopath?”

"There's more to McLaughlin's case than was reported in the media. Much of the story was covered up. For instance, when the authorities raided his house, they discovered a whole prison, full of holding cells and torture rooms right under his house. Did you ever wonder where a blue-collar worker like McLaughlin got the money and resources to build an underground prison complex in the middle of a St. Louis suburb?"

"Um, I never really thought about it. I try not to think about McLaughlin at all, if I'm honest. So, how did he build a whole prison under his house?"

"He didn't, he was just the man they left in charge of it. You have to realize that, for every Guantanamo Bay, and detention center, the public knows about, there's another, on home soil, that's secret and completely deniable. Many are in urban centers or suburbs, hiding in plain sight. Detention centers like the one McLaughlin ran."

Richard slapped his thigh in excitement. "I knew it."

Anna patted his knee. "You know lots of things, dear, and we're all very impressed."

"Are you mocking me?"

"Just a little." Anna gave him her last slice of pizza to make up for it.

Linda eyed her last two slices, but decided she was too full to eat either. "So, McLaughlin tortured Carver, as well as helpless women and children?"

"He tortured a lot of people."

"Did he find out how to separate the Midswégan?"

"By that point, events had overtaken them. Like I said earlier, shadow government cabals are always gaining and losing control of events. Sometimes they're on the ascendancy and sometimes they're not. After the fiasco in the desert and the loss of their most valuable asset, the Shadows in the Cave were vulnerable. Their enemies circled and effectively neutralized them."

McPherson made a low growl of disagreement. "I wouldn't say they were neutralized, or that they were vulnerable."

Linda and the others turned to regard him with surprise. Linda wondered what had promoted this interjection. He looked as though he took Anna's comment personally.

Anna shot him a scathing look. "You wouldn't say they were neutralized? Maybe you won't be so certain when you find out what happened next."

McPherson looked sheepish. "What I meant was that an organization like the Shadows in the Cave might lose a bit of power and influence, but they've been around too long to be neutralized."

Linda stepped in to spare him any more sharp comments. "What did happen next?"

"Most of this is conjecture, but the Shadowcasters were forced to give McLaughlin and his operation up. He'd kidnapped too many people and was becoming a liability.

"Their enemies sent in a S.W.A.T. team to clean things up, but that proved to be a major shitshow. The S.W.A.T. team took themselves out in a firefight, no one knows why. Police found the bodies along with the body of a woman who'd starved to death, and McLaughlin's body. No trace was ever found of Carver, or his body. About an hour later a six-year-old girl was found wandering the nearby streets, she was half starved, police believed she'd escaped from the complex. She was taken into protective custody and then put up for adoption."

Anna's words had rushed at Linda like an express train and they hit her with the same impact.

The case she was working had collided with her past life and Linda wasn't certain who she'd been investigating all along. Whose trail had they actually been following, Carver's, McLaughlin's or her own?

Linda tried to make her mouth work, to put these feelings into words, but after an infinity of mouthing silent phrases all she could manage was, "I don't understand."

Anna patted her leg. It was no less patronizing than her attempts to mollify Richard. "It's a lot to take in. But you deserve to know the truth."

Linda sighed, her stomach hurt. "I don't think anyone deserves to know a truth like that."

Anna narrowed her eyes, as if she didn't want to say what she had to say next. "I'm afraid there's more unpalatable truths. You mentioned the Shadows in the Cave put something called a Scwyrm on you and it ate one of your memories, right?"

"And dumped another one in my brain. Thanks for bringing that up, I love reliving traumatic experiences." Linda didn't bother to hide the irony in her voice.

"I'm sorry, but it was necessary. Are you aware of the memory the creature took?"

"Probably not, that's the whole thing about having one of my memories eaten, how would I know what they took? I mean I wouldn't recall it, would I?"

"Okay, I was trying to approach this delicately and I'm only making things worse. So, I'm just going to blunder in. You spoke about leaving your cell as a tiny child. You said there was another room with a closed door, there was lots of shooting, and there were strange colors you'd never seen before coming from behind the room's door. You knew you had to open the door and go into the room and it would change everything, forever. Have I missed anything?"

There was a cautious tone in Linda's voice. "No."

"That sounds, to me, like a child's description of a paranormal event. A paranormal event like encountering the Midswégan. An event like that would be impossible to put into any context as a six-year-old girl. So impossible you would have likely repressed the memory. That would explain your hysterical response when you tried to relive it."

"So you think that's why I broke down, why I couldn't answer you even though I was full of truth serum?"

"That's why I asked you if you knew what memory they lifted from your mind."

"You think it might be my memory of the Midswégan?"

"I think they were looking for it, but I don't think they found it."

"Why's that?"

"Because if they had, none of you would be alive right now. The Shadows in the Cave don't go revealing themselves to anyone. And if they do, that person usually ends up dead. You're not dead, so you still have something they need."

Linda took a deep breath, trying to process this bombshell. "You mean to say, we've been all over the country chasing down leads on Carver and . . ."

"The answer to it all, the key to the whole mystery of what happened to Carver and the Midswégan, has been buried in your memory all this time. That's why you're in such terrible danger."

Richard, McPherson, and Anna were all staring at Linda with something approaching awe. Linda didn't want to accept what she was saying. "No . . . no . . ."

Anna shot her a sad smile. "I'm afraid so. It's forty years since the last ceremony, and the continents are in the right position again. All the answers are in your memory and if you don't get to them before the Shadows in the Cave, it could be the end of everything. Not just for you, but the whole of humanity."

TO BE CONTINUED IN
DRAW YOU IN
VOL.3:
BEHIND THE MASK

SO, THERE YOU HAVE IT, GENTLE READER. THE CONTINENTS ARE IN ALIGNMENT, AND IF LINDA DOESN'T GET TO THE ANSWERS IN HER MEMORY BEFORE THE SHADOWS IN THE CAVE...
...IT MIGHT BE THE END OF EVERYTHING! WILL LINDA BE ABLE TO RECLAIM THOSE MEMORIES? WILL SHE, RICHARD AND MCPHERSON SOLVE THE MYSTERY OF CARVER'S DISAPPEARANCE AND LOCATE THE MIDSWÉGAN BEFORE IT'S TOO LATE?
I'M NOT GOING TO TELL YOU HERE, AM I? THAT WOULD SPOIL ALL THE FUN. YOU'LL JUST HAVE TO HUNT DOWN THE FINAL VOLUME TO LEARN EXACTLY WHAT LIES BEHIND THE MASK!

ACKNOWLEDGEMENTS

These three novels have taken up a good chunk of my life for the last few years. The story was originally supposed to be a single novel but it kept growing. It was Claire Matthews who suggested I make it into a trilogy when I complained I couldn't halt the book's relentless growth, so she's the first person I should thank.

The next people I'd like to thank are not only legends in the comics world, but two of the single nicest human beings you're ever likely to meet. I was introduced to Walter and Louise Simonson through our mutual friend Joel Meadows. I was originally going to base fictional characters on them both but, as the story developed, one theme became increasingly prominent—the way that fiction and reality often bleed into one another in the world of comics. So, I approached them both with the idea of them stepping into my novel. Thanks so much to them both for agreeing. You guys exceeded my expectations.

Fiction writing is a relay race. The first course is run by the author alone and it's a long one. Towards the end of the race the baton is passed back and forth quite a bit. That's usually when a whole team of talented professionals come in to turn your fault-ridden manuscript into a publishable text.

Chief among those people is Joe Mynhardt, head honcho at Crystal Lake Entertainment. I've been working with Crystal Lake for over a decade now, more or less since its inception and Joe and his family, Annemie, Jaco, plus daughter Cayleigh, have become close, personal friends. Joe in particular was great, not only when I blew several deadlines but also when I contacted him to say the novel I'd promised him was now going to be a trilogy. Without breaking a sweat he said, "okay" and kindly rearranged the whole of Crystal Lake's Publishing schedule. Now there's a publisher for you.

My editorial team for this book were incredible. My editor Heather Daughrity not only knocked the rough edges off my prose, she also challenged me where I needed to be challenged and, as a result, this book is so much better for her guidance and support. Jodi Shatz went above and beyond when proofing and even left me a lovely little note when she was done, something that's never happened to me before. I was most touched.

Laurels should also go to the art team. Ben Baldwin did an amazing job on the covers, especially as he had to completely redraw the cover to Vol 3 over from scratch, due entirely to my lack of foresight. He never ceases to astound and delight me with the covers he draws for the Bark Bites Horror line. Russ Leach did an incredible job with his depictions of Uncle Jasp for this trilogy. He leaped into the breach at the very last minute and excelled in his efforts.

As well as real life people crashing the fictional world of Draw You In, you may have noticed that R. L. Carver snuck out of the pages of this story and onto the internet with a series of pre-code and bronze age horror comics. He was helped in this great escape by the illustrious Mick Trimble, the colorful Aljoša Tomić and letterer-to-the-stars, Mindy Hopkins. I also have to thank Joel Meadows and Tripwire Magazine, John Freeman and the Down The Tubes website as well as old Groove himself, Lloyd Smith and the blog Diversions of the Groovy Kind for aiding Carver in his audacious prison-break from the confines of the fiction world.

I also have the charming Ali Vermeeren to thank for helping Linda Corrigan produce such excellent illustrations for her text prequel to *Doom Divine*. If you'd like to marvel at her and Linda's work then simply subscribe to my mailing list for this free, short novel, that you can't get anywhere else.

I should also thank writer and comic historian, Mike Howlett and editor extraordinaire, Jim Salicrup for also appearing as themselves in this work.

The comic history covered in these novels is 95% true. I am indebted to too many comics historians and writers for educating me about the great history of the 9th art. Apologies for not mentioning you all here and thank you for all your efforts.

Thanks finally to everyone who picked this book up and gave it a chance and especially for reading to the end of this awfully longwinded acknowledgements section. If I could recommend one thing, it's to go treat yourself to a horror comic as a reward for making it this far.

Jasper Bark
Wiltshire, 2024

THE END?

Not if you want to dive into more of Crystal Lake Publishing's Tales from the Darkest Depths!

Check out our amazing website and online store
or download our latest catalog here.
https://geni.us/CLPCatalog

Looking for award-winning Dark Fiction?
Download our latest catalog.

Includes our anthologies, novels, novellas, collections,
poetry, non-fiction, and specialty projects.

WHERE STORIES COME ALIVE!

We always have great new projects and content on the website to dive into, as well as a newsletter, behind the scenes options, social media platforms, our own dark fiction shared-world series and our very own webstore. Our webstore even has categories specifically for KU books, non-fiction, anthologies, and of course more novels and novellas.

ABOUT THE AUTHOR

Multiple award-winning author, Jasper Bark is infectious—and there's no known cure. If you're reading this you're already contaminated. The symptoms will manifest any time soon. There's nothing you can do about it. There's no itching or unfortunate rashes, but you'll become obsessed with his mind-bending books.

Then you'll want to tell everyone else about his visionary horror fiction. About its originality, its wild imagination and how it takes you to the edge of your sanity. We're afraid there's no way to avoid this. These words contain a power you're hopeless to resist. You're already in their thrall, you know you are. You're itching to read all of Jasper's bloodstained books. Don't fight this urge, embrace it. You've been bitten by the Bark bug and you love it!

WOULD YOU LIKE TO READ DOOM DIVINE BY LINDA CORRIGAN ABSOLUTELY FREE?

Of course you would. I mean, who doesn't like free books? And you can't get this one anywhere else!

That's right this is your exclusive chance to read a short novel written by a character in this book, based on the comic strip she draws. *Doom Divine—Vein Glorious Love* is a fully illustrated short novel and it's yours to own, free of charge as soon as you join Jasper's cult and sign up to his mailing list through the QR code below.

Don't worry, you won't have to shave your head or unalive any celebrities (for the first couple of years). But you will get all of Jasper's latest, videos, podcasts, blogs, breaking news on upcoming books and other crucial information to help you cyberstalk him. What's more, we'll throw in two more short novels, a graphic novel and a spoof picture book, just to sweeten the deal! That's five free books, that you won't get anywhere else, just for signing up.

Are we crazy? Of course we're crazy! We're asking you to join Jasper's cult!

And because we know you can't bear to miss out.

Don't be the only weird kid on your block to miss out. Don't delay. Sign up today.

Readers . . .

Thank you for reading *Draw You In Vol. 2*. We hope you enjoyed this novel.

If you have a moment, please review *Draw You In Vol. 2* at the store where you bought it.

Help other readers by telling them why you enjoyed this book. No need to write an in-depth discussion. Even a single sentence will be greatly appreciated. Reviews go a long way to helping a book sell, and is great for an author's career. It'll also help us to continue publishing quality books.

Thank you again for taking the time to journey with Crystal Lake Publishing.

Visit our Linktree page for a list of our social media platforms.
https://linktr.ee/CrystalLakePublishing

Follow us on Amazon:

Our Mission Statement:

Since its founding in August 2012, Crystal Lake Publishing has quickly become one of the world's leading publishers of Dark Fiction and Horror books. In 2023, Crystal Lake Publishing formed a part of Crystal Lake Entertainment, joining several other divisions, including Torrid Waters, Crystal Lake Comics, Crystal Lake Kids, and many more.

While we strive to present only the highest quality fiction and entertainment, we also endeavour to support authors along their writing journey. We offer our time and experience in non-fiction projects, as well as author mentoring and services, at competitive prices.

With several Bram Stoker Award wins and many other wins and nominations (including the HWA's Specialty Press Award), Crystal Lake Publishing puts integrity, honor, and respect at the forefront of our publishing operations.

We strive for each book and outreach program we spearhead to not only entertain and touch or comment on issues that affect our readers, but also to strengthen and support the Dark Fiction field and its authors.

Not only do we find and publish authors we believe are destined for greatness, but we strive to work with men and women who endeavour to be decent human beings who care more for others than themselves, while still being hard working, driven, and passionate artists and storytellers.

Crystal Lake Publishing is and will always be a beacon of what passion and dedication, combined with overwhelming teamwork and respect, can accomplish. We endeavour to know each and every one of our readers, while building personal relationships with our authors, reviewers, bloggers, podcasters, bookstores, and libraries.

We will be as trustworthy, forthright, and transparent as any business can be, while also keeping most of the headaches away from our authors, since it's our job to solve the problems so they can stay in a creative mind. Which of course also means paying our authors.

We do not just publish books, we present to you worlds within your world, doors within your mind, from talented authors who sacrifice so much for a moment of your time.

There are some amazing small presses out there, and through collaboration and open forums we will continue to support other presses in the goal of helping authors and showing the world what quality small presses are capable of accomplishing. No one wins when a small press goes down, so we will always be there to support hardworking, legitimate presses and their authors. We don't see Crystal Lake as the best press out there, but we will always strive to be the best, strive to be the most interactive and grateful, and even blessed press around. No matter what happens over time, we will also take our mission very seriously while appreciating where we are and enjoying the journey.

What do we offer our authors that they can't do for themselves through self-publishing?

We are big supporters of self-publishing (especially hybrid publishing), if done with care, patience, and planning. However, not every author has the time or inclination to do market research, advertise, and set up book launch strategies. Although a lot of authors are successful in doing it all, strong small presses will always be there for the authors who just want to do what they do best: write.

What we offer is experience, industry knowledge, contacts and trust built up over years. And due to our strong brand and trusting fanbase, every Crystal Lake Publishing book comes with weight of respect. In time our fans begin to trust our judgment and will try a new author purely based on our support of said author.

With each launch we strive to fine-tune our approach, learn from our mistakes, and increase our reach. We continue to assure our authors that we're here for them and that we'll carry the weight of the launch and dealing with third parties while they focus on their strengths—be it writing, interviews, blogs, signings, etc.

We also offer several mentoring packages to authors that include knowledge and skills they can use in both traditional and self-publishing endeavours.

We look forward to launching many new careers.

This is what we believe in. What we stand for. This will be our legacy.

Welcome to Crystal Lake Publishing— Tales from the Darkest Depths.